GOLDEN
GIRL

BOOKS BY DANA PERRY

The Silent Victim

DANA PERRY

THE GOLDEN GIRL

bookouture

Published by Bookouture in 2020

An imprint of Storyfire Ltd.
Carmelite House
50 Victoria Embankment
London EC4Y 0DZ

www.bookouture.com

ISBN: 978-1-83888-267-9
eBook ISBN: 978-1-83888-266-2

PROLOGUE

On a hot summer night in New York City, a policewoman named Maura Walsh walked into a strip club. She was pretty – maybe even more attractive than the dancers the men were paying to see. But the uniform made it clear she was there on business, and everyone gave her a wide berth. She walked directly over to the bar, pocketed a wad of cash the bartender handed her and left.

A short time later, the same scenario played out at a house of prostitution. It was located in a building where tenants had complained about male customers showing up at all hours of the day and night, but no one ever seemed to do anything about it. Maura Walsh went into the office of the woman who ran the business, closed the door and accepted more money.

The next stop was at a restaurant. It was a trendy singles place, and lots of young people were eating and drinking and having a good time. She sat down at a table, but didn't eat or drink anything. The manager came over, they had a brief conversation and money changed hands.

An hour after that, Maura Walsh was found shot to death on the street in the Little Italy section of Manhattan.

The news accounts the next day described her in glowing terms as a hero cop, a decorated five-year veteran of the force and the daughter of Deputy NYPD Commissioner Mike Walsh.

There was no mention of the strip club, the house of prostitution, the restaurant or the payoffs she took.

That would all come later.

CHAPTER 1

Crazy, senseless crimes always seem to happen in the summertime in New York City. Son of Sam was in the summer of 1977. The Preppie Murder Case, when Robert Chambers inexplicably strangled Jennifer Levin during sex after picking her up at a singles bar on the Upper East Side, happened in August of 1986. And I was attacked, brutally beaten and left for dead on a hot summer night in Central Park twelve years ago, just like the night when Maura Walsh was murdered.

"You should take some time off, Jessie," Danny Knowlton, the assistant city desk editor at the *New York Tribune* where I work these days as a crime reporter, said to me when I walked into the newsroom on this summer morning.

"I'm fine, Danny."

"A week, even a couple of weeks – no problem. It's summer. Go to the beach or something. Enjoy yourself for once."

"Maybe later."

I knew why Danny Knowlton was so concerned about me, and it wasn't because he was a warm, caring human being. Danny was a newspaper editor. And the words "warm, caring human being" and "newspaper editor" rarely belonged together. Certainly not in the case of an editor like Danny Knowlton, an ambitious young guy who was always looking for a big story to help him further his career.

No, my happiness and health was important to Danny because I'd been very good for him recently.

I had broken a huge Page 1 exclusive: the truth about what really happened to me during the attack in Central Park twelve years ago as well as the truth about the murders of several other women. It had implicated some of the most powerful people in the city. Since then, I'd been on the front pages of newspapers around the country; on the covers of magazines; and a regular topic of conversation by all the TV talking heads on the 24-hour news cycle.

Jessie Tucker, media superstar.

Just like I'd been after the first attack.

But the trauma and emotion I went through to get this sensational story – both now and in opening doors to fears I'd left behind me long ago – had taken their toll on me.

Danny Knowlton thought the answer to all this was rest and relaxation, but I knew better. I knew what I really needed now. I needed another story. So I decided to go after the biggest story around.

"I want to work on the Maura Walsh story," I told him.

Three weeks ago, Policewoman Maura Walsh was found shot dead on a Manhattan street. It was only the third time a female NYPD officer had died in the line of duty. Maura Walsh was also the daughter of Deputy Police Commissioner Mike Walsh, and the whole Walsh family had a long, honorable tradition with the NYPD. Despite a massive police investigation, no one had been able to find out any more since then about who killed her or why.

I'd been dealing with all the aftermath of my big Central Park story when it happened and hadn't been involved in the *Tribune* coverage.

But I was the paper's crime reporter, and now I wanted to write about Maura Walsh.

"We went really big on the coverage of that story at the time," Danny pointed out to me. "If there's an arrest in the case, we'll jump back on it. But there's a whole lot of other breaking news out there now which has pushed Maura Walsh off the front page…"

I looked over at the front page of the *Tribune* on his desk. The headline said: HEAT WAVE IN THIRD DAY: NO END IN SIGHT. I had an editor once who refused to run these kind of weather stories. He said it never made sense to make people buy the paper to tell them the weather they already knew. But the *Tribune* didn't follow that policy these days.

"We're going to keep telling people it's hot outside?" I said. "I think they already know that, Danny."

"Don't knock weather stories – they sell newspapers for us."

"So would a good story about the murder of a woman police officer."

"A lot of other reporters in town have already covered that story, Jessie."

"Not the way I'll do it."

That wasn't my ego talking. There were a lot of good reporters at the *Tribune* and elsewhere who covered breaking news, but my job at the paper was to be the crime specialist who went beyond the daily headlines to get the real story. I explained to Danny now how I wanted to do that with Maura Walsh.

"Let me do a deep dive into the Maura Walsh story. An in-depth look at how a woman cop from a legendary NYPD family like this lives – and tragically dies – on the streets of New York City. I'd talk to other cops, friends and family. I have a source in the department who might even be able to get me an interview with Maura Walsh's father. The deputy commissioner hasn't talked to anyone about his daughter's killing since a brief press conference right after it happened. If I could get him to really open up to me, it would be a helluva exclusive."

I could tell right away Danny liked the idea. And why not? It would be another feather in his cap as my editor if I could pull this off. We talked for a while about the logistics of how I would do it – and when it might run. Maybe a big Sunday piece for the *Tribune*. And we could break it first on the website Saturday night.

Then push it out on Twitter, our app and all the other social media throughout the weekend.

"And you're absolutely sure you want to keep working, Jessie? After all you've gone through recently?" he asked, even though I think he knew what I would say.

"Yes."

"What are you looking for? Even more Jessie Tucker headlines?" He smiled.

"No, I'd just like to get some answers about Maura Walsh."

I walked back to my desk in the newsroom and grabbed a granola bar from my desk drawer.

"How'd it go with Danny?" asked Michelle Caradonna, the reporter who had recently moved next to me.

"He wanted me to take some time off, but I said no."

"I've been trying for weeks to get a vacation, but he won't give it to me! That's not fair. You have all the luck."

"Yeah, too bad you couldn't get attacked and nearly killed in Central Park too, huh, Michelle?"

She looked embarrassed. "God, I'm sorry, Jessie. I wasn't thinking—"

"Don't worry about it."

Michelle was twenty-five years old, going on about fifty. She seemed to be trying to cram a whole lifetime of living into a quarter of a century. Her goal was to win a Pulitzer Prize before she turned thirty. She was absolutely fearless, and there was nothing she wouldn't do for a story. She'd parachuted from an airplane onto a private beach in the Hamptons to cover a celebrity wedding; gone undercover as a patient to do an exposé on medical malpractice; and even walked into a lion cage at the zoo to show how lax safety regulations were. I told her once that if she didn't slow down, she'd have nothing left to accomplish by the time she was my age.

I looked around the office. It was a little after ten a.m., and the newsroom was beginning to fill up. Within a few hours, it would be a maelstrom of activity as the staff raced to put out the day's news. There was an adrenalin in the room – an energy, a dedication – that I felt whenever I was here. It was what kept me working for the *Tribune* even after everything that had happened to me.

Even for a newspaper, the *Tribune* was a pretty eclectic place.

Take Danny, for instance. He had long, scraggly blond hair which he wore in a ponytail, was always dressed in T-shirts and jeans and pretty much looked like an exile from a heavy metal rock band. His temper tantrums are legendary. He once threw a chair though a plate-glass window. Another time he expressed his displeasure with a story by chasing a reporter down the street in front of the *Tribune* building and dumping a cup of coffee on his head. Much of this anger no doubt was fueled by his ambition to be the top man on the city desk. But his boss Norman Isaacs – the aged, longtime city editor of the *Tribune* – kept fending off retirement.

Isaacs was the exact opposite in temperament to Danny Knowlton. Plodding, cautious, and never wanting to make waves in the newsroom or the corporate hierarchy. He was known for announcing at the beginning of most workdays that he "just wanted to work a clean shift" without any problems, hassles or controversy. "No-Guts Norman" was what Danny called Isaacs behind his back because he rarely pushed hard on a story. But that careful approach had kept Isaacs as the city editor at the *Tribune* for more than a quarter of a century, so maybe he really did know what he was doing after all.

Occupying another corner of the newsroom was Peter Ventura. Peter was once one of the most legendary newspaper columnists in New York City – but now all the long nights spent in bars around town had caught up with him. He didn't break too many big stories anymore, but on the other hand he didn't seem particularly bothered by it. Right then, for instance, he was sleeping with his head on the keyboard of his computer. He slept a lot at his desk these days. No one bothered him much, although someone on the city desk had decided on a little fun a few weeks before by calling his extension while he was in the middle of one of his naps. When he sleepily picked up the phone, the person on the other end shouted: "Peter – your chair's on fire!" They say he jumped a mile, and the entire newsroom exploded in laughter. Maybe someday the paper will get rid of him, but I doubt it. He is an institution here and the paper owes him a lot.

The managing editor was a woman named Lorraine Molinski. Blonde, fortyish, a bit overweight, she'd been at the paper for only a few years. Before that, she had been a publicist and then an advertising woman and then spent a stint on the copy desk at the *New York Post*. When she was promoted to managing editor here, a lot of people wondered how she got the job with so little reporting experience. There was a rumor that it might have been because she was sleeping with a member of the owner's family. Maybe because of that, Lorraine always seemed paranoid about her job – she needed to constantly remind people that she was in charge. A lot of people don't like Lorraine, and the nickname they've given her was "Lorr-Reign of Terror". I'd never had a problem with her, though. She'd always been nice to me. And I liked the fact that there was something a bit – well – almost *dangerous* about her. There was also a rumor amongst my fellow reporters that she carried a gun. I remember a day when some of us were supposed to get White House security checks for a visit by the President, and Lorraine begged out. She said she didn't think doing a background investigation on her would be good for her or the paper. I liked that. Someday I knew I had to find out more about Lorraine Molinski.

OK, I don't have much of a life outside the *Tribune*.

I was an only child.

My mother was dead.

And I never even knew my father.

I was engaged once, a long time ago, but that fell through. So did the last big romance I had with a guy who lived on the West Coast. I had high hopes for that relationship for a while. But in the end there was just too much distance between us, both geographically and otherwise. So I'm alone these days.

All I have in my life is my job.

And the people around me here.

This newsroom…

Well, this newsroom *is* my life.

CHAPTER 2

Maura Walsh's body had been found on the street in the neighborhood known as Little Italy in downtown Manhattan.

She and her partner, a veteran patrolman named Billy Renfro, had begun their tour of duty at five p.m. that evening.

They were assigned to street patrol in a squad car out of the 22nd Police Precinct, which was located on 70th Street near Third Avenue.

Police records showed that Walsh and Renfro reported making five stops that night before calling in a Code 7 – police jargon for a meal break – at 10:30. Two of the stops were at restaurants or bars where disturbances had occurred; one at an apartment house; another at a bodega; and a fifth with someone listed as an "informant" on East 86th Street between Second and Third Avenue.

The explanation given for each stop was a simple "pursuit of citizen complaint". Of course, lots of cops called in or filled out paperwork with vague entries like that because they didn't have time to deal with all the bureaucratic details that were a part of the job. Most of the time it didn't matter. Unless something went wrong, like it had for Maura Walsh.

Her partner, Billy Renfro, said he'd left her in the squad car while he went into a pizza place to pick up an order for them. When he returned to the car, she was gone. He later discovered her body lying in an alley not far away. She had been shot two times in the chest with her own gun. The gun was missing.

By the time the paramedics arrived at the scene, Maura Walsh was already dead. It took her a long time to die though, the Medical Examiner's office later reported. The gunshot wounds had immobilized her and left her too weak to even call out for help, but she was still alive for at least fifteen minutes and maybe for as long as a full hour.

If she could have reached her police radio, maybe she could have signaled someone she was in trouble. But the radio wasn't on her body when she was found. It was discovered later in a trashcan down the street, dumped there by whoever killed her.

And so Maura Walsh slowly bled to death, alone in that dark alley.

Which made it all even more tragic.

This last part really got to me. I could imagine what it must have been like for Maura Walsh – lying there in the dark, terrified, in terrible pain and knowing she was going to die. I understood what she felt in those last minutes of her life because the same thing had happened to me when I'd been attacked in Central Park twelve years earlier. Someone found me in time to save my life, but Maura Walsh hadn't been so lucky. She'd remained conscious for fifteen minutes to an hour, the ME's office said. I just hoped it was closer to fifteen minutes and that she didn't suffer for the whole hour. A massive search of the area afterward turned up nothing. No suspect, no real evidence, no witnesses. The police had questioned known persons who were in the Little Italy neighborhood that night; suspects with a background that fit this kind of crime; ex-cons who might have had some sort of grudge against Maura Walsh – all to no avail.

The prevailing theory these days was that it was a random shooting. She stumbled into the midst of an ongoing crime or just ran into some lunatic looking for someone to kill. That person accosted her, stripped her of her gun, shot her and left her to die.

*

Back at my desk, I called up a YouTube video of the press conference the police had held the day after Maura died.

Her father, Deputy Police Commissioner Mike Walsh, was
front and center at the press conference. He was a tall, silver-haired
man who stood ramrod straight in his uniform, staring straight
ahead without any visible emotion as everyone talked about his
daughter's death.

I had come across a newspaper article about the Walsh family
when I was looking through all the materials on Maura Walsh's
background. It had run in the *Tribune* some time ago. The headline was: CARRYING ON A FAMILY TRADITION: MAURA
WALSH IS TRUE BLUE ALL THE WAY. There was a picture
of an athletic-looking, red-haired young woman standing in front
of a police station house. Maura Walsh, with her father standing
proudly next to her. It had been taken right after she graduated
from the Police Academy and received her first NYPD assignment.
I'd seen other pictures of her, but in this one she looked so young,
so pretty and so full of hopeful ambition for the future.

The article described how the Walsh family's connections with
the New York City Police Department went back for generations.
Maura Walsh's grandfather was a cop, his father before him and
so on. Some of them went pretty far up in the NYPD hierarchy
too. One had even been a police commissioner.

Maura Walsh had been following in that tradition. She
graduated Phi Betta Kappa from Baruch College with a degree in
criminal justice and then with honors from the Police Academy.
She had an exemplary record during her five years on the street as
a police officer and seemed to be on the fast track to becoming a
detective soon. She'd been transferred six months earlier to a new
post at the 22nd Precinct on the Upper East Side of Manhattan.
That was particularly noteworthy because it was the same precinct
where her father had once been the commanding officer.

I watched the entire press conference now about Maura Walsh's murder. Most of it was pretty standard stuff. Updates from police officials about the search for her killer and medical details about her fatal wounds and then more detail about her movements that night prior to the shooting.

At one point, a reporter asked Deputy Commissioner Walsh to describe his emotions at this painful moment. I was surprised Walsh was even there at the press conference, so soon after his own daughter had just died. But I was even more surprised by his reaction.

"I'm terribly proud of my daughter," he said, still staring straight ahead. "She always wanted to be a police officer. Always wanted to follow in the Walsh family's tradition of police service. There are no regrets. Maura knew the dangers involved in the job and accepted them. She was a street cop. She was risking her life every moment out there. A street cop is like a foot soldier in war – our first line of defense against the enemy. I'm proud of my daughter. Proud that she died heroically in the line of duty. Proud that she died doing what she loved best. Proud that she was so able to nobly carry on the tradition of police duty in our family. She was a Walsh. And the Walsh family is true blue all the way."

Wow, I thought to myself, *all the woman did was get herself killed.*

There was video and stories too from the funeral for Maura Walsh a few days later. It was held at a church on East 67th Street. Hundreds of cops attended in their dress blues. They listened to a procession of eulogies about what a wonderful person she had been – and the accolades, awards and acclaim she'd won as a police officer during her five years on the job. "Maura was an angel," one speaker said, "a shining angel who left us much too soon."

In the front of the church was the Walsh family. Maura's father and mother, her grandfather who'd spent four decades on the police force, assorted cousins and uncles and other relatives who belonged to the NYPD. I watched Walsh Sr. when the camera focused on him during the eulogies for his daughter. Not a tear, no emotion, nothing at all. Just like he'd been at the press conference the first day. Almost as if he was satisfied his daughter had died in the line of duty.

To find out more about Walsh, I googled some old newspaper articles about him.

There were a lot of them.

The New York City newspapers first made him a hero and nicknamed him "Prince of the City" during a big police corruption scandal years ago, when he was an up-and-coming young officer in the NYPD. *Prince of the City*, of course, was a hit movie at the time, which starred Treat Williams as a hero New York City cop battling crooked cops who were once his friends.

Just like in the movie, there was a real-life split going on in the department back then between the good cops and the bad cops. The cops who did their jobs honestly, fairly and by following all the rules versus the ones who ripped off drug dealers, took payoffs and brutalized people.

Walsh was one of the good guys. There were always a lot more good guys than bad ones on the force – *it was the few rotten apples who spoiled everything*, he was on record as saying. I knew from my reporting that it wasn't always easy being a good guy and a lot of cops tried to straddle the line – keeping their own noses clean but looking the other way when they saw corruption and wrongdoing happening around them.

Not him though.

There had always been an unwritten rule in the department known as the Blue Wall of Silence. That's not an official term, just an expression used to describe cops' unwillingness to testify against other cops. Never give up your partner, never give up any fellow cop. It was a long and deeply entrenched tradition in the police department, and most cops adhered to it in one form or another.

So, when a corruption scandal exploded – involving confiscated drugs that were being re-sold from the police evidence room back on to the street – no one wanted to talk. No one wanted to testify. No one wanted to cooperate. No one wanted to stand up and do the right thing.

The police commissioner at the time set up a special task force to investigate the matter, and Walsh was one of the top investigators on it, assigned to root out police corruption in the NYPD. Some people told him he was committing career suicide. He said he didn't care. He said you could never go wrong by doing the right thing.

There was a total of eighteen police officers arrested in the scandal. Another forty-two cops were either suspended, resigned or fired from their jobs before it was over.

One of the men who went to jail was Walsh's old partner. His name was Al Furillo, and he'd accepted about $10,000 in illicit money to not come forward about drug dealing by other cops in his precinct. It turned out that Furillo had a thirteen-year-old daughter who was dying of leukemia, and he desperately needed the money to pay medical bills.

Some people thought Walsh might go easy on him because of the extenuating circumstances and because of their past relationship.

But Walsh personally testified against Furillo at the trial, and it was that testimony which helped convince the jury to convict him. He was sentenced five to twelve years in prison. Six months after he went to jail, his daughter died. Nine months after that, Al Furillo was beaten to death by another prisoner.

If Walsh was shaken up or remorseful over what had happened to his old partner, he never talked about it publicly. I found a statement from him when he was asked about his actions during the corruption probe where he said:

"There are times in your life when you have to make decisions between what is right and what is wrong. You can never let outside influences confuse you. Not friends. Not career aspirations. Not fear of being unpopular or of being ostracized or even of physical violence. Nothing and no one is more important than your integrity. As long as you have your integrity, you can hold your head up high. Without integrity, you are lost."

No personal emotion of any kind in that statement… but then he hadn't shown any public emotion when his own daughter died. So why would he act any differently for his old friend and partner?

I picked up my phone and called my police source who was trying to set up an interview for me with the deputy commissioner. He said he was still working on it, but he would get back to me as soon as he could. He added that Walsh wasn't exactly the easiest person to work with. Thinking of the emotionless-sounding man I'd watched earlier, I could understand that.

"I just saw him at the press conference the day after the murder," I said. "I'm sure he really loved his daughter and all, but it was hard to tell from that."

"I think they had a very complicated relationship."

"Complicated how?"

"I'm not sure. But there was definitely some kind of weird dynamic going on there though. Maura never wanted to talk about her father. If you asked her about him, she immediately changed the subject."

"Why do you think that was?"

"Who knows? Just some kind of messed up father-daughter relationship. But that happens – hey, you know how father-daughter relationships sometimes have a lot of problems."

"Nope," I said. "I wouldn't know anything about that at all."

CHAPTER 3

My father died before I ever got a chance to meet him.

He was a fireman, and he was killed trying to rescue a family of five people from a burning building. The family got out, but it was too late for my father. He was hailed as a hero afterward for saving their lives and sacrificing his own in this brave and selfless effort. It was a memorable, moving story that brought tears to my eyes as a little girl every time my mother told it to me.

Except sometimes my father wasn't a fireman at all – he was a soldier who bravely charged an enemy bunker and single-handedly wiped out a machine gun that had been decimating the men in his platoon. He gave his life for his country. His body was buried with full military honors and his coffin wrapped in an American flag.

Or maybe he was a police officer who held off a gang of armed bank robbers so that a group of terrified hostages in the bank could escape, before he himself was gunned down. There was a full-dress police funeral afterward where the mayor and the governor and a lot of other important people extolled my father's actions as those of a courageous and dedicated servant to the people.

You see, all of these were things told to me by my mother when I was a little girl growing up and asked her why I didn't have a father like all the other children did.

I believed her then, never questioning the details or the facts or the variations in the story, because that was the kind of father I wanted to have too.

It wasn't until I was a bit older – and presumably wiser – that I discovered the truth about my father.

He wasn't gone because he had died heroically in a fire, or on a battlefield, or thwarting a bank robbery.

He was just gone.

It turned out that he had walked out on my mother – and abandoned me too – right after I was born.

And my mother made up all these stories about him because she never wanted to admit the truth to anyone, not even to her own daughter.

I was thinking about all that now – probably because of my discussion about the relationship between Maura Walsh and her father – while I did my morning workout in the bedroom of my apartment on Irving Place in the Gramercy Park section of Manhattan. It was a big bedroom, and I'd filled it with a lot of exercise equipment. Some days I went to a gym a few blocks away on Park Avenue South too for my morning workout regime. But I always did the workout either here or in the gym – and sometimes in both places when I really wanted to stretch myself out – without fail.

My workout routine varied, but I tried to do at least an hour before I left for work. I started with sit-ups and push-ups. Then twenty minutes of pedaling on a stationary bike. After that, I ran on a treadmill – generally while watching the morning news on TV. At the gym, I did leg curls and lifted weights and other stuff I couldn't do at home. I swam there too, doing laps in an Olympic-sized pool at the club.

Sure, all of this sometimes left me exhausted before I even got to my desk, but it was worth it for me. I'd started doing all these exercises during my long recovery period from the brutal attack I'd endured in Central Park. I hadn't even been able to walk then, but now I was almost healed, except for a stumble once in a while when one of my legs gave out, or the rare times when I needed to use a cane. But, all in all, Jessie Tucker was in pretty good shape for a woman who had almost died.

When I was finished exercising, I poured myself some coffee in the kitchen, toasted and buttered a bagel, then went back into the living room. I ate my breakfast in front of the TV – taking in the headlines about traffic tie-ups, fires, crimes, political controversies and, of course, the weather. The breaking news was it was going to be another hot one in New York City today. TV news loved to play up weather stories even more than we did at the *Tribune*.

I still had a bit of time before I needed to leave for work. So, after I finished the bagel, I took my coffee over to my laptop. Then I called up some of the old stories written about myself and Central Park. I did that sometimes. I wasn't exactly sure why. Maybe to show myself again how far I'd come since that terrible night.

There were two batches of stories.

The first was the story of my initial near-death attack. All about the heroic young woman – that was me – who bravely fought her way back to life and captured the city's heart. The arrest of the man who did it. His confession, his trial and his subsequent death in prison.

The second group of stories was from what had just happened to me a few months earlier. The truth about who had attacked me – and why. And how I'd broken that story myself in the *Tribune*, even though I almost died again in the process of doing so.

But I'd survived.

Twice now.

And I was stronger for it.

I closed the file on the computer about myself and called up the picture I'd seen of Maura Walsh – standing in front of a police station in her police uniform with her father and looking so full of life.

"I don't think she got along too well with her father," was what my source had told me.

I'd always felt sorry for myself because I had no father, but maybe having no father wasn't the worst thing in the world. Maybe even worse was having a father who didn't act like your father.

I had no idea what the problems were in Maura Walsh's relationship with her father and it probably had nothing to do with how she died on the street that night. But, looking at the picture of Maura Walsh again now, I felt a sense of real compassion for this woman.

I wished I'd had a chance to know her.

But it was too late to do that now.

Too late to save Maura Walsh's life.

All I could do for her now was find out the truth about why she died.

Just like I'd found out the truth about myself.

CHAPTER 4

I met Maura Walsh's partner Billy Renfro that afternoon at McGuire's, a bar on the Upper East Side around the corner from the 22nd Precinct.

It sure was another scorcher of a summer's day in New York City. The temperature had already hit ninety-eight, according to my iPhone. The latest forecast said it might reach a hundred. I wasn't quite sure why Renfro was drinking in the middle of the day around the corner from his precinct, but I suppose you have to cut a guy some serious slack to grieve when his partner has been murdered. I grabbed a napkin from the bar, used it to wipe the sweat from my cheeks and forehead and then plopped down on the seat next to him.

I knew Billy Renfro from my time on the police beat. I'd worked with him on a few stories over the years. He was probably between forty-five and fifty years old now, with a house in Queens and a boat that he talked about sailing to Florida the minute he put in his retirement papers. I always remembered Renfro as a good guy, a good cop.

"How's it going, Billy?" I asked.

"I've been better."

"Are you back on the street?"

"Since last week."

"New partner?"

"Yeah, some kid who barely looks old enough to be my son. Like I really need someone like that to watch my back out there.

They keep getting younger and younger every year. Or maybe I'm just getting too old for the job."

"Maura Walsh was young enough to be your daughter," I pointed out to him.

"Maura was different."

"Different how?"

"She was just different. She was good. A good cop. A good person. How could something like this have happened to her?"

We sat back and talked more about Maura Walsh over a few beers. I didn't have to ask Renfro too many questions, I just let him talk. He seemed to want to talk about her. As if talking about her made it feel like she wasn't really gone for good – just away somewhere for a while.

He explained how they'd been together on the street for six months. He told me about her first day with him; about the time she managed to slap handcuffs on a four-hundred-pound suspect who was sitting on top of him; about the time she walked into a bodega for a soda and broke up a robbery, capturing two gunmen single-handedly; about how she liked Chinese food and salted pretzels and those hot dogs with sauerkraut that street vendors sell in New York City; about the conversations they had together and the fun and the good times. The not so good times too – about Maura Walsh being a woman cop and how she had to deal with a lot of hassle because of that.

"Many of the guys at the precinct – well, they're not exactly the most politically enlightened people. Even after all these years, they still don't like the idea of a woman on the street. Made Maura's life pretty tough sometimes. They put tampons in her locker. Left obscene messages and pictures on her desk. Made her get coffee for everyone like she was an errand girl or something. I thought being Mike Walsh's daughter might have saved her from some of that, but it didn't. Lots of other people – hell, even my own wife – had trouble dealing with the idea someone like Maura was able to do the job. They thought she was there because she was Walsh's daughter and she was cute and the NYPD was under pressure to make a quota or whatever. Maura never complained though. Me, I got mad when people said stuff like that to her, but she just shrugged it off and said it came with the territory. She handled it really well."

I waited until I thought it was the right time to ask Renfro about her murder.

"Tell me about that last night on the street, Billy."

I could see how painful those memories were to him. I knew from all the previous stories I'd done about cop deaths that losing a partner was one of the most traumatic experiences that a police officer could face – almost the same as losing a member of your family. You felt guilty, you felt angry and you felt powerless. But I had to ask these questions. It was my job, just like his job was being a police officer and dealing with all the not so pleasant things that went along with that.

"There's not much to say," Renfro told me. "It was just like any other night. Our shift started at five p.m., we made maybe half a dozen stops at places – routine stuff, all of it – and then went on Code 7 to get something to eat at about 10:30. I left Maura in the car and went into a pizza parlor – a place called Delmonico's down in Little Italy, they make really good pizza – to get a pie. Sausage, extra cheese, but no anchovies – Maura didn't like anchovies. My God, I'll always remember that now. Anyway, that was the last time I ever saw her alive. When I got back to the car, she was gone."

"Do you have any idea how she wound up in that alley where she was found?"

"None at all."

"Something she saw or heard? Meeting with a contact? Responding to a call for help?"

"Who knows? Believe me, I've asked myself the same question over and over again too."

"What did you do when she wasn't there?"

"I waited by the car. I figured she'd just wandered off some-place to the can or something. After a while though, I began to get concerned. So I went looking for her. That's when I found her in the alley. I radioed the call in of an officer down, and the ambulance showed up right after that. But it was too late. She was already gone."

"What time was your call?"

"About eleven-thirty, I guess?"

He shook his head and stared down at his beer.

"It was just one of those things." He shrugged sadly. "Nobody's fault. It just happened."

"Right," I said.

But I think he was trying to convince himself of that more than me.

"Just one of those things," he repeated.

I nodded solemnly.

"Did you ever meet her father?" I continued. "The deputy commissioner?"

"Once. He stopped by the precinct in some official capacity, but he and Maura didn't spend much time together. Maura was really uptight about her family connections, always seemed to want to put a lot of distance between her and the Walsh tradition. She wanted to make sure no one ever gave her any special treatment. Besides, I don't think they got along that great."

"Maura and her father?"

"Yeah, she seemed to resent him for some reason."

Resented her father. Didn't get along with him. Interesting. This was the second person in the department who'd suggested that Maura Walsh and her father had a troubled relationship. That was an interesting idea to pursue for my profile about her. Maybe even to ask her father about – if and when I ever got an interview with him.

"Look," Renfro said, "I don't really feel up to talking about this anymore right now. It's still too fresh in my mind. You understand?"

"I understand."

"She was my partner, and I let her down. I'll have to live with that for the rest of my life. She's dead, and I blame myself for not protecting her better. A police officer is always supposed to be there for their partner. But I wasn't there when Maura needed me. I was off somewhere buying a pizza!"

He shook his head sadly.

"Helluva thing what happened to Maura, isn't it?"

"Helluva thing," I agreed.

There was something wrong here.

For one thing, Renfro never looked me directly in the eye the entire time we discussed the specific details of Maura Walsh's murder. Instead, he looked down at a beer he was drinking, across the bar at other people, at the floor – anywhere but me. This did not prove anything by itself, of course, but it was something I'd learned about people as a reporter. I called it lying eyes. Billy Renfro was lying to me about something, or at least he wasn't telling me everything.

Second, I didn't understand his story about the pizza. The 22nd Precinct – where they worked – was on the Upper East Side of Manhattan, maybe a twenty-minute drive from where Maura Walsh was murdered. There were pizza places all over the 22nd Precinct. So why did they go all that way downtown to Little Italy for pizza? Was the pizza really *that* good at Delmonico's? What the heck were they doing down there anyway?

Third, and most importantly, there was the problem of the missing hour of time. Billy Renfro said he'd gone into the pizza place at 10:30. He hadn't realized Maura Walsh was missing until he got back to the squad car – and radioed in the first call for help at 11:30. That was way too long. The first rule for a police officer was to always stay in contact with your partner. If a police officer can't reach their partner, he or she always expects the worst. But Renfro was out of touch with Maura Walsh for a full hour. A crucial hour in which she could have been saved, but died instead. It took Billy Renfro an awfully long time before he got worried about what had happened to her.

So what was Renfro hiding?

Who was he hiding it from?

And why?

CHAPTER 5

The heat hit me like a blast from a furnace when I left the air-conditioning of McGuire's.

Within a short time, I was drenched in sweat and wondering why I was still in this city during a heat wave. Maybe Danny was right. Maybe I should go on vacation. Go somewhere where I could sit on a beach and jump in the ocean and drink cold cocktails by the pool. Except I knew that was never going to happen. Not while I had a big story to do.

I headed back to the *Tribune* office. I took a Lexington Avenue subway down from the Upper East Side to 51st Street. Then I walked across town the rest of the way to the *Tribune*, which was located near Rockefeller Center.

It's really a terrific part of the city to work in. Rockefeller Center was where Jimmy Fallon, *Saturday Night Live* and NBC's *Today Show* had studios, so you'd sometimes run into celebrities on the street outside. Across the street was Radio City Music Hall with the Rockettes and all their holiday shows, plus the Rockefeller Center Christmas tree in December. In the other direction were the lights of Broadway and Times Square. No matter how many times I come here, I never get tired of the glamour and the excitement and the New York City feel of this area.

On my way into the newsroom, I passed Peter Ventura's desk. He was wearing an extremely wrinkled shirt and drinking black coffee. No one was exactly sure where he spent his nights these days. A while ago, his wife had thrown him out of the house when he finally returned home after an unusually long bender. Now Peter probably just drifted from hotel to hotel or spent the night with friends or whatever women he met in bars.

He once told me about an emergency plan he'd devised for when he couldn't find a bed: he'd simply go to a hospital emergency room and complain about chest pains. The standard procedure was for the medics to give him a cot in the ER and monitor his vital signs throughout the night. In the morning, when they couldn't find anything wrong, he'd simply get up and be on his way. This plan worked well a number of times, Ventura said, until one night he was woken up by the sounds of doctors frantically pounding on the chest of a patient lying next to him. It turned out that guy really was having a heart attack. "I had nightmares for a long time after that – in fact, it scared me so much I almost gave up drinking," he said in telling the story. "Almost."

"Do you know Billy Renfro?" I asked Ventura now.

"Maura Walsh's partner. Sure. I've worked on a few stories about him."

"What do you think?"

"Good cop. Why?"

"No reason. I interviewed him for my story."

"How's he doing?"

"He's pretty upset about what happened to his partner."

Even with all his drinking, Peter Ventura probably had better police sources than any reporter in the city. Cops liked him, they talked to him, they confided in him.

I perched on the edge of his desk. "Say, what do you know about Maura Walsh?"

"Everyone said she was a good cop too. Even if her father is a real prick. The people who knew her, who worked with her, said she was okay. Real shame about what happened to her. I'll tell you one thing I do know, though. The police brass are very worried about the lack of progress in the investigation. I found out they just shook things up and put somebody new in charge of investigating the Walsh case 'cause they're getting nowhere. He's called Lieutenant Thomas Aguirre. Hey, that could be a break for you! You must know Aguirre pretty well from what happened in Central Park?"

Oh, I knew Lieutenant Thomas Aguirre, all right.

I had mixed feelings about Homicide Detective Lt. Thomas Aguirre.

On the one hand, he was an arrogant, egotistical blowhard; a sexist charmer who routinely treated women as objects for his own amusement; and a media hound who would do anything to get his name and face all over the newspapers or on TV news.

On the other hand, he'd saved my life just a few months earlier.

So that last item probably trumped all the rest, I told myself as I went to see him in his office at the Midtown East Precinct, which had taken over the Maura Walsh murder investigation as of this morning.

That was the attitude I went in with anyway, but it didn't last long.

"Jessie Tucker!" he boomed when he saw me. "The woman who made me a star! What can I do for you, honey?"

Yes, I'd made the guy famous. He'd shot and killed the person who was trying to murder me when I uncovered the true story of what had happened to me in Central Park more than a decade before. It put him on the front pages and certainly gave him a huge boost in his career. Probably one of the reasons why he was in charge of such a high-profile murder investigation now. But I still didn't like him. Go ahead, call me ungrateful. But the guy just grated on me.

"Don't call me 'honey'," I said.

"Why not?"

"It's not appropriate in today's world to refer to a woman doing her job in those kinds of terms. You can call me Ms. Tucker. Or Jessie, if you prefer. But not 'honey'."

Aguirre just shrugged and sat down behind a desk in his office. I sat down too.

"What brings you here today, *Miz Tucker*?" he said, exaggerating the "Ms. Tucker" for effect.

"Maura Walsh."

Aguirre shook his head sadly.

"A terrible tragedy." He frowned. "I feel so badly for her father." He said it like he meant it too. Then I remembered reading somewhere that Walsh had been one of Aguirre's mentors in the department, who'd helped him advance to the rank of detective lieutenant. Maybe Aguirre had some feelings after all.

He brought me up to date on the investigation. Not that there was much to tell. There had been very little progress in the case so far, he said, which was one of the reasons he'd been brought in to take it over during the last few days.

I asked him about Billy Renfro.

"He didn't have anything to help us," Aguirre said.

"Don't you wonder what he was doing while Maura Walsh was killed?"

"He was eating pizza."

"For an hour?"

"What are you suggesting?"

"That he must have eaten a lot of pizza?"

"C'mon…"

"His story doesn't sound right, Lieutenant."

"So what do you think? Billy Renfro shot her himself? Or else he deliberately went off to eat pizza so someone else could shoot his partner? My goodness, the guy feels terrible about what happened. He knows he screwed up by being out of contact with her for so long, but nobody follows the regulations all the time.

You're barking up the wrong tree on this, Tucker. There's nothing going on there."

"Any possible suspects or motive at all?"

"Not yet. We wondered about her boyfriend at first. Well, her ex-boyfriend. They broke up a few months ago. He's a cop too, name of Charlie Sanders – works out of the Bronx. Breakups can get nasty, especially when both parties are armed like Sanders and Walsh were. But Sanders has got a pretty airtight alibi. He was on some stakeout in the Bronx the entire night of the murder.

"Look, Maura Walsh was probably killed by a junkie or crazy person or someone like that. He took her gun, killed her and then fled. Probably didn't even have a real motive or reason for it. Just a random act of violence – she was in the wrong place at the wrong time. Those are the toughest kinds of murders to solve. We'll catch the killer – hopefully one day soon – when her gun turns up on a hopped-up addict shooting up in another alley somewhere."

Aguirre shook his head. "Summertime blues, Tucker. Summertime blues. D'you know what I'm saying?"

I understood. "Summertime blues" was a term cops used for the spike in murders – many of them senseless ones – during the summer months in New York City. It always happened: when the temperature soared, so did the violent crime on the streets. Maybe it was because there were more people outside during the summer months. Or maybe it was the heat that made people crazy enough to kill for no apparent reason. But it made the job of a police officer even tougher than it usually was. Which was why many of them referred to July and August as "the summertime blues" from the old rock song sung by Eddie Cochran and The Who and a lot of other people. That's the way police officers sometimes felt about it too.

"And so, Lieutenant, you're sure it was just some crazy person – a senseless crime with no real motive – that cost Maura Walsh her life?"

"What else could it be?" Aguirre asked.

CHAPTER 6

The first place Walsh and Renfro had been to that last night together on the street was an Upper East Side strip club called Hands On.

I went to visit the place. I had no reason to think that what happened there had anything to do with Maura Walsh's murder a few hours later in an entirely different part of Manhattan but I decided to check it out anyway. Because that's what a reporter does. We check things out, we check out everything. It was a newspaper rule I'd learned a long time ago, and I'd followed it faithfully since on every story I did.

And since Maura Walsh had visited there first on the night she was killed, I decided to start there too.

I pushed open the door and walked inside. It was only the middle of the day, but the place was already crowded. I guess there must be a big audience for watching scantily clad women dance for men. Who knew? There was a stage, complete with poles for the dancers to slide up and down on, in the center of the room. Next to that was a long bar where men sat drinking and watching the entertainment. There were a few other women in the room, but because of the way they were dressed (or, more accurately, not dressed) I assumed they were working. Me, I had on a tan V-necked blouse I'd gotten on sale at Macy's and an old pair of dark brown slacks – I definitely stood out like a sore thumb. Or, as Raymond Chandler once put it in a book I read a long time ago, I was "about as inconspicuous as a tarantula on a slice of angel food cake".

Sure enough, the bartender hurried over and asked me what I was doing there. I told him I wanted to talk to the manager. He said the manager was busy in a back office, but would be out in a few minutes.

"Hey, sweetie!" some guy yelled at me. "Aren't you on the wrong side of the bar?"

"Yeah," another one laughed. "Get up on stage and let's see what you've got."

I ignored it all until a door opened in the back, and the manager came out to see me. He was a balding, trim man of about sixty in faded jeans and a leather vest.

He cleared his throat nervously when he reached me. "Ma'am, I think you may have inadvertently wandered into the wrong place? I really don't think you want to be here."

"And who are you?"

"My name is Martin Clauson. I'm the manager here."

"Hey, that's great, Marty. You're just the person I want to talk to."

I introduced myself and handed him my press card. He looked at it carefully, then shook his head and handed it back to me.

"Sorry," he said, "I don't like talking to the press."

I grunted. "Right. I'm sure you get a lot of media interview requests, huh?"

Next to me I heard a woman snicker. Clauson whirled around and glared at her. "Shut up, Bubbles!" he snapped.

The woman was a freckle-faced young blonde who looked barely old enough to have graduated high school.

"Look," I told Clauson, "I don't care about you. I want to talk to you about Police Officer Maura Walsh and her visit to this club on the night she was killed. It's listed in her police log as one of the stops she made."

"Sure, I remember her," he said. "I wondered if it might be the same woman when I heard about it on the news. Yeah, she was here that night."

"What was she doing?"

"What do you mean?"

"Well, she was on duty at the time. It was an official visit. There must have been a reason she came here?"

"Oh, right… we had a little problem."

"What happened?"

"Someone just got a little too boisterous with the girls. It happens sometimes."

"And that's all it was?"

"Yes. She left right afterward. It's a shame about her getting killed like that, but it had nothing to do with my place."

I rolled my eyes but I wasn't surprised. I didn't figure a guy like Clausen was going to tell me anything significant – even if there was anything to tell me. I wasn't picking up on anything out of the ordinary here, but still, I wanted to check out the other places from Maura Walsh's log that night.

When I left the Hands On club, I saw a woman standing on the street outside the front door smoking a cigarette. I recognized her. It was the woman that Clauson had called "Bubbles".

"That was pretty funny," she called over to me now.

"You mean my remark about how he must be a real media celebrity in this job?"

"No, the load of BS he was giving you about why the police-woman was here that night."

"He didn't tell me the truth?"

She laughed. "Ol' Marty's not a big believer in the truth."

I walked over to where she was standing. Up close, she looked even younger than she had in the bar. I told her who I was and she said her name was Nancy Wesley. Bubbles was the name they'd given her to use for the customers in the club.

"Why do you…?"

"You mean, how did a nice girl like me wind up working in a place like this?"

"Something like that."

"I need the money to pay my tuition."

"Tuition?"

"I go to NYU. I'm a business management major. I go to classes full-time, then work here part-time to pay the bills. It's only for a little while until I graduate. Believe me. I'm not going to be doing this any longer than I have to."

I nodded.

"Were you working the night Maura Walsh came in?"

"Sure. I saw her a bunch of times."

"She was here more than once?"

"The two of them were – her and her partner. They came twice a month. It was like clockwork. Then they would do business with Marty."

"What kind of business?"

"What do you think?"

"I have no idea."

"Picking up their money from Marty."

"Wait a minute… Clauson was paying them?"

"Yep. The Walsh woman picked up her five hundred dollars from him that night. The way she always did. That was the deal."

Damn. Not that cops taking payoffs was a new phenomenon in New York City. That kind of corruption has been going on for years. What was startling was that the daughter of the deputy police commissioner – the man known as the "Prince of the City" because he was so squeaky clean – was doing it.

But that sure might explain why Billy Renfro was reluctant to be entirely truthful with me about the details of that night.

"You know, she was a piece of work, that Walsh woman," Nancy continued, grinding her cigarette under her heel. "I mean, she looked like an angel but she took the money like a pro. Icy cold, no nerves, totally businesslike about it. She knew exactly what she wanted. Hey, I understand that – it's just the way things are. She's not the first cop on the take, she won't be the last. I'm not naïve. Anyway, it's a shame how things worked out for her. Getting blown away like that by a drug dealer or crazy person or whatever. Real bad luck."

It didn't take long after that to confirm Maura Walsh was definitely not the hero cop her family and everyone else had made her out to be.

The story at the apartment house where Maura Walsh and Billy Renfro had gone next was pretty much the same. There was an escort service – or, more accurately, a prostitution service calling itself by a fancier name – operating out of the first floor.

At first, the woman who ran it was reluctant to tell me anything about why Maura Walsh had been there. But when I told her what I already knew – and threatened to write an article about what kind of business she was really running – she agreed to talk off the record about Maura Walsh and Billy Renfro.

"It's the cost of doing business," the woman told me. "I understand that. I take care of the police, and they take care of me."

"You realize, of course," I said, "that paying off a police officer is illegal?"

"Yeah, well, try telling that to a cop who threatens to shut you down if you don't pay up. Besides, everyone does it."

"Who told you that?"

"She did."

I had no idea who the "informant" was who Walsh and Renfro had met with on the Upper East Side, but – based on the rest of their activities – it seemed likely that something illicit had gone down there.

And the bodega owner who was another stop on that night admitted to making payoffs to Renfro and Walsh too. He said they had threatened to write him up for all sorts of violations if he didn't pay them what they wanted. He paid.

The bodega owner then added a new piece to the puzzle for me.

"Are you working with the other guy?" he asked me, crossing his arms over his belly.

"What other guy?"

"The private investigator."

"I'm a reporter, not a private investigator."

"Well, he was asking me lots of questions about them too."

Why would a private investigator be checking up on Walsh and Renfro's activities?

"Do you remember the private investigator's name?" I asked.

"Uh, Walters… no, Walker… no, it was Walosin. That's it. Frank Walosin? He left me his card. Told me to call him if I remembered anything else on the two of them. Let me see if I can find it for you."

He came back a few minutes later and handed me a small white business card. It read: "Walosin Private Investigations – Friendly operators, friendly service, friendly rates." There was a picture of a smiling man below the words. Friendly seemed to be the key theme here.

But what did it all mean?

Was it possible this corruption thing had something to do with Maura's death? That it wasn't just a random killing, as everyone assumed? But, even if she was on the take, why would anyone want her dead? And why was a private investigator involved in it? I rolled all that around in my head for a while, looking for an answer… and got nowhere.

Also, the police investigating her murder must know about this too. I mean, I'd found out about all the payoffs she was taking pretty quickly. Apparently, so had Walosin, the private investigator. Maybe the police were aware of the corruption angle, but they didn't think it had anything to do with her death? They were probably trying to keep it under wraps to protect the reputation of her father and the department.

After I left the bodega, I took out my phone and called the number of the private investigator listed on the card the owner had given me.

"Yeah," a voice rasped on the other end.

"Frank Walosin, please."

"You got him. Start talking, but make it fast. Otherwise I'll have to bill you for my time, lady."

Friendly. Just like the ad promised.

"My name is Jessie Tucker, and I'm a reporter for the *New York Tribune*. I'm working on a story about Maura Walsh, a police officer that was murdered recently. I've been told you might have some information about her."

"Oh, I've got information. I've got a whole lot of information about Maura Walsh and her partner. Pictures. Video. Audio recordings. The works. It's all there for the right buyer, honey."

"Information for sale?"

"That's the only kind I deal in."

"What's your connection to her? Why are you looking into what she was up to?"

"I'm not telling you anything for free. Let's just say for now I was doing another job for someone. A personal matter. Anyway, I stumbled on this funny business going on with the Walsh woman while I was checking it out, and I figured it might be worth some money. Now the *Tribune* is a big newspaper. You must have plenty of money. So if you want to make me an offer…"

"How much? I suppose I might be able to give you a little something, if it checks out."

"Big money. You want to find out what I know about Maura Walsh, you'll have to pay plenty for it. It's the law of competitive bidding."

"What do you mean?"

"I mean I've got another potential buyer for this information."

"And you want us to get in a bidding war against each other?"

"Something like that. I'm offering that buyer the same deal as you. I'm open to the best offer. It's a seller's market."

No way the *Tribune* was going to pay big money for this kind of information, we didn't work that way. But I didn't want to tell Walosin that. Not yet, anyway. I decided to string him along a bit and see where that took me.

"How about we get together and talk about this?" I suggested.

"Sure. Talk's cheap."

"When?"

"Give me your number."

I did.

"I'll get back to you," he said.

"I could meet with you today, Mr. Walosin—"

But he'd already hung up on me.

CHAPTER 7

The final spot I knew Maura Walsh had visited before she and Billy Renfro stopped at the pizza place was the restaurant on the Upper East Side.

It was a place called The Hangout in the East 70s. It was already half-filled when I got there, even though it was only four o'clock in the afternoon. It looked like a popular drinking and meeting up place for singles. Everyone was laughing and having a good time. I was the only woman there who wasn't standing with a man. No big deal. I was used to being by myself.

I sat down at the bar, ordered some wine and told the bartender I wanted to talk to the manager.

While I was waiting, a guy slipped on to the barstool next to me.

"Hi," he said.

"Hi."

"You know, a pretty girl like you really shouldn't be drinking alone."

Terrific, the local Romeo.

"Yeah, well I have impetigo. Very contagious."

"Is that terminal?"

"Just itchy."

"I can live with that." He smiled.

I swiveled around on the barstool to face him. He was maybe thirty-five years old, with a shaggy beard and long sandy hair that hung down to his shoulders; wearing blue jeans, a gray T-shirt and sandals. He was looking at me with an eager, puppy-dog kind of expression. Under different circumstances, I might have been mildly interested. But not now. I didn't have time for this now.

"I'm waiting for someone," I said.

"Me too."

"Good luck."

"Thanks."

"Now, goodbye?"

He didn't move from his seat.

"Look, I'm here to meet the manager of this place," I said. "If you don't go away, I'll tell him you're hassling me."

"You'd do that? After all we've meant to each other?" He chuckled at his own joke and put his elbows on the bar.

"I'm serious."

"Okay, then I'll find the manager for you myself."

He made a big show of looking around the place, then turning toward me with a big grin on his face. "Well, Goll-darn! I almost forgot – that would be me."

"You're the manager?" I raised my eyebrows.

He nodded. "I'm Sam Rawlings."

"Jessie Tucker."

We shook hands.

"Why didn't you just tell me who you were in the first place?" I asked him.

"Oh, I was enjoying myself too much."

I explained to Rawlings why I was there. How I was a reporter at the *Tribune* working on a story about the murdered policewoman who had been to the restaurant on the night she died. He seemed very interested in the fact that I worked for a newspaper.

"I'm a writer too," he said.

"I thought you were a restaurant manager."

"I'm a restaurant manager *and* writer."

"That must keep you pretty busy."

"I'm actually a lawyer as well."

I looked at him quizzically.

"I went to law school and graduated and passed the bar, then decided that I didn't want to be a lawyer," he said. "I got a job doing corporate law, and it was b-o-r-i-n-g. What I really wanted to do was be a writer, but I learned pretty quickly that writing unpublished novels doesn't pay all that well. So I got involved in this restaurant. I manage it during the day, then go home and work on my Great American Novel at night. It's only a matter of time, I figure, until I become rich and famous."

"How's it going so far?"

"The novel or the restaurant?"

"Both."

"The restaurant's doing pretty well. I guess there's a lot of thirsty or hungry or lonely people in Manhattan looking for a place to go. The writing is kind of a different story. I'm a good writer, I really believe that. And a good writer can make it with a bit of luck and good connections. Everyone's looking for the next Stephen King or Lee Child or James Patterson. There's a lot of money being paid out to a lot of writers these days."

"But not to you?"

"It's a world gone mad." He grinned.

I asked him about Maura Walsh. He said that she and her partner came into the place about nine-thirty p.m. or so. They ordered something to eat and then they left.

"They weren't responding to any complaint of trouble here?"

"Not that I'm aware of."

"Did they talk to you?"

"Just for a minute."

"What'd they say?"

"They wanted to know if the chicken cutlet special was any good. I said it was a bit dry. My chef had an off day. They went for the hamburger platter instead."

"And that's all that happened?"

"As far as I can remember."

Billy Renfro and Maura Walsh had called in a Code 7 – a meal break to go to the pizza parlor – at 10:30. That was barely an hour later. Why would they eat dinner here, then go out for a pizza an hour later?

"Do you have a receipt?" I asked Rawlings.

"Huh?"

"The receipt for their meal. Do you have it?"

"Somewhere."

"Could I see it?"

"That's a lot of trouble to try and find—"

"I'll wait."

Rawlings started to get up from the barstool, then sat back down again.

"There was no receipt," he said.

"I figured there wasn't."

I told him what I had found out at my previous stops. He listened silently, playing with a swizzle stick on the bar in front of him. When I was finished, I asked him if the same thing had happened to him. He nodded his head yes.

"How much?" I asked.

"A thousand dollars each time."

"And what did you get in return?"

"They made sure we didn't have any trouble with the law. Look, it's a cost of running a restaurant in this city. Sometimes you pay off the cops, sometimes you pay off the mob –sometimes both. A couple of thousand dollars a month really isn't very much. Especially if it protects you from unpleasant hassles."

No, a couple of thousand dollars a month wasn't that much. Unless you were getting it from a lot of different places. Then it could really add up to some nice money.

"Was it always just the two of them?" I asked.

"Recently. For the past six months or so. Before that, it was Renfro and some other guy. I don't know what happened to him."

Probably Billy Renfro's former partner. It was six months ago that Maura Walsh got transferred to the precinct and became Renfro's partner. Did she have any idea what she was getting into? Or had she been already involved?

"Did you tell this to anyone else?" I asked Rawlings.

"No."

"Why not?"

"Who was I going to tell?"

"You could have filed a complaint with the police?" I told him. I picked up my wineglass and drained it.

"But the police were the ones asking me for the payoffs."

When I left, Rawlings walked with me out the front door and onto the street. He hailed a cab for me.

"Stop by again next time you're in the neighborhood," he said before I got in.

"I'm not in this neighborhood very often."

"How about lunch then tomorrow wherever you are?"

"I'll be busy working on this story tomorrow."

"Another time?"

"I'm busy a lot."

"Is that a no?"

"Maybe." I smiled.

"Well, at least now you know where to find me." He smiled back.

CHAPTER 8

"So what do you think is going on with the Maura Walsh story?" said my best friend Ellen Robbins as we pedaled away next to each other on a pair of exercise bikes at the gym where I worked out.

I'd just told her about the payoffs and kickbacks and bribes I'd discovered Maura Walsh was taking.

"I don't know, Ellen. This started out as a routine profile piece about the Walsh woman. But once I started asking questions… well, it turned into something a lot more complex and confusing."

"So why did you ask the questions?"

"Because I'm a reporter. And that's what reporters do. Ask questions to find out the truth. Someone taught me that a long time ago."

"Good girl." Ellen smiled. "You learned your lessons from me well."

Ellen was a high-powered book and movie agent now, but she used to be a reporter. She was a helluva reporter too. In fact, she was the reporter at the *Tribune* who covered the original story of my recovery from the attack in Central Park. We wound up becoming best friends – and it was her who later got me a job on the *Tribune* and mentored me as a crime reporter. I still valued her advice.

"Okay, I see three possible scenarios here as far as the corruption angle goes," she panted, easing up on her pedaling. "First, she was working undercover. Assigned by her father to root out dirty cops like it sounds her partner Renfro was. I'm sure you already thought of that possibility too?"

"Of course I did."

"Except it really doesn't make much sense if you think about it. Every dirty cop involved – especially Renfro – would be suspicious that the daughter of the deputy commissioner was a plant unless they were convinced she really was taking the money for herself. Also, once she got murdered, there would be no reason to keep that secret. The only reason for the cops not to talk about it was if she really was a dirty cop and they didn't want that to become public in order to protect her father's reputation."

"That's the way I figured it too," I said, standing up to pedal harder. "So she's not working undercover for her father. What else you got?"

"Second scenario, all the people who told you she was taking payoffs were lying. They were trying to set her up for some reason, maybe to get back at her father for something he'd done to them. Mike Walsh must have made a lot of enemies in his years on the force. But that seems like a reach too. You had a lot of people – different types, different locations – saying pretty much the same thing. That can't be a coincidence.

"Scenario three – and this is the one I like the best – Maura Walsh was taking payoffs, but she wasn't doing it for her own personal gain. She was doing it to embarrass her father. Maybe she even wanted to get caught. You said she had a lot of issues with her father, people told you they didn't get along. What better way to get back at him than tarnishing the hallowed Walsh name in the NYPD with a scandal like this? Sounds crazy, I know. But daughters do get crazy sometimes over their fathers. I mean, you know that better than anyone, Jessie."

I hadn't really talked about my father in much detail with anyone, even Ellen. But she knew enough to be aware that I never had a father – and that it bothered me.

"Of course, the bottom line is," I said, "that the corruption angle probably had nothing to do with her murder. It's just interesting information that emerged when I started to peel back the layers of her life."

I kept pedaling away furiously on my bike. Ellen was still on hers too, but she was barely moving her legs now. I could see she was ready to quit. Ellen didn't take exercise as seriously as I did, but then the stakes were much higher for me. Exercise had helped me to walk again after all the injuries from Central Park and exercise kept my body in decent working order now, even if I'd never be in perfect physical shape again. So I was fine with doing as much exercise as I needed to make that happen.

The gym where we were was actually a pretty massive health club facility in the middle of Manhattan. It was located on the fifth floor of a big building on Park Avenue South, near Union Square, not far from where I lived. The place had everything I needed: a large workout area filled with free weights, dumbbells, barbells and other equipment like that; a cardio/exercise room with rowing machines, stationary bikes and treadmills; and a swimming pool on the floor above the main gym. This place was my home away from home.

"Have you told Norman or Danny or anyone else at the *Tribune* about Maura Walsh being on the take on her beat?" Ellen asked.

"Not yet."

"Why not?"

"I want to find out more first. I don't want to smear Maura Walsh's reputation – or the reputation of her family – until I get all the facts."

"I wouldn't wait," Ellen said.

"I know you wouldn't. But I want to do the right thing."

"That's the trouble with you, Jessie. You have a conscience. That's the one thing I was never able to teach you as a reporter. Having a conscience about a story always complicates things."

She laughed and got off her bike. The workout was over for Ellen. Me, I kept going. I figured I'd do at least another fifteen minutes, then maybe swim some laps in the pool.

"Anyway, how's the love life, Jessie? Is it definitely over with that Logan guy from the West Coast? I really thought something might come of that."

I had too. Logan Kincaid had worked with me on a story about his dead sister that came out of all the Central Park stuff I'd written about… and we'd wound up in bed together. It lasted for a few weeks, but then he went back home to California. After that, the distance between us had pretty much doomed the relationship.

"We decided we would be better off just being friends," I told Ellen.

"Friends?"

"Yes, it was a very amicable breakup. I might even go out there to see him sometime later in the year."

"Three thousand miles is a long way to travel for a new 'friend', Jessie."

I shrugged.

"Anyone else in the picture?"

I told her about Sam Rawlings asking me out when I went to see him about Maura Walsh.

Ellen seemed dubious.

"And he's the manager of this restaurant you went to?"

"At the moment, yes."

"Do you really want to go on a date with some long-haired guy in sandals who runs a restaurant? You can do better than that. Strike one against Sam Rawlings."

"Well, he's also a novelist."

"Really?"

"Well, you know, an aspiring one."

"Strike two."

"He's also a lawyer."

"Practicing anywhere?"

"Uh, no… he said he didn't like it."

"Strike three and he's out! This guy really sounds like a loser." I sighed.

"I dunno, he seemed nice, Ellen."

"Nice?"

"Yes, there's a lot to be said for spending time with a nice person."

"Are you going to have sex with this guy?"

"I haven't even gone out with him yet."

"Not always a prerequisite for sex." She smiled.

CHAPTER 9

The 22nd Precinct – where Maura Walsh worked and where her father had once been the commanding officer – was familiar territory for me. I'd covered plenty of stories from there over the years since I'd become a crime reporter: murders, robberies, sexual assaults and a lot more.

But it had been a while since I'd been there, and some of the faces at the 22nd had changed. They were younger too, and there were more African Americans, Hispanics and women. There used to be a time when a woman cop was a rarity. That wasn't true anymore.

But it didn't mean the life of a woman cop was any easier. I remembered Billy Renfro telling me about the harassment that Maura Walsh had to put with. How he was surprised at how many male cops still didn't think a woman – even one who was the daughter of the deputy police commissioner – belonged on the force.

"Boys will be boys" was the excuse that was always given for how they behaved. I wondered if that would ever change.

Even now, there were probably cops in this precinct who said privately that Maura Walsh's murder simply proved that women weren't tough enough to be out on the street.

The commanding officer of the 22nd Precinct was a captain called Lee Florio. He'd worked at the 22nd for a long time, starting way back when Mike Walsh was in charge. Florio was supposed to be a protégé of Walsh, and he'd kept climbing rapidly in the ranks.

No doubt, his close association with the deputy police commissioner had helped that ascent. I hadn't been there in a while and I wasn't sure he'd recognize me at first, but he did.

"Jessie, Jessie," he said when I walked into his office, "you're a sight for sore eyes. You look great!"

Always nice to get a compliment. I'd lost a few pounds since I'd seen him last, so maybe that was it. Or maybe Florio was just being polite.

"I guess I'm getting better, not older," I said.

"The newspaper business must really agree with you."

"Actually, I think it's not drinking that lousy coffee you used to brew downstairs when I was hanging out here more often covering stories."

"We send out for cappuccinos now." He chuckled.

"Gee, if I'd known that, I'd had come back to see you sooner."

I do this kind of banter with people all the time, and I think I've gotten pretty good at it. The idea is to put them at ease, make them feel good – and then ask them the questions you really want to ask. Sometimes it works, sometimes it doesn't.

In this case, Florio brought up Maura Walsh before I did.

"We're all in a state of shock here. It's always tough to lose someone on your squad. But especially someone like Maura. She was so young, she was so good and she had so much to live for."

He shook his head sadly.

"Yeah, exactly. I mean, there are some things about her murder that don't make sense to me," I said to Florio. "Like the fact that her partner, Billy Renfro, goes to buy a pizza and Maura Walsh walks away from the squad car on her own for no apparent reason. Why would she do that?"

"Hey, things happen. Believe me, you're asking the same questions we've asked ourselves a thousand times in the past few weeks. Especially Renfro. The poor guy's a wreck. He's going to have to live with this for the rest of his life. Losing your partner is a terrible thing for any of us on the force. And because it was Maura and because of the way it happened… well, this was even worse for him."

"Is Renfro around?" I asked. I had been hoping to grab him for a few more questions while I was there.

"He's on sick leave. Still dealing with everything that happened."

"I thought he came back on duty?"

"He did. But he wasn't quite ready. Like I said, Maura's death really affected him pretty badly."

"How long is the sick leave for?"

"Not sure yet."

"That does sound pretty bad."

Then I put my next question to him as delicately as possible to see what his reaction might be.

"Was there anything going on with Maura Walsh that could have played a role in her murder, Captain?"

"What do you mean?"

"You know, personal problems?"

"She'd broken up with her boyfriend, but it seemed pretty amicable. They still talked, I'm told. And, as I'm sure you know, he was on the other side of the city when she died. So he was immediately ruled out as a suspect."

"Anything else?"

"Such as?"

"Drinking problems? Drugs? Gambling?"

"No, nothing at all like that with Maura."

"What about corruption?"

"Huh?"

"Is there any possibility at all that Maura Walsh could have been involved in some kind of illegal activity on the street – bribes, payoffs, extortion – that got her killed?"

"What in the hell are you talking about? She was a clean cop. I mean *squeaky clean*. She had to be. She was Mike Walsh's daughter, for goodness' sake."

"Yeah, I guess so."

Everyone seemed to say that.

"Maura was a wonderful police officer and she was a wonderful person too, Jessie. That's why this is all such a senseless tragedy for us to deal with here."

I spent some time talking to a few other people in the precinct who I knew, and I introduced myself to some of the new ones who I didn't. None of them told me anything particularly interesting.

Until I talked to one woman cop who said she'd been a friend of Maura's.

"It's a shame about Maura and her father," she said.

"What are you talking about?"

"Their fight?"

"Maura and her father had a fight?"

"Sure, a real blowout. It happened right in the middle of the precinct. God, everyone was talking about it. And why not? The deputy police commissioner himself standing screaming at his daughter at the top of his lungs, right here in the station house. He kept yelling at her, 'How can you do this? How can you embarrass the Walsh family name like this?' I'm not sure what it was about. Maura wouldn't talk much about it afterwards, even to me, and I was pretty close to her. But she did tell me at one point that her relationship with her father had been really strained for a while. It's such a shame – I imagine her father feels so badly about that argument now that she's gone."

"Do you have any idea at all what they were arguing about?"

"Maura never told us. Believe me, I tried to find out. But she kept it a secret until the very end."

Maura Walsh had kept a lot of secrets. I was finding that out the more I dug into her background.

The question was if any of these secrets had gotten her killed.

*

On my way out of the precinct, I stopped to look at a plaque that had been put up on the wall in honor of Maura Walsh. There was a picture of her standing in front of the precinct building – looking jaunty and confident in her blue uniform. Nearby, there was a picture of her father from when he'd been the commanding officer here at the 22nd.

"The thing is, we're like a family here," a voice said behind me.

I turned around. There were two uniformed police officers standing there. One of them was older, and the other one looked no more than thirty. I didn't recognize either one, but I looked down at their name tags over their badges. The older one was named Shockley, the other one Janko. Janko didn't say anything, Shockley was clearly the one in charge here.

"A family doesn't tell its secrets to outsiders," Shockley said, his voice low and serious. "A family doesn't dishonor its dead. The bond between the police officers at this precinct – and on the whole force – is something very special. We watch out for each other, we protect each other and, most importantly of all, we make sure that whatever happens in this family always stays within the family. You've been asking questions about Maura Walsh. You need to make sure that you don't do anything to dishonor her memory. It's very important that you understand that."

I had a feeling at that moment he was trying to send me a message. Or a warning.

I'm not sure which.

"Maura Walsh was a *good cop*," he continued. "That's what your newspaper story should say about her. That's what you should write about in your article."

"I just want to tell the truth."

Shockley looked over at Janko, then back at me and nodded.

"I'm sure you'll do the right thing, Ms. Tucker," he said.

CHAPTER 10

I had a decision to make.

I was sitting on what seemed to be a big story.

The prevailing theory so far by law enforcement authorities was that Maura Walsh was the victim of a random murder. She accidentally ran into someone or some unrelated crime on that street in Little Italy that resulted in her death. Wrong place, wrong time. That left the police with a lot of potential suspects.

But what if she was the target of the killer all along? What if the killer was someone she was doing business with – the illegal business of payoffs and graft – and something had gone terribly wrong between them? That meant the people she had come into contact with on that last night of her life took on a new importance in the scheme of things.

I sat in front of my computer in the *Tribune* newsroom and thought about the lead for a story I could write about it all, based on the information I'd uncovered.

> Three weeks ago, a woman police officer named Maura Walsh – the daughter of NYPD Deputy Commissioner Mike Walsh – was gunned down in Lower Manhattan.
>
> At first, it seemed to be simply a random murder.
>
> But now a *Tribune* investigation has uncovered a secret web of police bribery, payoffs and extortion that could have led to Walsh's murder.
>
> Here is the story as we know it:

At a little after eight p.m. on the night of July 12, Police Officer Maura Walsh walked into the Hands On club on the East Side. According to sources at the bar, she was there to shakedown the owner for a payoff. She was paid $500 – and then left. She then went through the same procedure at several other locations in Manhattan, collecting many hundreds more.

According to numerous people the *Tribune* talked with, it wasn't the first time Police Officer Walsh had taken payoff money.

But it was the last.

A few hours later, she was murdered while her partner was ordering pizza at a nearby location.

There are many questions about the circumstances of Maura Walsh's death.

And more questions about her life before that.

Who killed Maura Walsh? And why was Maura Walsh killed? And why are police apparently holding back on revealing some of the details of this tragic murder, only the third female police officer to die in NYPD history…

I stopped writing and stared at the words on the screen in front of me.

The truth was, I was uncomfortable going with a story like this. It still didn't make sense to me. Why would someone from such an esteemed NYPD family background like Maura Walsh turn her back on all that for some easy money? Why weren't the cops all over this as a motive for her murder? And, maybe my most immediate concern of all, what would be the fallout for me as a journalist if I printed a story like this?

I was a police reporter. I needed police sources to do my job. I would become the most unpopular reporter in town with the NYPD for smearing Maura Walsh's reputation (and the reputation of the Walsh family) by making this public – even if it was true. Just like the two cops at the 22nd, Shockley and Janko, had warned me about. I'm sure there were many other police officers who felt the same way.

And what if it wasn't really true?

What if I was missing something important here?

I also thought about the interview I still wanted to do with Deputy Commissioner Walsh, Maura's father. No way I'd get to talk to him if I wrote a story like this about his daughter.

Granted, this story might be better than an interview with the father at this point. But I still wanted to hear what he had to say. Especially before I blew the lid off this whole scandal his daughter was seemingly involved in with my story. Maybe he could fill in some of the missing pieces about his daughter's life – and death – for me.

On the other hand, Maura Walsh's secret life of corruption couldn't stay hidden for long. There were trained investigators trying to find her killer who were presumably taking her life apart as I sat here. Someone else must have found out the same things I had. They'd been working on the case for three weeks. I stumbled across the damning information on the first day.

So why hadn't they said anything about it? Why hadn't they done anything about it? Or maybe they had. Maybe they'd already told Walsh what they'd found out about his daughter. Maybe that's why he seemed so emotionless and seemingly uncaring at the press conference afterward. Maybe it wasn't just his daughter's death, but the circumstances about her life that caused the bottom to drop out of his own existence?

I needed to make absolutely sure my story about Maura Walsh's corruption was accurate before I printed it. Or even before I told Danny or Norman or Lorraine or anyone at the *Tribune* about what I'd uncovered. I still needed more confirmation about what Maura Walsh had been doing before she was killed.

I made a list of people and places to check out further.

First, there was Charlie Sanders, the cop who was Maura's ex-boyfriend. Normally, he would be a key suspect in her death. Romantic breakups are rarely completely amicable, and sometimes turn violent. Except Sanders had the perfect alibi. He was on duty in a squad car in the Bronx, miles away from Maura Walsh, when she was killed. Still, he might have known about some of the secrets going on in her life at the end.

Then there were the X-rated businesses she'd visited for payoffs: the strip club and the escort service in the apartment building. I didn't believe that the people running those businesses at both places were the actual owners. There's usually some kind of big money man – albeit an unscrupulous one – behind these kinds of shady businesses. It took me a bit of digging, but I eventually found out that both the strip club and the escort service were owned by a man named Dominic Bennato. Also known as Fat Nic Bennato. Fat Nic was a longtime mob figure in New York City, which I found interesting. Of course, mobsters don't very readily grant interviews to the media. But I wanted to try to talk to Bennato.

And finally I still had Frank Walosin out there, the private investigator who seemed to know something about Maura Walsh and was trying to sell that information. I hadn't heard back from Walosin, even though I'd tried calling him again a few times. But I did find an address for Walosin Investigations on the West Side just off of Times Square. I could go to the address and knock on his door.

I thought again about Aguirre using the "summertime blues" term to describe Maura Walsh's murder – and I wondered if that was the way this story would turn out at the end. Nothing to do with any of the information I'd uncovered. Just a senseless crime for no reason.

When I was a young reporter, I interviewed a detective who had handled the infamous Preppie Murder. That was before my time, but he told me how that case still haunted him. On a sweltering August night, a handsome, nineteen-year-old named Robert Chambers met pretty seventeen-year-old Jennifer Levin at an Upper East Side bar. Both had big plans for the future. Levin was headed to college in Boston in the fall, while Chambers' family had aspirations of him one day becoming a U.S. Senator. They left the bar together, walked into Central Park and made love under a tree. When it was over, Chambers strangled and beat her to death. The papers quickly dubbed it the Preppie Murder Case. In his confession, Chambers claimed Levin had forced him to have rough sex – that she had, in effect, raped him. He said he was only trying to protect himself when he accidentally killed her. Since he stood 6 foot 4 and weighed 200 pounds, while Levin was 5 foot 4 and 135 pounds, the cops never believed his self-defense story. But Chambers stuck to it through long hours of questioning. "Why didn't she just leave me alone?" he kept saying. To this day, no one knows what really happened to set off Chambers' murderous rage on that hot summer night in New York City.

"Summertime in New York City," the Preppie Murder cop told me, "you can't believe how much crazy stuff like that goes on out there on the streets during that time."

Why were there so many senseless murders like that in the summertime?

Some cops claimed it was simply the heat, a simmering inferno that rose relentlessly out of the concrete canyons, the streets and the subways of New York during July and August – and somehow drove otherwise sane people crazy enough to commit such horrendous acts.

Others argued it was just a matter of chance that so many big murder cases happened in the summer. They pointed out that terrible crimes happened at other times of the year too. It was simply the luck of the draw that so many of the worst ones had been during the summer months, they said. These crimes could have just as easily have occurred in November or March or January.

Then there were those people – and I was one of them – who believed there were sometimes greater forces of nature at work here. The cop in the Preppie Murder Case even compared it to those unexplained happenings in the Bermuda Triangle. Or like The Perfect Storm, he said – the story about three storm systems converging together to create a once in a lifetime storm of such ferocity and violence that it consumed everything in its path.

After years of covering crime on the streets of New York, I was convinced that there were indeed times when everything came together like that in a freak occurrence that superseded all the laws of logic and science.

A perfect storm.

Like Son of Sam.

Or the Preppie Murder.

Or maybe even Maura Walsh.

CHAPTER 11

I had the dream again that night.

The dream about being attacked in Central Park. At first, the dream was the same as it had been in the past. I was being chased through the dark woods of the park by someone wearing a New York Yankees baseball cap. Of course, I know now who it was in the park with me that night, I know who did all those terrible things to me.

I wondered how long I'd keep having this dream. The original attack on me was twelve years ago, and yet I continued to replay it over and over again in my sleep. Even after I finally found out the truth about what happened to me. Would the dream ever go away? I remembered when I was younger having a recurring nightmare about my college finals. I was supposed to take my final exams, but I didn't know where to go or even what courses I'd taken. I'd wake up in a panic thinking about that, but eventually that dream stopped happening.

Maybe that would happen to the Central Park dream too. Of course, what happened to me in Central Park was a lot different than hypothetically missing a final exam.

I was running in my dream again this time. Like I always do. Trying to get away. But then the person in the baseball cap is on top of me. Hitting me, beating me, doing awful things to me until I lose consciousness.

It always happens that way.

Except this time something was different.

Just before everything went dark, I saw a face. Not the face of the person in the baseball cap. I saw my face. Beaten and bloodied as I fought for my life. Except slowly, strangely, it became the face of someone else.

Maura Walsh's face.

I woke up with a start then and I looked at the clock. It was only a little after nine p.m. I'd fallen asleep on the couch in my living room in front of the TV. I was too wound up to go back to sleep now, so I got up and went into the kitchen to look for something to eat. I grabbed a bag of potato chips and took them back into the living room with me.

You didn't have to be a rocket scientist to figure out why I was suddenly seeing Maura Walsh's face in my usual dream. I'd come to identify with Maura Walsh, especially after pulling together all that stuff about her and her relationship with her father.

I wandered over to the office area of my apartment, munching on a handful of chips, and sat down at my desk. Even in Manhattan, with its notoriously small apartments, I had a pretty spacious place – enough for a separate office area to do my writing in. Newspaper reporters don't make a lot of money, certainly not in comparison to plenty of other occupations these days. But I'd become a national media star twice and all that publicity had translated into a bestselling book and even a made-for-TV movie at one point. Hey, I had never wanted to become famous this way, but becoming a celebrity crime victim (and surviving it) had helped me to live a comfortable life now.

Of course, the office in my apartment wasn't technically supposed to be an office. It's actually listed in the description as a "dining alcove", and I'm told that's what the previous tenants used it for. They apparently even had regular dinner parties there. But since I always had a lot of paperwork at home for stories I was working on (and never planned to throw any dinner parties), I figured a desk and filing cabinet would be a lot more useful than a dining room table.

There were printouts scattered around the desk at the moment. The printouts weren't about a story, they were about me. Or, more accurately, about my father.

I'd thought for much of my life about looking for the man who was my father, but I had never really done anything about it. Then, after I finally got some sort of closure about the Central Park attack on me by finding out the truth after twelve long years of lies, I began thinking it might be satisfying to find out the truth about my father too.

So I'd googled his name off and on when I had time, just to see if anything showed up.

I looked down now at some of the stuff I'd downloaded. My father's name had been James Tucker. Yes, my mother had kept his surname after he left – no doubt part of her effort to perpetuate this myth of him leaving us in some glorious and heroic fashion instead of dealing with the reality that he slipped out like a thief in the night.

James Tucker was a pretty common name. There was a long list of possible hits when I made my initial checks. But there were ways to narrow it down with his birthday, last known address (where he'd lived with my mother when I was born) and things like that. I just hadn't decided whether or not to do that yet because I wasn't sure if I wanted to know the answers that were out there.

My image of my father – no matter how flawed he was in it – might not be accurate. I'd only seen one picture of him – it was one that my mother kept. He was a good-looking man – very handsome with a roguish kind of smile that made him even more attractive. Maybe he didn't look like that anymore. After thirty-six years, how could he?

Did I want to see him as an old man now?

Or worse, find out he was dead? Or in prison?

Wasn't it better to just remember him the way he was in that picture and leave it at that?

I still remembered the day I found out the truth about my father. I was a little girl, in second grade, and we'd been assigned to write an essay about our dads for Father's Day. I based mine on everything I knew about my father. All of which came from my mother's story – or stories – about him dying a tragically heroic death.

The next day, after I handed the essay in to the teacher, I was ordered to go to the principal's office. The school counselor was there too. They asked me questions about why I had made up such an outlandish story. I had no idea what they were talking about. Finally, they asked my mother to come to the school. Eventually, the truth came out.

I was never sure about all the details of what really happened between my parents. All I knew was that my mother had given birth to me in the hospital, and my father had been there for that. Sometime soon afterward, when they had brought me back home, my father went out for a pack of cigarettes or something and never came back. He sent my mother a note explaining why he had left, which she found later. But she never told me exactly what was in that note.

I always wanted to ask her about what happened – to find out the truth about him leaving so suddenly and abandoning us like that.

But I never did.

You see, my relationship with my mother was a very troubled one too, even before I'd found out about the lies she'd told me.

My mother had decided that if she couldn't have the perfect marriage, she'd have the perfect daughter. And that's what she demanded of me in every aspect of my life when I was growing up: perfection. School grades, swim team competition, piano lessons, even the boyfriends I had – you name it. I had to be the best. Not for me. For her. That was an awful lot of pressure to put on a young girl already struggling to deal with missing father issues. And so, as soon as I was old enough, I moved away from her and never went back.

The final disillusionment with my mother came after I'd been brutally beaten – and nearly killed – during that horrendous attack on me in Central Park. She flew to New York and was sitting by my bed when I woke up from the coma I'd been in. Her first words to me were: "How could you be so stupid as to go walking through the park by yourself like that at night?"

I was in tremendous pain. I couldn't walk or hardly move, and my face had been bloodied and bruised. I needed love, not criticism from her. But I never got that love. Soon after, she went back home and left me to recover from all that had happened to me on my own. I knew why too. I wasn't perfect anymore.

My mother was dead now.

The only family (if you could call him that) I had left would be my father.

Assuming he's still alive.

I took another bite of potato chip now as I looked again at the printouts of information in front of me. Lots of James Tuckers there. Maybe one of them was my father. Yep, the answers were out there somewhere, if I really wanted to learn about my father. All I had to do was go find them.

CHAPTER 12

The next morning I was drinking coffee in a Bronx station house with Charlie Sanders, the police officer who'd been dating Maura Walsh until just a few weeks before her death. I'd drunk a lot of coffee in a lot of station houses with a lot of cops over the years. It was a tradition if you were a police reporter: you bought the cop a cup of coffee and hoped that would be enough for him to open up with you. It usually worked. The coffee/cop bond was a very important one for a police reporter like me.

Charlie Sanders was a youngish-looking guy – probably no more than thirty. He was good-looking, had an infectious smile and curly red hair, not unlike the red hair I'd seen in pictures of Maura Walsh. I thought about how they must have made a cute couple.

"When did you and Maura break up?" I asked him.

"Right before Memorial Day weekend. I remember because I expected to take her to the Jersey Shore for our days off, but she said she didn't want to go. Then she also told me it was over between us, at least for a while. She said 'we just need to take a break'."

"What was the issue that led to it?"

He shrugged.

"There's always a lot of issues in a relationship."

"Name one between you and Maura."

"Commitment."

"Meaning marriage?"

"That's right."

"She wanted to get married, and you didn't?"

"No, it was the other way around. I loved Maura, I wanted to marry her. I wanted to spend the rest of my life with her. But I guess she wasn't that into me. For a while now, we'd been growing more and more apart."

"Any idea why that was?"

"If I did, I would have tried to fix it. But I think it was about more than just me or anything I was doing or not doing. She seemed to be having doubts about everything in her life. I asked her what was wrong and she just told me she was 're-evaluating things'. When I asked her what she was re-evaluating, she said: 'everything'. I guess that included me. But it even included her being a police officer too."

"She was thinking of leaving the force?"

"I'm not sure. But she kept talking about how her father had pushed her into joining the NYPD. How he'd pushed her into everything in her life. And that she was tired of being pushed into doing things by him, now she was going push back on her own. I had no idea what that meant. And she wouldn't tell me."

"Tell me more about your actual breakup," I said.

"Why? What does that have to do with what happened to Maura?"

"I'm just trying to get a good picture of her for the story I'm writing, Charlie. I'd like to write something that can help people remember her for the kind of person she really was. Not just another crime statistic."

Which was almost true.

"Well, there's not much to tell about our breakup," Sanders said. "There was no big dramatic moment. It was more gradual. She got more irritable and stressed out and defensive about anything I asked her toward the end."

"Do you think she was seeing someone else?" I asked.

He seemed uncomfortable with the question.

"I don't know."

"Did you ask her?"

"Yes."

"And?"

"She denied it. She said it was all about her. She needed to be alone to deal with some things going on in her life. Whenever I tried to press her about what those were, about what was bothering her, she'd snap back at me that it was none of my business. But I guess the final straw came when I tried to get answers from her about the money."

"What money?"

"She'd suddenly started spending a lot of money on stuff for herself. I couldn't figure out where this money she had was coming from."

Aha. The money from illegal payoffs. Did Sanders have any suspicions about that? Probably not. Maybe with someone else he might have. But, like everyone else, he would never believe something like that was possible with the daughter of an NYPD icon like Mike Walsh.

"She traded in her car for a fancier new one," Sanders said. "She bought a lot of expensive clothes and jewelry. I found out she even put a down payment on a condo. I couldn't understand it. She'd never had that kind of money before."

"Do you think she might have been getting the money from her father?" I asked, playing dumb about my own knowledge of her financial dealings.

"Not likely. She never took money from her father before. She always made a big deal about wanting to live on her own, not as a member of the Walsh family. That was very important to her. Besides, she seemed really angry at her father. I don't think they'd even spoken in a long time."

"Did you know him?" I asked.

"Deputy Commissioner Walsh?"

"Yes. I heard he could be... well, somewhat officious."

"That's a nice way to put it. Walsh is a real piece of work. Ice-cold, no emotion. At least none that I ever saw. He knew who I was and that I was seeing his daughter, but he never acted friendly or asked me questions about myself or anything. I thought at first that he didn't like me. But then I discovered he's like that with everyone. I don't think he likes many people. Except maybe himself."

I nodded. I might not know much about what was going on in Maura Walsh's life at the end, but I sure had a pretty good take on her father. Everyone seemed pretty much in agreement on him. The guy was a prick.

"It sounds like she was going through a lot of stuff at the end," I said. "Anything else you remember?"

"Just the trips."

"Trips?"

"She used her off days to go on a bunch of trips before we broke up. All to the same place. She went upstate to this town called Saginaw Lake, a couple of hours north of here. It turned out she and her family used to spend summers up there when she was growing up. I figured that it was just some kind of nostalgia, but she got really weird when I asked her about it. Then someone told me she had a lot of bad memories from that place. Apparently, her brother died there one summer."

"When was this?"

"Oh, when she was a teenager and her brother was much younger. Some kind of an accident. The whole thing was so traumatic that the family sold the house and never went back until she started going recently. I figured she'd explain to me what was so fascinating for her up there whenever she was ready to do it. But then..."

Sanders teared up now. I felt bad for putting him through this. He seemed like a nice guy. I wondered why Maura Walsh would walk away from a relationship with a man like him.

"The last time I saw her I told her I loved her," he said. "I told her I wanted to help her with whatever troubles she was going through. She said I couldn't help her. She said no one could help her. But I told her I'd always be there for her, no matter what. All she had to do was ask. I truly believed that Maura and I belonged together, that she would come back to me at some point later. Except there was no later…"

Charlie Sanders began to cry now.

I tried to comfort him the best I could, but he was still in tears when I left.

Sometimes being a newspaper reporter isn't such a fun job.

CHAPTER 13

There was a message from Sam Rawlings on my voicemail at the *Tribune*. It was the latest in a series of messages from Rawlings. He'd been sending them since we met that afternoon at his restaurant. I'd listened to them all, but never called him back. Not yet anyway.

I told myself it was because I was too busy working on the story. But I also realized I was avoiding him. Yes, I found him interesting and… well, okay, attractive too. But I just wasn't emotionally prepared to go down that route with any man again right now.

Now, when I got back to the office after my meeting with Sanders, I found that Sam had left me another message. The messages all asked me to call him and left a number. I was still trying to decide whether or not to do that when my phone rang. It was Rawlings.

"Ah, the elusive Jessie Tucker," he said.

"Hi."

"Did you get my message?"

"Actually, I got five of them."

"Too many?"

"It might have been a bit of overkill."

"I'm persistent."

"If by persistent you mean acting like a stalker…"

"You got something against stalkers?"

"They're okay – from a distance."

"But you wouldn't want to date one, huh?"

"No, it makes breaking up so hard to do."

He laughed. It was a nice laugh. If a woman felt like laughing, she could probably do a lot worse than Sam Rawlings, but timing is everything when it comes to dating, at least for me. And Rawlings' timing was awful.

"How about we meet up for lunch?" he asked.

"I've already eaten."

"Then maybe a drink later? Or dinner?"

"I don't think so."

"If you go out with me, Jessie, I promise to stop calling you. Now that sounds like a fair deal, doesn't it?"

He laughed again.

"Sam, you seem like a really nice guy—"

"Uh-oh."

"What?"

"That doesn't sound good. There's a 'but' coming now, right?"

"Well, yes. The thing is I'm in a weird place right now with my life. I've got a lot of things going on. For whatever it's worth, I do think you're an interesting guy. I enjoyed talking with you. And I appreciate all the effort you've put into this. But I'm just not interested at the moment. OK?"

"You're sure you won't change your mind?"

"Maybe another time."

"So there is hope…"

"Listen, I gotta get back to work."

I told myself after I hung up with Rawlings that I'd done the right thing. The last thing I needed was a romantic relationship in my life right now. I was already on emotional overload and I just couldn't deal with anything more. I told myself that Sam Rawlings might be a charming, attractive guy, but there were lots of charming, attractive guys in the world. I told myself that I really didn't mind being alone.

I almost convinced myself of all that too.

Almost.

CHAPTER 14

"Have you heard anything about me?" Lorraine Molinski asked.

"Like what?"

"Like that I'm on my way out at the *Tribune*?"

"Um… no."

"You're telling me the truth, Jessie?"

"Absolutely."

I had this conversation with Lorraine every few weeks or so. That's about how often she became convinced the *Tribune* was about to fire her. Some of the reporters in the newsroom thought she was just being paranoid. I thought others deliberately spread the rumor to fuel her paranoia. If that was true, it really had worked. Lorraine Molinski was a walking bundle of nerves and insecurity.

"You're sure Norman hasn't been bad-mouthing me to the higher-ups? I mean, he's been here a long time. He probably thinks he should have my job. I'll bet he's out to get me. I'll bet Norman Isaacs is bad-mouthing me every chance he gets."

"Norman never bad-mouths anyone," I said. "You know that as well as I do."

"What about Danny then?"

"Danny Knowlton bad-mouths *everyone*. Not just you. You're being a little bit paranoid."

"I am not paranoid," she insisted.

"What do you call it then?"

"I just think there's a lot of people around me here that are out to get me."

"Uh, that's the definition of paranoia, Lorraine."

She smiled now. "Thanks, Jessie. I know you're the one person here I can always count on."

I assured her that was true. In any case, I had a reason for being so nice to Lorraine Molinski. I needed her on my side right now.

"I want to go to Saginaw Lake," I told her then.

"What's Saginaw Lake?"

"A small town in upstate New York."

"Why?"

"I think there could be an angle to the Maura Walsh story there."

I'd done some checking on the Walsh family and Saginaw Lake after my conversation with Charlie Sanders. On a summer day in 2009, seven-year-old Patrick Walsh – Deputy Commissioner Walsh's son and Maura's brother – had died in a shooting accident. The Walsh boy had apparently somehow found his father's service revolver in the house, began playing with it and the gun went off, killing him with a fatal shot to the head. Like Charlie Sanders had said, the Walsh family – which had been a familiar sight in Saginaw Lake during the summer months until then – left town afterward and sold the house they owned there. They never returned to Saginaw again, as far as anyone knew.

And yet Maura Walsh had made multiple trips there in the weeks leading up to her murder. Why?

Charlie Sanders didn't know and neither did I, but I figured that any answers I might find would be up in Saginaw Lake.

I told Lorraine now about the little seven-year-old Walsh boy's tragic death back then.

"What does that have to do with Maura Walsh's murder?"

"Nothing. But I think it would make a great human-interest story. 'Tragedy strikes the Walsh family twice.' First they lose their little boy in a tragic shooting, now their daughter is dead too. I go up there and tell the story in detail of that death, then I segue into the family having to deal with this second tragedy now. I think it would really tug at people's heartstrings, Lorraine."

"Have you talked to Norman about going to this Saginaw Lake place?"

This is where it got tricky. For me to go to Saginaw Lake, I'd need to rent a car to drive up there, stay in a hotel for at least one night and bill the *Tribune* for whatever other expenses I incurred along the way. It wasn't a long trip, but it was still an out-of-town trip. And Norman Isaacs was the person who usually had to approve any out-of-town trip for a reporter.

The problem was Norman Isaacs was one of the cheapest editors you'd ever meet. Maybe that's why he'd lasted so long in his job. He always kept the paper's expenses down to a bare minimum. Getting Norman Isaacs to approve a trip out of town for a story was like pulling teeth.

And Danny Knowlton wasn't much better. He was so ambitious for Norman Isaacs' job that he didn't want to do anything Isaacs could use against him with the top brass to show he was too young and too reckless and too irresponsible to take over the job. So Danny wound up being as tight with spending money on trips by reporters as Isaacs was.

I figured I had a better shot at working Lorraine on this one.

"Why do I have to go to Norman?" I said to her. "After all, you're the managing editor."

"I know, but—"

I stood up and sighed. "Of course, if you don't have the authority to approve a road trip for one of your reporters…"

"Who says I don't have the authority?"

"No one. Well, I mean it was just a rumor I heard. Probably nothing to it…"

"If I want to send a reporter out of town, I'll do it. I don't need to talk to Norman or Danny or any other goddarned person here! You tell that to everyone, okay?"

"I sure will."

Lorraine signed the forms approving my rental car, hotel and expenses. I felt a little badly afterward about pushing the buttons of her paranoia like that. But not that badly.

Next, I went back to Danny Knowlton and told him what I was going to do.

"But if you go out of town, you won't have time to file the piece for Sunday's paper, like we talked about," he said.

"I want to hold off a bit longer before I write it."

"Jessie, I've already penciled it in for the Sunday lead feature!"

"Even if I didn't take this trip upstate, I wouldn't be able to have it done in time for that, Danny."

"C'mon, Jessie, you know how to meet deadlines, just send me what you have."

"Look." I searched for some excuse. "I've… um… I've been having some health issues. They've slowed me down a lot on this. Like you warned me about, the attack affected me more than I wanted to admit. Both physically and emotionally. I'm not walking so good, I've got a lot of aches and pains and I've been having trouble sleeping too. Just give me a few more days on the story, Danny."

He sighed. I hated to play the victim card like that, but it did work most of the time.

"Okay," he said. "I know we owe you that. I'll go with something else on Sunday – and we'll push your piece back until the following week."

I mean, I knew I should tell Danny – and Lorraine and Norman and everyone else at the *Tribune* too – about everything I'd found out on Maura Walsh being a dirty cop. But for some reason I wasn't ready to do that yet – maybe because I harbored some kind of faint hope that I'd come across a wholesome explanation for her actions if I kept looking at her life.

"Make sure you give me the story as soon as you get back from this trip you're taking, Jessie."

"Absolutely," I said.

When I got back to my desk, I made some calls trying to get more information on the Maura Walsh story. I'd done the interview with Charlie Sanders, but I still wanted to talk to Dominic Bennato, the mob guy who owned the escort service and the strip club where she'd been that last night. Plus, the private investigator Frank Walosin who'd been looking into her activities for some reason.

I found a telephone number for the company Bennato ran – or at least was listed as chief executive officer for – and called it. I told the woman who answered I was a reporter for the *Tribune* and we were doing a story that might involve one of his business enterprises. She said she would pass the message on to him, and he would call me if he wanted to respond. I didn't get the feeling from the way she said it that was very likely.

After that, I called Walosin again. I still wanted to get some idea of what the private investigator had come up with about Maura Walsh. But there was no answer there. The phone just kept ringing. Probably out on some top-secret stakeout. Why didn't this guy have voicemail?

I'd have to try again when I got back from my trip upstate.

I shut off my computer and went home to pack.

CHAPTER 15

It was warm in Saginaw Lake, but not as bad as it had been in New York City. Less humidity or whatever it was that made the hot weather so uncomfortable. Probably because Saginaw Lake was near a… well, near a lake. That must be one of the reasons people lived in a small town like this.

The first thing I did when I got there was to meet with Dale Palumbo, the Saginaw Lake Police Chief.

I brought him some coffee from a Starbucks down the street as an inducement to talk to me. Not exactly original thinking, I know. But, since bringing a cop coffee was one of my tried and true traditions for getting police cooperation in New York City, I figured it might work just as well here.

Palumbo liked the coffee, except it turned out I needn't have bought it. He was happy to talk to me. I guess they didn't get a lot of big shot New York City reporters coming to Saginaw Lake, and he seemed to enjoy the unexpected media attention.

Palumbo was younger than I expected, early thirties. It was only a six-man police force in Saginaw, so I guess you could get promoted quickly. He had blond curly hair; was good-looking in a sort of pretty boy way; and had a picture of his wife and family face-out on his desk, just in case I had any ideas about mistaking his friendliness for anything more.

I told him how I was there to find out more about the death of seven-year-old Patrick Walsh when the well-known family had a summer home in the town.

"Why?" he asked.

"I'm doing a story on the Walsh family."

"But why now?"

"Well, because his sister just died in New York City where she was a police officer. I thought it would be a good human-interest angle to talk about the tragedy involving her brother too."

"That was her? Maura?"

He looked shocked. More shocked than I would have expected.

"I heard about a woman police officer being killed there. But I never really paid a lot of attention to the details of who it was. Otherwise, I would have recognized her name right away."

"Were you involved in the investigation into the death of her little brother when it happened, Chief Palumbo?"

"No, not me. I was barely out of high school. My father was the police chief here back then."

Ah, I thought to myself, *that might help explain how Dale Palumbo had risen to the rank of police chief so fast.*

"So why would you have recognized her name so quickly if you'd heard it?" I asked him.

"From when she was here."

"Back then when she was a teenager?"

"No, it was about six months ago. She returned to Saginaw Lake. Sat right in that chair where you're sitting now and asked me a lot of the same kind of questions as you. She wanted to know more about her brother's death."

"Did she tell you why she was so interested after all this time?"

"No, we never got around to that. She just asked me if she could go through the police files on her brother's death. I was happy to cooperate with her. I mean, she was a member of the family and all. Plus, of course, I knew she was a New York City police officer now and that her father was a big shot in the NYPD. So I showed her what we had."

"Did she tell you afterward whether or not she found out anything significant from it?" I asked.

"Not really. She read the file, asked me some questions and then we talked a bit about my father being the chief back then. After that, she thanked me and she left. She was a real nice person though. She seemed especially interested in how I dealt with following in my father's footsteps as a police officer. I guess we kind of bonded over that since she had the same thing with her own father. But that was the last time I talked with her."

"And you say this was about six months ago?"

"Right. It was during the winter. I remember because she was worried about driving back to New York in a snowstorm."

Six months ago.

It was six months ago too that Maura Walsh had transferred to her father's old precinct and become partners with Billy Renfro.

Was there some connection?

"Could I talk to your father about the Patrick Walsh death?" I asked Palumbo. "Since he was the police chief when it happened, maybe he could fill in a few more details about it for me."

"Oh, he's dead. About five years ago. From a heart attack."

"I'm sorry to hear about that. Was he still the chief when he died?"

"Yep. He left the force here briefly to join the NYPD himself. Not long after the Walsh boy died. But then he came back to Saginaw Lake and finished out his career as chief here. I took over from him. All I really know about the Patrick Walsh death was what I heard from him. And he didn't talk about it very much. I guess because it was so tragic. Can't imagine what it's like for Walsh now to lose his other child too. He's had all this success with the NYPD, but all this sadness in his life too. I guess I've been lucky. I have a good job and a good family. You really appreciate that when you hear about all the bad fortune that happened to the Walshes."

"Didn't you ever think of leaving this town? Maybe joining the NYPD, like you said your father did?"

"Not me. I'm staying right here. No NYPD for me."

"Why not?"

"My father's experience down there was pretty bad."

"What happened?"

"Not sure. He never told anyone. But he didn't stay there very long. Like I said, he came back here and went back to being chief until the day he died."

I thought about everything I'd just learned.

That his father had left the force to take a job with the NYPD after he investigated the death of the seven-year-old son of Walsh, who was a prominent police official with the NYPD.

And that six months ago, Maura Walsh had come to Saginaw Lake to ask questions and read the police file about her little brother's death – at the same time as she was starting a new assignment at her father's old precinct.

Was that all a coincidence?

Two coincidences?

Seemed hard to believe.

But then I had no other idea either about what any of it meant.

"Can I read through the police file you have on the Patrick Walsh case too?" I asked Palumbo. "It might have some details I can use in my story about the Walsh family and the loss of both of their children."

"Sure." He smiled. "I don't see why not."

CHAPTER 16

The Saginaw Lake police file on the death of Patrick Walsh wasn't very long and much of it seemed pretty routine at first glance. Like you'd expect with an incident that wasn't a crime, simply a terrible tragedy.

First, there was the police investigation – the report of the officers on the scene, interviews with family members or possible witnesses and evidence and photographs from the incident. Then the medical findings: summaries from the EMT responders who got there first; plus records from the hospital and doctors and other medical personnel there.

I read through the opening pages quickly, looking for something – anything at all – that I could use for my story.

I stopped at the report from the first officer at the scene, filed by Dale Palumbo's father, Police Chief Walter Palumbo.

At 16:37 hours, this department received a 911 call of a shooting at 221 Magic Leaf Lane. Myself and Deputy Greg Stovall arrived at the location at 16:46 hours. The lights were on, the front door was open and a TV set was playing inside.

We entered the domicile. In the living room, we found the victim – Patrick Michael Walsh, 7 years old. He was lying unconscious on the floor where paramedics were engaged in what turned out to be a futile effort to revive him. Also in the living room – standing over the paramedics as they worked – was the father of the boy, Mike Walsh, and his wife Nora.

It was determined that the boy had suffered a gunshot wound to the head, from a single bullet fired by a 9 mm pistol lying next to the boy on the floor. The pistol belonged to the father, who was a police officer with the NYPD in New York City.

A few minutes after we arrived, the medical team on the site pronounced the boy dead.

The parents – particularly the father – were extremely emotional, almost hysterical. The father threw himself on the boy's body crying at one point and talking to him. I and Deputy Stovall were forced to pull him away and comfort him so that the body could be removed to the morgue by the ambulance team.

The mother was also very emotional – which was understandable given the situation – and needed to be sedated by the medical personnel at the scene.

There was no one else in the house at the time of the shooting, the parents said. A sixteen-year-old daughter, Maura Walsh, was out with friends and had not yet been told about the death of her younger brother. An officer was designated to attempt to contact her to break the news.

Walsh and his wife Nora said seven-year-old Patrick apparently climbed onto a shelf in a closet and found a service revolver belonging to his father, according to the report. He then must have begun playing with it and accidentally pulled the trigger, shooting himself in the front of his head.

No one knew the exact details of what happened. But the little boy was dressed in a Superman T-shirt with a tiny cape – and the family said he loved that costume. One investigator speculated that the little seven-year-old believed that bullets would bounce off him like they did for Superman in the movies and TV and comic books. And that's why he had begun playing with his father's gun.

The final police report concluded that the boy's death was a tragic accident – and it was ruled accidental death by firearm.

All of that made sense.

There was a notation from Deputy Stovall – Palumbo's partner that night – in the file about the victim's sister. Stovall said he wanted to interview Maura Walsh to see if she could shed any more light on the events leading up to the deadly incident. But there was no indication if – or how – that was ever done.

It was an accidental death, plain and simple.

No questions really needed to be asked.

Except I had a few questions.

Like why was Walsh so emotional that night, according to the account I'd just read? He showed almost no emotion a few weeks ago when his daughter was murdered. But, on this night, he was so hysterical they had to pull him away from the body. Two totally different reactions to losing a child. Sure, the circumstances of the first death were different than the second, but not *that* different – it still bothered me.

Also, how did a seven-year-old boy manage to get his hands on a loaded gun? The police officers I knew who had kids kept their weapons unloaded at home. Or, if they didn't, they made sure they were stowed away carefully so no one in the family – most of all, young children – could get access to them. And yet little Patrick Walsh did just that.

Did this Deputy Stovall ever track down Maura Walsh and talk to her about everything from that day? If so, what did she tell him? And why wasn't it in the report?

Finally, and most importantly, why was Maura Walsh up here asking questions about her brother's long-ago death at the same time she transferred to the 22nd Precinct, her father's old precinct?

I didn't have any answers to those questions.

Patrick Walsh's death came before Dale Palumbo's time on the Saginaw police force. And his father, who had handled the case, was dead. That left the deputy, Greg Stovall, who Palumbo now told me had left the force not long after the incident. All I knew about him was that he had wanted to talk to the teenaged Maura Walsh after her brother's death.

Maybe he had some answers.

CHAPTER 17

When I left the Saginaw Lake Police Department, I called the *Tribune* office and asked for Michelle Caradonna.

"*Tribune* newsroom!" she said when she picked up the phone. "You make the news, we break the news."

"Do you always answer the phone like that, Michelle?"

"What the hell, it never hurts to advertise. How are you doing upstate there in Red Butt or wherever you are?"

"Saginaw Lake."

"Whatever."

"I need some help. I want you to track down some information for me in the *Tribune* library, or on our online information service or anyplace else you can think of."

"C'mon, Jessie, I'm not your secretary."

"This is really important. I need someone smart working on this stuff, not just a clerk in the library or whatever I can google up here on my phone. I promise I'll owe you big time if you do this for me, Michelle."

"You sure will," she muttered.

I told her I was trying to locate a Greg Stovall who had been a Saginaw Lake Police Officer in 2009 – then quit the force and moved away. I gave her the details I knew about Stovall, including his approximate age and description I'd gotten from Chief Palumbo – as well as his original hometown of Elmira, New York.

"So, how's everyone there?" I asked Michelle when I was finished.

"Well, Lorraine quit this morning."

"Again?"

"Right, she's already resigned three times this month."

In addition to worrying about getting fired, Lorraine periodically announced she'd had enough and was handing in her resignation. Then she'd go back to work. No one took it very seriously.

"She's still there, right?"

"As we speak, Danny is in her office. He's screaming at Lorraine. And Lorraine's screaming at him. Something about wanting to be treated with the kind of respect she deserves. Oops, Danny just kicked a wastebasket across the room…"

"Anything else going on?"

"Well, Danny's got a new girlfriend. This one looks like she's about seventeen years old. I met her last night, and I wanted to ask her if it was all right for her to be out on a school night."

I should probably explain here that Danny was not just an ambitious editor, he was also an ambitious – and amazingly successful – pickup artist when it came to attractive women.

Especially young women.

He'd been divorced once – a few years ago – and now he moved from one woman to another, never staying in a relationship for more than a few months. All of them were very young. Danny never went out with a woman who was over thirty. And he preferred his women to be under twenty-five.

No one quite understood how he was so successful with the ladies. He wasn't particularly good-looking, he was a bit overweight and his personality could be abrasive. But Danny – well, he just had this incredible way with them. He picked them up everywhere. Bookstores. Museums. Department stores. His favorite targets were struggling artists, actresses and dancers. He'd wine and dine them and somehow get them into bed.

Danny never messed around in the office though. He told me once that was a hard and fast rule of his. His breakups were usually quick and ugly, and I think he knew it would be a disaster if he ever tried anything in the newsroom. So he was never anything but professional with me and all the other women at the *Tribune*.

"Sounds pretty routine," I said to Michelle.

"Just another day in the *Tribune* newsroom." She laughed.

"Listen, Michelle, I really need this information about Greg Stovall in a hurry. So if you could—"

"Yes, ma'am," she said sarcastically. "I'll get right on it, Ms. Tucker."

I was definitely going to pay for this when I got back.

After I finished with Michelle, I called Peter Ventura.

"Peter, I'm out of town on an assignment. Upstate in a town called Saginaw Lake. Could you just make some checks for me with your sources about someone who came from here?"

"Yeah, I've got a little time on my hands, Jessie. The bars don't open for another hour yet."

He was kidding, I think.

"Who are you looking for?"

"His name is Walter Palumbo, and he was the police chief of Saginaw Lake about eleven years ago. After that, he joined the NYPD. But he only lasted there for a short time. He quit after that, then returned to Saginaw Lake where he wound up getting back his old job as police chief. But that was a while ago."

"You want to know where Walter Palumbo is now?"

"I know where he is. He's dead."

"What exactly are you looking for then?"

"I want to know why a man makes a big career move like that, leaves a little town for New York City, uproots his entire life – and then, very quickly afterward, changes his mind and goes back again. I'm not going to find that in the official records, Peter. But maybe you can track down someone who's still around who might had crossed paths with Palumbo back then when he was with the NYPD. Albeit, very briefly."

"What's this story all about, Jessie?"

"Maura Walsh."

"What does a small-town police chief have to do with Maura Walsh's murder?"

"That's what I'm trying to figure out."

CHAPTER 18

Greg Stovall didn't turn out to be hard to find. He owned a landscaping business about a hundred miles away in Elmira, New York – where he was originally from. It was situated over several acres on a road about a mile outside the center of the town.

Stovall said he'd started the landscaping company after he left the police force. It had grown so much in recent years that he had a dozen employees now. They did landscaping work for people in town – cutting grass, trimming trees, maintaining flowers and gardens – and also had a wide variety of plants and trees and shrubs for sale at the store.

"I always loved gardening," Stovall explained to me as he gave me a tour of the place. "Except I was never able to do much of it when I was a Saginaw Lake police officer. Then, after I left the force, I decided I wanted to do something that I really loved doing. So I started this business. We do pretty well. Especially in the spring when everyone wants to plant stuff and make their gardens look beautiful. Then in the summertime we do lawn mowing and hedge trimming and all that. In the fall, it's picking up leaves. And even in the winter we keep going by selling Christmas trees and wreaths and other decorations. But you didn't come all the way up here to ask me about growing grass and plants, did you, Ms. Tucker? What do you want to ask me?"

"I have a few questions about an old police case you worked on – the death of a little seven-year-old boy named Patrick Walsh from a gun accident."

If I expected him to be surprised, I was wrong. He nodded.

"I wondered when someone might come around to ask me questions like that," Stovall said. "Especially because of what happened."

"What do you mean?"

"The death of the sister. In New York. Maura Walsh."

"You know about it?"

"Sure. I might not be a police officer anymore, but I still relate to other people doing the job. It's a tricky thing about being a cop – you tell yourself you're not anymore, but there's a big part of you that still bleeds blue, if you know what I mean. The death of any police officer is especially difficult for me to hear about. But this one was even worse for me. Because I knew her."

"You knew Maura Walsh?"

"Of course I did. She and her father and the family came up to Saginaw Lake every summer. She was just a teenage girl then. I saw her and the mother and the little boy around town a lot. I didn't see the father as much, he was working in the city and coming up on weekends and vacations. But I knew all about him. For a police officer in a small town like me, it was pretty impressive having a NYPD big shot around. I tried to talk to him a few times, but he wasn't very receptive."

"What did you talk about with him?"

"Oh, I had dreams about joining the NYPD then. Becoming a real police officer, not just some guy directing traffic or whatever in Saginaw Lake. But he wasn't much help. He was kind of a cold fish, as I recall."

Yep, that sounded like Walsh.

"What do you remember about that night his son died?"

He told me pretty much the same story I already knew from the police file. The 911 call; the little boy lying on the floor with his father's service weapon next to him; the emotional scene with the parents; and the paramedics and EMT people declaring Patrick Walsh was dead.

I brought up the fact I'd found out from the file that Maura Walsh wasn't in the house when it happened.

"What did she say when you contacted her later?"

"I don't know," he said.

"You don't remember?"

"I never talked to her."

I was confused.

"The police report said you were attempting to track her down after the shooting to break the news to her and find out if she had any information on the events leading up to what happened."

"Chief Palumbo did that," he said.

"And what did she tell him?"

"He said she didn't know anything."

"That's all?"

"All he told me."

I started to ask Stovall what he meant, but I didn't have to. He told me more without any prompting at all. I figured out afterward that he'd been troubled by this for a long time himself, and the news of Maura Walsh's death had brought it all back to him again.

"Look, there were a lot of things we never got answers for about what happened that night," he said. "Or at least I never did. That's why I wanted to talk to the teenaged sister Maura. Even though she wasn't there when it happened. I really thought she might know something more about the events leading up to it if we talked to her. But Chief Palumbo insisted she didn't, that she had no new information – and was as shocked as everyone else when she heard about her little brother's death. Me, I wanted to question her some more. But Palumbo ordered me to stand down and leave her alone. Instructed me that I was not to bother the girl – or the father and the rest of the family – in any way. He said the investigation was closed."

I wasn't sure where he was going with this, but I was about to find out.

"What do you think happened that night?"

"Well… this is all speculation on my part, but I think it didn't happen exactly the way we were told. But the chief, Walt Palumbo, took me out of the picture. Never let me talk to anyone in the Walsh family, including the sister. Then the family left Saginaw Lake. After what happened, nobody blamed them. Too many bad memories in that house. But I always wondered about the sister and what she knew or didn't know."

"Did you ever ask Walter Palumbo any more about it?"

"Walt refused to speak to me about the Walsh boy's death. And then, not long afterward, he left to take a job with the NYPD in New York. Which was a job he had always wanted. I figured Walsh had helped set that up for him. In return for him not pushing further about the Walsh boy's death. Again, I have no proof of any of this. But that's when I quit the force. If that's what being a police officer was all about, I didn't want to be one anymore."

"And you never confronted Palumbo about any of it?"

"Once I did. When he came back to Saginaw Lake on the force again as chief. He only stayed with the NYPD for a very short time. I'm not sure what happened. But I always had a feeling he had a guilty conscience about the way he had gotten the job.

"He said that pretty much to me that time we talked when he came back to Saginaw Lake again as police chief. I thought maybe I could get him to talk more, but then he died. Anyway, all of this came back to me when I heard about how Maura Walsh had died. What a terrible tragedy for that family. The accident that killed the boy. Then the daughter's death like this.

"Completely different circumstances, of course. But it still made me realize the enormity of the tragedy that enveloped that family."

Different circumstances, all right.

Obviously one death had nothing to do with the other. I kept reminding myself of that as Stovall talked about it.

But I heard another voice too, one inside me. The voice of my reporter's instinct. That voice was telling me something else.

It was a helluva coincidence the brother and sister both dying from gunshot wounds, even if it did happen years apart.

And coincidences don't happen that often, I'd found during my years covering crime stories for a newspaper.

"Do you have any idea why Maura Walsh would have come back to Saginaw Lake after all this time to ask questions about it?" I asked, telling him about her trips and visit to Chief Walt Palumbo's son, who now ran the police force.

"No idea whatsoever."

"Did she ever try to contact you?"

"No, I never heard anything about her until I saw her on the news."

If Maura Walsh had been investigating the circumstances of the death of her little brother, she presumably would have tracked down Greg Stovall in Elmira, just like I had. Sooner or later, she would have had the same conversation with Stovall that I was having now. Except Maura Walsh just ran out of time.

Before I left, I asked Stovall if he ever missed being a police officer.

"Every day of my life," he said. "It gets in your blood, I guess. I haven't been a police officer for more than a decade, but I still feel like I'm a police officer inside. That's why I get so upset when I hear about something bad that happens to one of my brothers or sisters in blue, like Maura Walsh. I just hope they find out who did it."

"Me too," I said.

CHAPTER 19

When I got back to the city, I went to see Lt. Thomas Aguirre again to find out if he had anything new yet from his investigation. He said he did. He said that he'd solved the Maura Walsh murder.

Well, sort of…

"See that guy sitting in front of my desk?" Aguirre said, pointing to a short, nervous-looking man there. "His name is Elmer Tate. Elmer Tate just confessed to murdering Maura Walsh."

I was stunned.

"That guy really confessed to killing her?"

"Among other things."

"Huh?"

"Well, he also confessed to a kidnapping, three bombings and the murder of a top mob boss."

"Oh, Lord!"

"No kidding, I'm thinking we can clean up a lot of other unsolved murders on our books with him. Maybe he even did the John F. Kennedy assassination? I don't think he's got an alibi for that."

Whenever a murder gets a lot of attention like Maura Walsh's did, crazy, confused people like this come out of the woodwork to confess to it. I've never been sure exactly what motivated them to do that. Maybe it gives them some sort of purpose in their lives to live out this bizarre fantasy, since their real lives didn't have much purpose.

"No possibility that Elmer Tate here is telling you the truth?" I asked.

"He doesn't know anything about the crime. He couldn't describe her or the gun. And he wasn't even sure where the murder took place. Other than that, he's a perfect suspect."

"What are you going to do with him?"

"What else? I've called someone to take this fruitcake away to a hospital ward or whatever. I can't waste any more time with him."

A short while later, two EMS officers strode in. A young guy who looked like he didn't need to shave yet and a woman with long blonde hair she had bundled up inside her hat. They started to take Elmer Tate away, but he began to protest violently. Said they were supposed to put handcuffs on him.

"Other people get handcuffs," he said in a whiny voice. "I see it on TV. Why can't I get handcuffs?"

The two young cops looked over at Aguirre for advice. He shrugged and told them to put the cuffs on. The blonde-haired woman took a pair of handcuffs off of her belt and cuffed Elmer Tate's hands behind his back. Then they took him away. He looked happy.

"Does that answer any questions you have about how the investigation is going?" Aguirre asked me when they left.

"I've turned up a few leads that might help you."

"Lucky me."

"Do you want to hear what I found out or not?"

"Go ahead."

"First off, did you know Maura Walsh had been making regular trips in the weeks before her death to Saginaw Lake in upstate New York? That's where her family had a summer house when she was growing up. And where her little brother died in a gunshot accident when she was a teenager. She was asking a lot of questions up there about her brother's death."

I gave him a rundown of what else I'd found out up there.

"So what?" he asked when I was finished.

"It seems like very unusual behavior."

"How could the accidental death of a little boy years ago have anything to do with the murder of a police officer on the streets of Manhattan today, Tucker?"

"I don't know, I'm just flailing around here."

"Gee, I sure hope the other leads you want to tell me are better than this one."

I decided to run the payoff stuff past him and see what his reaction was.

"I've heard rumors that Maura Walsh may have been corrupt – taking bribes and payoffs and kickbacks from businesses."

"The deputy commissioner's daughter? That's crazy."

"I got a call from a private investigator. He said he'd been trailing her for some reason and had evidence of illegal things she was doing. He offered to sell me the information."

"That doesn't mean anything," Aguirre said. "He was probably just talking, trying to make a quick buck for himself. Sounds like a real shady operator."

I told him then about people at the various spots she'd been on her last night who said Maura Walsh was taking payoffs, but I didn't give him any specific names. Not without checking first with Rawlings or any of the others. So he pretty much shrugged that off too as hearsay evidence.

"You haven't found out anything at all about the angle that Maura Walsh might have been a corrupt cop?" I asked.

"No, and I'm not going to go around talking about something like that in this building either. Not with the deputy commissioner himself breathing down my neck on this case. He wants results, and that's what I'm looking for. I don't have time to chase down crazy rumors like that. Especially irresponsible ones that might ruin the reputation of his daughter and his family."

But these weren't just rumors. The evidence was there. I'd found it out pretty quickly. So had Walosin. Why couldn't the police find the evidence that Maura Walsh was dirty? Or maybe they had and they were all trying to cover it up to protect the reputation of the Walsh family. Would they really do that? Maybe, if they believed the corruption had nothing to do with her murder. Which seemed so far to be the case, from what Aguirre told me.

"Look, it's like I told you before. Maura Walsh was probably killed by a junkie or crazy person or someone like that. He took her gun, killed her and then fled. Probably didn't even have a real motive or reason for it. Just a random act of violence for no reason at all. Those are the toughest kinds of murders to solve."

CHAPTER 20

"I need your advice on something," I said to Ellen.

"Personal or professional?"

"Personal, I guess."

"Yikes!"

"What does that mean?"

"Just that whenever you come to me for advice about your personal life, it usually gets messy. Like it did with Logan. This isn't about Sam Rawlings, is it?"

I shook my head no. "There's nothing happening between Sam and me. It was just a few minutes of flirtation between us. That's all."

"So, what did you come here for my advice on?"

We were sitting in Ellen's office in a skyscraper downtown not far from Wall Street. It was an impressive office. Ellen had done well for herself since leaving journalism. She'd done well for me too, helping to guide me through the media onslaught that threatened to envelop me during all the publicity over the Central Park attack. Both in the years after the original attack – and then the latest one where I broke the big story about it all.

But this time I was there about something different. I remembered a few years ago Ellen had made a lot of money representing an author who'd tracked her family roots back to the days of being a slave in the Deep South – then written a moving, very emotional and highly acclaimed book about what it meant to her life today. It wound up being a bestseller; she was interviewed on *Dr. Phil* and a lot of other programs; and the book even got turned into a TV movie. Ellen mentioned to me back then that she'd been so intrigued by the idea that she'd signed up for Ancestry.com or one of those services to look into her own background. I didn't ask her a lot of questions about it at the time, but now I was interested in finding out as much as I could about the whole process.

"Genealogy," I said now.

"Genealogy?"

"More specifically, finding a parent through genealogy."

I thought she might laugh or make a smart-ass remark or at least act surprised. But she didn't bat an eye or do any of those things.

"I'm listening," she said.

I talked about the genealogy stuff she'd told me in the past. "I was hoping you could tell me more of what you found out. How to go about it. What should I do or not do. How much it costs. Anything you can still remember…"

"I assume this is about you looking for your father?"

I'd told Ellen some stuff about what happened to my father and how he fell off the face of the earth after I was born. But I'd never gone into much detail with her. This time I did. I went through it all – including my recent efforts to find some trace of my father on the Internet.

"Do you think your father wants to be found?" Ellen asked when I was finished.

"Probably not."

"That makes it harder."

"Or he could be dead."

"Even more difficult."

"Are you saying it's impossible then?"

"I'm saying it wouldn't necessarily be easy. And it may not be successful. And, on top of that, it can cost a lot and take a lot of time. But, if you're determined to hunt down your father, I'll take you through what I know about the process."

She said the first step was to find out whatever information I could through the biggest genealogy sites out there. She also told me to send a DNA sample to them. You submitted your DNA to them, she explained, then they tried to match it with other DNA samples in their database.

"The problem is that there's a separate DNA base for each site. So if your father submitted his DNA at some point to Ancestry, and you're on another site, you won't be able to find a match. You'd have to sign up for all the sites to get a real shot at finding someone. Or at least the biggest ones.

"Now if your father never submitted DNA to any of the sites – which he probably didn't, unless he went looking for you too – then there's still a chance you might find other relatives who will help you find him. Still, I wouldn't get your hopes up."

We talked more about my preliminary efforts on Google to get names that could be my father – and how difficult it was to narrow that long list down to real possibilities.

"I'd suggest going to a genealogy investigator," she said. "They use a lot of methods – including old-fashioned investigative ones – to track down relatives. Maybe they could do it with your father? Or at least tell you what happened to him. I'll give you some information to contact one of them. Let me warn you about one thing though: a genealogy investigation like this can take a long time and eat up a lot of money. Take my word for it, Jessie."

"Wow, you know a lot about this," I said.

"I should. I spent a lot of time on it. I hired a genealogy investigator myself after that book deal. I really got hooked on the idea."

"Who were you looking for?"

"My birth parents."

Now I was the one who was surprised.

"I'm adopted," Ellen told me. "Given away at birth. Sorry if I never mentioned, but the thing is, my adoptive parents are great. I didn't need to find my biological parents for them to tell me they really loved me or any of that crap. No, my reason was more practical. I learned that my biological mother had a lot of health problems, even at a young age. The kind of thing that's genetic so I wanted to know what my medical background was. From what I was able to find out, I had a bad family history. Lots of relatives dying very young. I could too if the pattern holds. Maybe that's why I do some of things I do – why I'm in such a hurry to make money and make a name for myself in this business I'm in now. I don't know how much time I have left. So I want to take advantage of every minute of it I can."

I nodded solemnly. This was all news to me, but clearly Ellen hadn't wanted to share it until now.

"Did you ever find out all the answers you were looking for?"

"Oh, I found both of them."

"What happened?"

"Nothing. I decided I didn't want to contact them. I didn't want to find out any more about them. I was afraid the answers would be something I didn't like. Sometimes you're better off not knowing about your past. Did you ever think about that with your father? Maybe you don't want to find out he's dead or sick or whatever really became of him."

I knew exactly what Ellen was saying. It was why I never went looking for him in the past. But that had changed now.

Maybe because finding out what really happened to me in Central Park had finally given me a sense of closure (or at least as much closure as I could ever have) about that horrific event – but still left me wanting answers now about the rest of my life.

Maybe because all the things I'd learned about Maura Walsh and her troubled relationship with her father had unleashed long-buried feelings and emotions inside of me about my own family past.

Either way, and it was probably a combination of these two things, I had decided it was time for me to confront the one truth I'd been running away from all my life.

"I want to know about my father," I told Ellen.

CHAPTER 21

I was back at my desk in the newsroom the next morning, reading through the *Tribune* to catch up on any news I might have missed while I was out of town, when I saw a story that almost made me spill my coffee.

It wasn't on Page 1. Not Page 2 either. Or Page 3 or 13 or even 23. It was a column the *Tribune* ran called The Crime Blotter, buried at the back of the paper between the crossword puzzle and horoscope. The article was three paragraphs long and said only:

> A man was found shot to death in a Times Square office building yesterday.
>
> The victim was identified as Francis (Frank) Walosin, who operated a private investigation service on W. 47th Street.
>
> Police said Walosin had apparently been dead for several days, possibly for as long as a week. There was no known motive for the shooting, according to authorities.

Frank Walosin, private investigator. Friendly rates, friendly service. He had some information about Maura Walsh, he said. Wanted to sell it to someone. And now here he was murdered.

Of course, there was no way to be certain his death had anything to do with the information about Maura Walsh. Walosin's murder could have been about anything – robbery, personal dispute, another case he was working on. To suggest anything more than that at this point was just supposition, hypothesis and jumping to conclusions on my part.

Still, I was ready to jump to those conclusions.

And it sounded like he'd been killed soon after his phone call to me where he said he had "another customer" for the Maura Walsh secrets he knew.

He probably was already dead the last time I'd tried to reach him, when the phone just rang and rang in his office.

Did Walosin see what went down that last night in Little Italy with Maura Walsh? Did he know who her killer was? If he'd offered the material to the person who actually murdered Maura Walsh, the killer might have decided it was easier to eliminate Walosin instead of paying him. That all added up to a possible motive for murder in the Maura Walsh case too.

The police didn't realize that though because they didn't have the information I had – there was no reason to connect the private investigator's murder to the death of a hero woman police officer the way I did.

But I still had to figure out where that link led.

Or if it led anywhere.

The biggest question I had was this: why would a sleazy private investigator like Frank Walosin, who specialized in keyhole peeping and cheating spouses and other low-level cases, be chasing after a police officer like Maura Walsh?

Blackmail?

Maybe. Maybe that's who Maura Walsh had gone to see on that last stop. Frank Walosin. To pay him to keep the evidence of all the payoffs quiet and not alert the authorities to her illegal activities. Could that mean Walosin killed Maura Walsh? But why would he do that if he hoped to make money out of it from her? And if Walosin killed Walsh, then who killed Walosin?

None of this made any sense at all to me – no matter how many ways I tried to approach it.

Okay, I needed to look at it from a different angle.

Frank Walosin made a living getting paid by people to do sleazy snooping jobs. That meant someone must have hired him to snoop on Maura Walsh. There had to be a client. Maybe if I could track down the client, I could find out more about the connection between Walosin and Maura Walsh's death.

I went through all the possibilities I could think of.

First, the people on Maura's beat that were being shaken down. The escort service, the strip club – hell, even Sam Rawlings. Maybe one of them wanted proof of what she was doing. Except they already knew she was taking payoffs, so why would they need more corroboration beyond that? Maybe someone in the police department that was out to get her? But they would presumably just go through Internal Affairs or some other official agency, not go to a PI like Walosin.

Then there was Charlie Sanders. Walosin specialized in cheating spouses and girlfriends and romantic entanglements like that. Sanders said Maura had ended her relationship with him because she said she had "other things she wanted to pursue". Maybe one of those other things was another man.

What if Sanders had hired Walosin to spy on Maura to find out if she was seeing someone? Walosin took the job, but then stumbled onto the payoff angle and figured he could get an even bigger payday from that than Maura Walsh's sex life.

Yep, Charlie Sanders sort of made sense as Walosin's client.

Except he didn't really.

Sanders was a police officer. A pretty respected police officer from what I'd found out about him. He would never have gone to someone like Walosin no matter how much he wanted information about Maura Walsh and a new man.

The one name that intrigued me the most in all this was Dominic Bennato. I'd found out earlier that the mob boss owned two of the businesses – the strip bar and the escort service – where Maura Walsh had taken payoffs before her murder. And Bennato, from everything I'd heard about him, was certainly a man capable of murder. More than capable of it. He'd been linked to dozens of murders over the years, even though he'd never been convicted of any of them.

I asked Michelle Caradonna, who sat next to me, what she knew about Bennato. Michelle had done a big series for the paper a while ago called "Real-Life Tony Sopranos" – about all the mob bosses in the New York City/New Jersey area. Bennato had been one of the bosses she focused on.

"Scary guy," she said to me.

"How scary?"

"Well, he seems like a decent and personable guy when you meet him. Almost likeable in a bizarre kind of mobster way. But then you find out the things he's done – murders, kidnappings, beatings and a lot more. That's the scary thing. The fact that you don't realize how scary he is makes him even scarier when you find out about the real Dominic Bennato."

I called Bennato's number again, and I left another message that I wanted to talk to him. I didn't really expect to get a response from this one – any more than with the previous messages I'd left there. And, even if I did manage to get an interview with Bennato, I didn't figure he was going to admit knowing anything about Maura Walsh's murder to me. So why was I wasting my time trying? Because that's what a reporter like me does. I just keep asking questions, even if I don't get any response. You never know. Sometimes it leads you to the right answers in the end.

Meanwhile, I still hadn't heard back from my NYPD source about getting an interview with Deputy Commissioner Walsh.

I wanted that interview more than ever now because of all the things I'd found out were going on in the Walsh family – and also this new development with the murder of the PI Walosin.

Walosin's death might have nothing to do with Maura Walsh. He was a sleazy PI who could have been killed because of some sleazy client or some sleazy case or some sleazy enemy he'd made along the way in his snooping. But I wouldn't know that for sure until I found out more about what was going on with Maura Walsh at the end of her life.

Which was why I wanted to talk to her father.

Even though I was pretty sure Walsh – given everything I'd found out about his uptight personality – would never really open up emotionally to me or shed much light on most of those questions I had about his daughter's murder or the death of her little brother in Saginaw Lake or anything else.

But maybe there was another member of the family who would.

His wife.

Maura's mother.

Her name was Nora Walsh, and they'd been married for more than thirty years. But she barely had been mentioned in anything I'd read about the Walsh family, except for that police report in Saginaw Lake. I could make a formal request through the NYPD to interview her, but I didn't think that would get me any further than my own efforts to meet with the deputy commissioner.

And I'd learned a long time ago as a reporter that the best way to score an interview was not to sit back and wait for it to happen – but instead to use some old-school journalism methods by just showing up and knocking on the door.

So I decided to go knock on Mrs. Walsh's door.

CHAPTER 22

Deputy Police Commissioner Walsh and his wife lived in Roslyn, an upper middle-class community in Nassau County out on Long Island.

It's about a forty-minute ride on the Long Island Railroad to get there under normal conditions. But it took me nearly an hour and a half because of a lot of train delays at Penn Station. I used the time to think about the questions I was going to ask her, assuming she would even talk to me.

A little before eleven a.m., I stood in front of the Walsh address. It was a pleasant-looking two-story red brick house at the end of a cul-de-sac. There was a long green lawn sloping down to the street, with two mid-sized maple trees standing near the house. Near the front door were two metal swans along with a welcome mat that said, "Welcome to Our Home."

The swans looked beautiful, but battered – as if they'd been standing at their posts in front of the house for a long time. They'd probably been here ever since the two young Walsh children were growing up, and the swans were once supposed to signify the joy inside this house.

But now both children were dead, and I didn't figure anyone inside cared much about the swans anymore.

I stared at the house for a few minutes before I went to the door. The sun was beating down on me. I wanted to get out of the sun, go into an air-conditioned house for a bit of relief. But I still dreaded what I was about to do. This was the part of the job

I hated. *Excuse me, Mrs. Walsh, but I'd like to talk to you about how your daughter was murdered. Oh, and I just found out your daughter was a crook and a shakedown artist too. What do you think about that? Our readers want to know.*

Then I walked past the two metal swans, climbed up the steps and rang the doorbell.

The door opened and a woman of about fifty stood there. She had freckles on her face, traces of red mixed with gray in her hair – she looked like an older version of pictures I'd seen of Maura. Obviously her mother, Nora Walsh.

"Hello, can I help you?" she asked.

"My name is Jessie Tucker, and I'm a reporter with the *New York Tribune.*"

Nora Walsh stared at me and said nothing.

"It's about your daughter. There are some things I'd like to discuss with you."

More staring.

"Look, Mrs. Walsh," I said finally, "it's really hot out here. And I had a long trip out from New York City so I'm tired and thirsty. I really could use something to drink. Do you think maybe I could come inside for a few minutes? If you want me to leave after that, I'll leave. Okay?"

She smiled slightly. "Okay."

We went into the living room. It was a large, airy room, decorated in Early American style, with a big window overlooking the trees and the swan figures outside. On the wall were pictures of people in police uniforms. Mike Walsh. The grandfather. Lots of other relatives. And a big one overlooking the fireplace of Maura.

"Is your husband home?" I asked.

Mrs. Walsh shook her head. "Oh, no, he's at work. He never misses a day of work. Even when… well, even with what happened with Maura, he still went to work the next day."

Of course. I remembered him and the way he looked at the press conference. Standing tall, erect – almost proud. *Daughter died in the line of duty, you know. Good for the family tradition. Police blue through and through.*

"You said you'd like something to drink?" Mrs. Walsh asked.

"Sure. Iced coffee would be good."

"I'm sorry. I don't have any."

"Okay, maybe just some regular coffee then?"

"Er… no, we don't have that either. You see, my husband doesn't believe in any kind of stimulants. Alcohol. Drugs. Even coffee. So we don't have any in the house."

Wow! Living with this guy must be a real bundle of laughs.

"We do have some juice," she suggested. "Or herbal tea."

"Tea would be fine."

She returned a few minutes later carrying a silver tray with two cups and a teapot. I poured some tea into a cup and looked around for the sugar. There didn't seem to be any. I asked Mrs. Walsh for some.

"We don't have sugar," she said.

"Don't tell me – your husband doesn't approve of it."

"He feels sugar is unhealthy," she said.

"Right."

I took a sip of the tea. It tasted bland. There were several slices of lemon on the tray next to the teapot. I took one and squeezed it into the tea for flavor. I hoped that was okay with her husband.

"I'm trying to do a profile on your daughter for the *Tribune*," I told her. "How she got on the force, her accomplishments, her aspirations. Sort of a life story."

"It wasn't much of a life, was it?" Mrs. Walsh said. "Only twenty-seven years. That hardly qualifies as a life at all."

I nodded sympathetically. "She accomplished a lot of admirable things in those twenty-seven years." I pushed the payoffs and the corruption out of my mind. "More than most people do in a lifetime. That's what you should remember."

"Thank you." Mrs. Walsh smiled.

I decided I'd said a good thing, I was proud of myself.

She did start talking then about Maura. She talked a lot. As if she didn't get a chance to talk that much with her husband around. She talked about Maura's childhood, about raising children in a police family, about all kinds of things. Here and there, I would ask her a question along the way. One of them was about the death of her young son Patrick at the house in Saginaw Lake a long time ago.

She wouldn't say much about that, just mumbled something about it being a "terrible tragedy". I was hoping she might shed some light on why Maura was so interested in it again recently, but I didn't want to push her too much. Just the mention of Patrick Walsh's name upset her, even after all this time. So I focused instead on the other thing I'd found out about Maura.

"I've been told by some people that there was tension between Maura and your husband," I said as diplomatically as I could. "She apparently refused to talk about him with anyone. And I've heard your husband and Maura weren't even speaking to each other at the end. Can you tell me why?"

Mrs. Walsh stared down at her now empty teacup for a long time.

"My husband can be a very difficult man sometimes," she said finally. "A good man, but very stubborn. Very rigid."

I wasn't going to disagree with that.

"Did he put a lot of pressure on Maura to become a police-woman, to follow in the Walsh family tradition?"

"Yes, it was very important to him. He wanted a son so badly. And when Patrick was born, he was already talking about him growing up to join the NYPD. But then after Patrick was…" she hesitated, the tragic death of her young son was clearly still difficult for her to deal with "… after he was gone, my husband convinced Maura to do it. The Walsh family has always put its children on the force. He wanted to continue that tradition."

"Is that what Maura wanted to do?"

"Oh, she was very happy in her work. She loved being a police officer."

I thought again about my conversation with Charlie Sanders, who said she was re-thinking her career with the NYPD.

"Are you sure about that?"

"What do you mean?"

"I don't know. Didn't she ever say she might rather do something else with her life?" I wasn't sure where I was going with this line of questioning, but somehow it seemed like something I wanted to know. "Maybe be a firewoman instead? Or a lawyer? Or a brain surgeon? Anything else besides being a policewoman?"

"Well, I really don't—"

The telephone rang, cutting her off in mid-sentence. She walked over to a phone in the dining area, about fifteen feet away, and picked it up. Close enough so that I could hear what she was saying. And figure out who she was talking to.

"Hello, dear, how are you?" she said.

There was a brief pause while the person on the other end said something.

"Oh, no, Mike, everything's fine." Her husband. "Yes, there's a very nice lady visiting with me. Her name is Jessie. She's from the *New York Tribune* and she's very interested in Maura and—"

The tone of the conversation changed then. Whatever her husband was saying at the other end wasn't good. When she spoke again, her voice sounded strained. Tense.

"I don't know why you would say that. It's just a little conversation about our daughter."

Another pause.

"All right, I know she works for a newspaper. But I don't really see why… Hello! Hello!"

Mrs. Walsh stood there, holding the phone in mid-air, almost frozen like a statue. She wasn't talking anymore Obviously her husband had hung up. Finally she put the receiver down and walked back to where I was sitting.

"I hope I'm not causing you a problem," I said. I felt uncomfortable.

She sat down on the couch across from me.

"If you'd like me to leave now, I understand."

"Marine biologist," Nora Walsh said.

"Pardon me?"

"You asked me before if Maura ever wanted to be anything else besides a policewoman. Well, she wanted to be a marine biologist. Talked about it all the time. Read everything she could get her hands on. Even had this big aquarium in her room that she filled with all sorts of exotic fish and sea plant-life."

"What happened?" I asked.

"Her father wouldn't hear of it. Especially after we lost our son. So, he went to work on Maura. Discouraged her from wanting to study marine biology. Berated her for even talking about it. And then one day, while she was at school, he went into her room and threw away that aquarium and everything in it. Maura cried for days over it."

I nodded. "So, in the end, she gave in and became a policewoman."

"In a manner of speaking, she gave in. But I was never really sure if she gave in or not. Sometimes I think she just did it to prove something to him – to show him she could do it. And that sometime – somehow – she planned to throw it all back in his face."

Nora Walsh began to cry then. Her body heaving and sobbing as if she'd held it inside her for all this time. Maybe her husband didn't allow crying in the house either. I comforted her as best I could, then made my way out the door. When I turned around and looked back at her on the couch, she was still crying. In a way, I felt glad about that. After all I knew about her husband, it was good to see some kind of emotion coming out in this family.

I walked down the steps, across the lawn and past the two metal swans again. They didn't look any happier than they had the first time I saw them.

"Yeah, I know how you feel," I said softly to the swans. "This house is trouble."

No question about it, the Walsh family was hiding a lot of secrets.

I'd found out about some of them.

But I had the feeling I had only begun to scratch the surface.

CHAPTER 23

Norman Isaacs wanted to see me in his office. There was a message telling me that when I got to work at the *Tribune* the next morning. Getting called into the city editor's office like that is generally not a good thing. Especially when the city editor was Norman Isaacs, who hardly ever talked to reporters unless there was something wrong. I suspected that Isaacs was *not* going to give me a pay raise or a promotion or a pat on the back.

No, this was about my visit to Deputy Police Commissioner Walsh's house.

"I got a call from Jonathan Larsen," Isaacs told me when I sat down in front of his desk. Larsen was the owner of the *New York Tribune*. "He was not happy. He got a phone call from NYPD Deputy Commissioner Walsh complaining that one of my reporters showed up at Walsh's door and invaded the privacy of his home."

"I can explain, Norman."

"Did you push your way into the house and confront Mrs. Walsh, Jessie?"

"No, not at all. She invited me in. Even made me tea. It was all going fine until Walsh called and found out I was there."

"Why were you there?"

"To try to find out what she and her husband knew about the death of her daughter."

"You should have formally asked Walsh for an interview at his office."

"I did."

"And?"

"He never responded."

"So you took it upon yourself to just go to his house and knock on the door? A house where the people inside have recently lost their daughter to a violent crime?"

"We knock on the doors of crime victim families all the time."

"Not when the crime victim family is the Walsh family."

I sighed.

"Not to mention he happens to be a personal friend of the owner of this newspaper."

"I wasn't aware of that when I went to Walsh's house."

"Would it have made any difference if you were?"

"Probably not."

Isaacs shook his head.

"What the hell did you think you were going to find out about the murder anyway from Walsh and his wife?"

"I'm not sure, but I have a lot of questions."

"What kind of questions?"

I told him. I told him everything. Well, almost everything.

About Maura Walsh's troubled relationship with her father. About her ex-boyfriend Charlie Sanders saying how she'd been acting strangely and seemed upset for the past few months. About her trips back to Saginaw Lake where the family had spent summers when she was growing up to look into the death of her young brother. About some of the questions and inconsistencies I'd discovered in the circumstance surrounding Patrick Walsh's death back then.

And, most of all, I told Isaacs about the payoffs to her that had been reported by people at the places she visited that last night. I wrapped it up by including my speculation that maybe Maura Walsh had gone rogue as a dirty cop as a way to embarrass and get some sort of bizarre revenge against her father for whatever reason they'd grown apart.

"Is there any official confirmation about these alleged payoffs?" he asked when I was finished. "Are the police investigating that angle as part of the murder investigation?"

"Not that I could find out. Or, if there is anything to it, they're not talking."

Isaacs sighed.

"We can't go with the payoff stuff in your story, Jessie," he said.

"I agree."

"You do?"

"Yes. We don't have any official confirmation from the police, just hearsay from people on the street. There's no indication that the investigators on the Walsh murder are looking at the payoff angle or think anything like that might be the motive for her death. And, maybe most important of all for me, I have no desire to be the reporter who accuses a cop, especially one from a revered family like Maura Walsh, of being corrupt. Calling out dirty cops doesn't make you very popular with the other members of the force. Being on good terms with the police is very important for me if I'm going to be able to do my job well. I could lose a lot of my sources and my access and my credibility with the NYPD. I'm not saying I wouldn't want to go with the story if I really had it nailed down. But I'm not prepared to risk my police reporting career with what I've got right now."

I also knew I didn't want to go with the payoff story because I felt some sort of empathy for Maura Walsh and whatever she'd been going through that might have pushed her into doing something like that. That I wanted her to remain a hero in her death. But I didn't tell that part to Isaacs.

Isaacs looked relieved when I was finished talking. I was relieved too. I'd held onto the secrets I knew about the Maura Walsh payoff activities for too long. If it came out publicly at any point now, I was covered. I'd reported it to my boss. I could have told Danny

Knowlton or Lorraine Molinski, instead of Isaacs. But, despite all his faults, I trusted Isaacs. He'd been a stand-up guy for me on the last big story I'd done. Every once in a while, No Guts Norman showed me something.

"Are you ready to write about what you have now?" Isaacs asked me.

"Absolutely."

"Okay, let's go with it in tomorrow's paper. 'Baffling Questions Remain in Hero Woman Cop's Death.' That way you can get in all the other stuff you told me about. And maybe you can even drop a few hints that there might be more to come."

"Okay, but Danny said he wanted to hold it for a Sunday edition lead feature."

"I'm the city editor here, not Danny Knowlton," Isaacs snapped. "If I want to run this story tomorrow, that's what we're going to do!"

Like I said, sometimes Norman surprised me.

I went back to my desk and started writing from all the notes I had. It was easy to do because I'd made such detailed notes over the past few days. Plus, I'd been thinking about it a lot. So it didn't take long to put all that into a story on my computer screen.

I used the interview with her partner, Billy Renfro. The one from her former boyfriend, Charlie Sanders. The previous tragedy in the Walsh family of losing their son at an early age. I even threw in a few quotes I got from Mrs. Walsh (assuming Norman would let me use them) about her daughter dying too young at twenty-seven – and not getting a chance for a real life.

I ended it by writing:

> More than three weeks after Maura Walsh's murder, there are still many baffling questions about who took her life.

A life that had been filled with many exhilarating high moments as well as some tragic ones for her and the Walsh family.

A life that – as Maura Walsh's mother said – ended far too soon at the age of twenty-seven.

CHAPTER 24

"Now that was a pretty good story you came up with, Jessie," Danny Knowlton said to me.

"Yeah, it worked out okay in the end."

We were in a bar near the *Tribune* where a group of us had gone after closing up the paper with my front-page story about Maura Walsh. Michelle was there, Peter Ventura and Lorraine and maybe a dozen or so other reporters and editors.

"So what are you going to do for a follow-up tomorrow?" Danny asked me.

"I haven't thought about it yet."

"Start thinking about it."

That's the thing about being a newspaper reporter – you're only as good as your last story.

No matter how many big stories you've written, a reporter – especially a woman reporter – has to prove herself over and over again each day on the job. People at newspapers have very short attention spans. By the time the paper is on the stands or your story is up on the website, everyone in the city room has already moved on to the next story.

The bottom line at any newspaper is *what have you done for us lately.*

Tonight I had a story on the front page.

Tomorrow I'd have to start all over again.

We talked about pursuing the corruption angle I'd uncovered but hadn't been able to write about; about the mysterious PI Frank

Walosin who claimed he had information for sale about Maura Walsh; about Dominic Bennato, the mob boss who owned two of the businesses Maura had gone to on that last night; and even about the possibility of going back to try for an interview with Deputy Commissioner Walsh, although that one would be tricky because of his close relationship with the *Tribune*'s owner.

Peter had told me earlier what he'd found out about Walter Palumbo, the dead Saginaw Lake Police Chief, which wasn't much. Yes, he'd joined the NYPD not long after the death of little Patrick Walsh in Saginaw Lake. He was assigned to a good job at the 22nd Precinct, where Mike Walsh had once been precinct commander. But he later resigned and went back to Saginaw Lake to be chief there again. "He wasn't around long enough for anyone I talked with to get to know him too well," Peter said. "But one of them said he was very unhappy at the 22nd and complained that working for the NYPD was not what he thought it would be. He regretted leaving Saginaw Lake." It was interesting information to know, and it did seem likely that Palumbo had gotten the job as a result of the way he handled the investigation into the Walsh boy's death back then. But I had no idea what any of it meant – if anything at all – for my Maura Walsh story now.

In the end, nothing got decided that night.

Danny eventually lost interest in me when a young waitress asked him to tell her about the newspaper business. She said she was taking a journalism courses at NYU, and she wanted to get a job in the media when she graduated. She said she'd really appreciate it if Danny could give her some career advice. Danny took her off into a quiet corner for some one-on-one guidance counseling.

I walked over to a table where the others were sitting. They were all laughing about Lorraine, who'd left in a panic a few minutes earlier after checking the time on her phone and seeing how late it was. Except it wasn't really that late. Peter Ventura had set the time on her phone ahead an hour and a half when she left the phone on a table while she was in the ladies' room. She would discover this later, of course, and she would be furious in the morning.

"Aren't you afraid that one day Lorraine's going to go postal on you?" I asked Peter. "Totally lose it, walk into the city room and shoot you."

"It's just a practical joke."

"She carries a gun, Peter."

"That's a legend, not a fact."

"You don't think she's packing heat?"

"No."

"Are you sure about that?"

"Well, not completely."

"It'll be a tough way to find out if you were wrong."

Michelle had brought a date. I found out later the guy was a young doctor she'd met while trying to break a story about health care violations at a big city hospital. She didn't get the story but she got the doctor. Michelle never did like to waste her time.

The two of them said they were leaving. So did Danny and the young waitress, whose shift was over. The others drifted away too, until finally it was just me and Peter Ventura and a few other hangers-on left at the table. Peter was holding court the way he did late at night whenever he'd had a few drinks, which was pretty much every night.

"My top five favorite newspaper movies of all time!" he announced to us. "Number one: *Deadline – U.S.A.* Humphrey Bogart is the city editor of a New York City newspaper that's about to fold, but he wants to break one more big story before they go out of business. Simply the greatest newspaper movie ever. End of discussion.

"Number two: *All the President's Men*. Okay, an obvious choice, but how can you go wrong with Robert Redford and Dustin Hoffman as Woodward and Bernstein.

"Number three: *His Girl Friday*. The remake of *The Front Page*, starring Cary Grant as the managing editor and Rosalind Russell as his ace woman reporter. She and Lois Lane were journalism's first true feminists. I'd give an honorable mention to the original of *The Front Page*, but forget the later version with Jack Lemmon and Walter Matthau. Go watch *The Odd Couple* instead.

"Number four: *The Paper*, which was directed by Ron Howard of Opie and *Happy Days* fame. Not a great movie in itself, but makes the list because of a terrific performance by Michael Keaton as the metropolitan editor of a New York City newspaper. Watch the scenes of him chugging Coca-Cola at eight in the morning to get himself going – he looks like he's on a caffeine high for the whole movie.

"Number five – and this one may surprise you – is a movie called *30*. It has Jack Webb – yes, that Jack Webb from *Dragnet* – as the city editor and David Nelson from the *Ozzie and Harriet* show as an eager young copyboy. Take my word for it, it's a camp classic. Very underrated.

"My favorite moment in any newspaper movie? That's easy. Humphrey Bogart talking to a journalism school graduate who comes to him looking for a job on the paper the day before it's supposed to shut down forever.

"Bogart says to the kid: 'So you want to be a newspaper reporter, huh? Well, let me tell you something about the newspaper business. It may not be the oldest profession in the world, but it's the best.'" Peter shook his head in admiration. "God, I love that sort of stuff."

At some point in the night, I'm not sure exactly when, Peter announced that he was going to another bar to continue his drinking. He asked me if I wanted to go with him. *No thanks*, I said. Bar hopping with Peter generally meant drinking until dawn. Never a good idea. The others went with him though.

So there I was alone in the bar, trying to figure out what to do.

I didn't have any idea where to go next on the Maura Walsh story or how to pursue the angle of the troubled relationship she had with her father in the months before she died.

I didn't have any idea what to do about my looking for my own father.

I didn't have any idea what to do about much of anything.

So I left. I walked for a while. It was a nice summer night out, the first one we'd had in a while. The humidity was way down. The temperature was hovering around only eighty. Finally, I got on a subway. Only instead of going downtown toward my own neighborhood, I took an uptown train. I got off at the East 72nd Street station. Then I walked around some. I tried to pretend to myself that I was just walking aimlessly on a pleasant summer night. But I knew where I was headed.

Eventually, I found myself in front of The Hangout, the restaurant where Maura Walsh had gone the last night of her life.

I pushed the door open and walked in.

CHAPTER 25

Sam Rawlings was sitting at the end of the bar, reading a newspaper. As I got closer, I realized it was an early edition of the *Tribune* with my article about Maura Walsh on Page 1. There was an empty seat next to him. I slipped onto it.

"Hi," I said.

"Hi."

"You know a good-looking guy like you really shouldn't be drinking alone."

He smiled. "Yeah, well I got impetigo. Very contagious."

"I can live with that," I said.

Rawlings ordered drinks for us from the bartender. Wine for me, and a beer for himself. He pointed down to my article in the *Tribune*. He said he thought it was very good. But he pointed out that I hadn't mentioned anything in it about her trip to The Hangout that last night or the money she took there. He seemed happy about this, but surprised.

"Not yet I haven't."

"Why not?"

"I need more information. She was the daughter of a high-ranking NYPD official and from a revered family in the department. I don't understand why she'd be taking money under the table. I wondered at first if maybe she was working undercover or something for the force. But if that was the case, it would have come out by now. No, she was taking payoffs on her beat, no question about it. I believe what you told me and the other people she visited that last night too. But it still doesn't make sense to me. I guess I'm looking for something that makes more sense before I put a story in the *Tribune* about it all. Not all reporters would do that, but that's the way I work."

"You sound like a good reporter," he said.

"I have my moments."

Rawlings nodded.

"I checked up on you, Jessie – googled you." He shrugged. "I was curious. There's a lot of stuff – not just everything you've written, but everything that's been written about you. You've been in the headlines a lot."

"I almost died a couple times. I'm the poster girl for crime victims. Not the best way to become famous. I wouldn't recommend that approach for fame to anyone."

"Tell me more about yourself."

"Like what?"

"Is there a 'Mr. Tucker'?"

"Not yet."

"Good to hear."

He smiled.

I smiled back. Okay, this guy was flirting with me, but I was flirting with him too. Maybe I needed a bit of flirting at the moment. Maybe I needed someone who actually seemed interested in me.

"How about you?" I asked him. "Is there a Mrs. Rawlings in the picture?"

"Oh, there was a Mrs. Rawlings."

"Past tense?"

"We got divorced."

"When was that?"

"About two years ago? But the years before that weren't so hot. We should have done it – gotten divorced, that is – a lot earlier."

"What went wrong?"

"A lot of things. Mostly, she had very expensive tastes, and she pushed me into trying to do a lot of things with my life I didn't really want to do – and wasn't very good at – so she could indulge them. That's why I went to law school and tried for a while to become a lawyer. Even though I realized early on I wasn't that interested in the law. By the time I realized what I really wanted to do – write a novel – she was gone. So here I am working in a restaurant until I become the next John Grisham."

Rawlings finished off the last of his beer and stared at me without saying anything for a few seconds.

"I didn't offend you or something, did I?" I asked. "You've suddenly gone very quiet."

"No, I was actually thinking about you."

"What about me?"

"Everything you went through that night in the park. Do you want to talk about it?"

"What's there to talk about? You read the articles. You know everything there is to know about it."

"No, I meant do you really want to talk about it? That must have been quite an ordeal you went through. How are you doing with all that?"

"I'm fine," I said, taking a big sip of my wine.

"*Fine,*" he repeated.

"Yes."

"Really?"

I took another huge gulp of the wine now. Pretty much emptying the glass.

And thinking about what to say next to Sam Rawlings.

No, I'm not fine. I still think about it all the time. I have nightmares about it. I have friggin' nightmares about it that are so bad I don't want to go to sleep again. So I sometimes stay awake for hours at night. Does that answer your question? And no, I don't want to talk about it anymore.

Except I did. I realized it wasn't the smartest thing to open up with all your fears and emotions to a guy you barely knew. Especially if the guy was someone you might be interested in pursuing a relationship with. But I needed to talk to somebody. And Rawlings was the somebody I was with right now. So in the end I totally unloaded on Rawlings. About everything that happened to me in Central Park. About everything that had unfolded after that until I'd discovered the truth. About how I now found myself identifying with the dead Maura Walsh, that I couldn't get out of my mind the horror of her dying scared and alone in that alley – just like I'd been scared and alone in Central Park. And even about how Maura Walsh's troubled relationship with her father raised questions for me about my own father, who I'd never even met.

By the time I was finished, I figured he'd want to run away from me as soon as he could.

"I'd really like see you again, Jessie," he said instead. "How about reconsidering that offer of mine for a date?"

"Why are you so interested in me? A guy like you must have a lot of beautiful women who would love to spend time with you."

"I like talking with you."

"Talking? That's all you want from me?"

"Well," he smiled, "we can start out talking – and see where that leads."

CHAPTER 26

"What's your endgame here?" Ellen asked me.

"What are you talking about?"

"This whole Sam business. Where do you want it to go?"

"Like I said before, I just think he seems very nice."

"Let me get this straight. You meet a guy you're attracted to. He asks you out, but you say no. He keeps asking, and you keep saying no. Then out of the blue you go to this guy's bar to find him, and he asks you out again. But you still haven't said yes. All you can tell me is that he's… well, nice."

"There's nothing wrong with me just thinking he's nice. It doesn't have to be any more than that."

"Of course it does. Sooner or later, you're going to have to make a decision on this guy, Jessie."

"I know." I sighed.

We were back at the gym on Park Avenue South. Well, Ellen was back. I'm pretty much always there. Like my apartment, this place was my sanctuary from the uncertainty of the world outside. All I had to do here was worry about how many reps I did on the machines or how many minutes I spent on the treadmill.

That's what I was doing right now.

Running on the treadmill.

With Ellen beside me.

"If you like this guy, go after him. Call him up yourself. Ask him to go out with you this time. Hell, show up at his door again and make it clear you want to see him. This is the twenty-first century, kiddo. We women can do a lot of things now we never did before. Take advantage of that."

"I'm not sure I want to have a relationship with Sam. I'm not sure I want a relationship with anyone, ever."

"That's crazy talk."

"I don't seem to do very well in relationships," I said. "Like with Logan. I don't know that I want to go through all that again with someone else."

Ellen sighed. The kind of sigh she gives me when she's exasperated with me, but knows there's no point in pushing the argument right now.

"Let me ask you another question," she said as we continued to run side by side on the two treadmills.

"Sure."

Around us the health club was beginning to fill up with more people. Men and women all trying to get in some early morning exercise before starting their workday. I looked at their bodies bathed in sweat – some fit, some less so – all around me. There was music blaring out of one of the loudspeakers in the room – something by Katy Perry, I think. I ran even faster on the treadmill as I listened to the music and felt the adrenalin from my running flow through my body.

"Have you done any more about that genealogy stuff we discussed the other day?"

"Not yet."

"But you're thinking about it?"

"Yes."

"Do you want the name of the genealogy investigator I used?"

"Later. I'm too busy right now working on the Maura Walsh story. I just don't understand what was going on with her during those last weeks and months of her life. There's too many moving parts here. My God, her life was a mess. I feel sorry for everything she must have been going through. Even if she was a dirty cop at the end, I don't think she was a bad person. I think she just got messed up by a lot of things – including her father and the hallowed Walsh family NYPD tradition."

Ellen didn't say anything for a few minutes. Finally, she stopped running, got off the treadmill and began using a towel to dry herself off. I did the same thing, even though I knew I'd be sweating again the minute I left the air-conditioned gym – no matter how long I stayed in the shower – and went out onto the hot New York streets.

"Jessie, we talked about this. You're getting too personally involved in this. You always need to separate yourself from a story, put up an emotional barrier between it and yourself so you stay objective."

"This is just another story for me, Ellen."

"No, it isn't. You've established some kind of personal connection between Maura Walsh's life and your own. You just admitted that to me. It's almost like the two of you were soul sisters or something. You believe you feel her pain and understand all the problems she went through. The reason for that is pretty obvious: all the troubles she was having with her father. You don't know exactly how to deal with your own daddy issues so you're throwing yourself into this story instead. It's too late to save Maura Walsh, but you think maybe if you can find out the answers to what happened to her, maybe it can save you now. This isn't just about Maura Walsh, Jessie. It's about you."

That's one of the problems when you have a best friend like Ellen.

You can't hide anything from them.

They know you too damn well.

CHAPTER 27

For twelve years after the night I'd been attacked and left for dead in Central Park, I never went back to the place where it happened.

The nightmares were all still too real for me.

And returning to the spot where my ultimate nightmare happened seemed just... well, it was a door to the past that I never wanted to open up.

But that had all changed now.

What was once a symbol of my weakness as a crime victim was now a symbol of my strength as a survivor.

I'd returned there – to that infamous place in New York City that I once dreaded – time and time again over the past several months for inspiration and hope and optimism for my future.

The location of my original attack had been on the south side of Central Park, near the 79th Street Transverse Road leading out to Fifth Avenue. I'd been walking through the park on my way home twelve years ago – I lived just a few blocks away then – when my attacker jumped me.

I stood at this spot now and looked around at it all in the daylight of a hot New York City summer day.

Everything was still there. The path I was walking on when I'd been attacked. The clump of trees I'd been dragged behind. A hilly ravine I'd been pushed down after the attack and where they found me unconscious the next morning.

For a while, people had left flowers and prayers and cards wishing me well in my recovery at this site. But that was a long time ago. Back when I was front-page news as a victim, not as a crime reporter. Now there had been other crimes and other stories that had replaced me on the front page. Many of them I had written myself.

Today everything here seemed perfectly normal. There were joggers, cyclists, children playing and people enjoying a summer day in the park.

But twelve years ago, I'd been left for dead in this same spot.

Just like Maura Walsh was left for dead in an alley a few weeks ago.

Except I'd somehow survived.

And she didn't.

I thought about that and a lot of things as I stood there now under that hot summer sun in Central Park, where the unthinkable had once happened to me. I thought about the pictures of Maura Walsh I'd seen – so young, so pretty, so full of hopes and dreams for the future. I thought about her father and how cold and aloof and unfeeling he'd appeared to be. I thought about the cruelness of her father in throwing her aquarium filled with fish away and how she cried for days afterward.

I thought about my own father too and the tears I'd shed over a man I never even knew.

I needed to find out the truth.

About everything.

Maura Walsh.

Her father.

And my father too.

CHAPTER 28

The police didn't seem to know or care much about the murder of Frank Walosin, which made sense since he was just a small-time PI with no apparent link to the Maura Walsh case.

Even after I went back to Aguirre to tell him that Walosin was the private investigator who had called me trying to sell information he claimed to have about Maura, Aguirre still figured it was more likely that Walosin had been murdered over a sleazy case he was working on for one of his sleazy clients.

Aguirre was probably right, but I couldn't shake a feeling they were connected.

Frank Walosin's murder was still a loose link for me in the story. And I hate loose links. So I used all my training and experience and skills as a reporter to come up with a sensible way to find out more about what Walosin was working on when he was killed. I couldn't think of a sensible way to do that.

Instead, I decided to try something that made no sense at all. And wasn't exactly legal either.

But, on the positive side, it was the only option I could think of.

I checked back in my notes, found the address I'd located for Walosin's office after he'd called me and headed over there.

It turned out to be a run-down-looking building on W. 47th, between Ninth and Tenth Avenues. I let myself into the lobby and checked the directory. Walosin's name was still there. That was good, maybe the landlord hadn't moved out his stuff yet. The rest of the businesses seemed a bit on the shady side – mail-order houses, sex equipment distributors, an escort service or two. That was good too. I found a buzzer that said, "Building Mgr." and pushed it.

A minute later a squat, middle-aged man appeared. He was wearing green work pants and a white T-shirt and carrying a cigar. The T-shirt had a reddish stain down the front that looked like spaghetti sauce. The end of the cigar was wet with saliva. He put it back into his mouth, chomped down and said to me between his teeth:

"What can I do for you, lady?"

"I'm looking for some office space. You got anything available?"

He nodded. "Yeah, something did open up recently. The previous tenant… uh, suddenly relocated."

Sure. He *relocated*. No sense in telling a prospective tenant he was murdered in your building. Might hurt the place's spotless reputation.

"Can I see it?" I asked.

"I haven't had time to move all of the previous tenant's stuff out yet."

Perfect. Of course, I still had to hope the police hadn't spent too much time going through Walosin's office when it was a crime scene. But, based on Aguirre's reaction, I was betting they hadn't.

"That's fine," I told him.

"Okay, let me get the keys."

He disappeared into a little cubbyhole off the lobby. Inside I could see a small unmade bed, a hot plate and a small TV. The TV was tuned to one of those daytime courtroom shows where the people were yelling back and forth at each other. He got the keys, and we went up to the third floor where he said the office was.

"What's your business?" he asked as we climbed the stairs. "You with an escort service or something?"

I looked at him sternly. "You from the Better Business Bureau?"

He shrugged. "Nope, it's nothing to me. You pay your rent, don't do anything to bring the law here – hey, it's fine. That's the way me and the landlord like it."

"Great."

We got to Walosin's office and he let us in with the key. It looked pretty much the way I expected it would. Small and cramped. Dusty file cabinets. Paint peeling from the walls.

"Like I said, I haven't had time to move the previous tenant's stuff out yet. He left in a hurry without it. If you're interested, I could probably make you a good deal on some of it – assuming no one shows up to claim it."

"I might be interested in that," I said, pretending to think it over. "Say, do you think I could have a few minutes to look around here? To help me make up my mind for sure?"

"No problem," he said. "Just close the door on the way out. I'll be downstairs in my place."

After he was gone, I went through Frank Walosin's drawers and files. What I found was about what I expected. Bedroom pictures. Tapes of lovemaking. Eavesdropping equipment. Walosin was clearly one of those private investigators who operated on the very edges of the law. And, more often than not, he went over the edge. Divorce dirt. Blackmail. Extortion. You name it, it was available for a fee at Walosin Investigations.

One thing about Frank Walosin though: he was organized. All the filth was neatly accounted for and labeled. Except I couldn't find anything in Walson's files about Maura Walsh. Nothing in the W file or the Ms either. Of course, if that really was what Walosin's murder was about, the killer would have made a point of getting his hands on that before he fled.

Still, he might not have had time to do a thorough search.

And the police probably didn't spend too much time looking through the stuff in this office either, a low rent killing like this didn't get a lot of attention from them any more than it did in the media.

So maybe there was still some other clue in Walosin's files about what he knew or what he was doing in regard to Maura Walsh. It took about ten minutes more of looking, but I finally found something. A file folder that contained documents on all his cases from the current year. There were a lot of them, too many for me to go through before the building guy might come back to check on me. But Maura Walsh must be in there somewhere. So I took the file, stuffed it in my purse and got the hell out of there.

Back down on the ground floor, I could hear the sounds of the TV still coming from the little cubbyhole. It was tuned to some kind of Jerry Springer show now. A woman was screaming at her boyfriend, accusing him of sleeping with both her sister and best friend. He admitted that and then revealed that he'd slept with her mother too. The audience howled with laughter, and I could hear the guy with the T-shirt and cigar laughing too.

I slipped quietly past the open door, through the dingy lobby and out onto the street. When I got there, I noticed a police car sitting at the curb across from Walosin's building. When I started walking toward the subway station, it began moving in the same direction as I was. Were the cops watching his office for some reason, even though Aguirre had dismissed the idea of a link to Maura Walsh's murder? That made me a bit paranoid since I had just stolen documents out of there. I quickly ducked down into the nearest subway station. As I got off the train again at Rockefeller Center, I looked around on the street there for the police car. But it was gone. Just my imagination running wild, I guess.

CHAPTER 29

I didn't read the Walosin file right away when I got back to the *Tribune* office. Partly because I got busy doing a lot of other stuff there for the rest of the day, but also because I didn't want anyone to see me reading the file and asking me questions about what it was. I was very aware that I had not obtained this through normal journalistic channels. What I had done to get it was not strictly ethical. I didn't want to reveal that to my bosses or anyone else at the *Tribune*. Not yet anyway, until I knew more about exactly what was in the file. So I put it in my bag to take home with me to read in private.

When I did finally get back to my apartment on Irving Place later that evening, I pretty much collapsed onto the couch for a few minutes before I did anything else. It had been a long few days for me working on this story, and I was exhausted. Both physically and emotionally. My right leg – it's the weaker of the two, and I still on occasion had to use a cane – was really bothering me now. That was why it felt so good to just sit there in the peace and quiet of my apartment like this.

I got up, poured myself a glass of wine and went back to the couch. Below me, I could hear the sounds of traffic on the streets of Manhattan. Outside my living-room window, I saw the Empire State Building and other parts of the New York City skyline. I turned on the TV, drank some wine and snuggled more comfortably into the couch. Ah, this was the life. My happy place. Oh, it might be better if I had a man to share it with. Or a dog or a cat or even a goldfish. But, for now, this would do just fine.

I eventually got up and went back into the kitchen. I made myself scrambled eggs with sausage and toast for dinner. I know that probably sounds weird but I'm one of those people who hardly ever eats a big breakfast, so sometimes I like to eat breakfast at night. I also make terrific scrambled eggs. Lots of milk and butter and usually cheese melted in it. I can't fry an egg or make an omelet worth a damn, but I'm great at scrambled eggs.

I took my meal back into the living room, eating in front of the TV while I watched a news show about everything happening in the world today. My God, how did people live before there were 24-hour news channels? I realized as I was eating and watching TV so contentedly how comfortable I'd gotten living – and mostly being – alone. In other words, without a guy in my life. I thought about Logan, the last guy I'd been with. I even thought about Gary Bettig, my long-ago fiancé who had callously abandoned me while I lay close to death in a hospital bed. And mostly I thought about Sam Rawlings. What the hell was I going to do about Sam? I wasn't sure about that.

It was easier to think about the story I was working on. So I was glad to finally pull out the file I'd taken from Walosin's office and start going through it, looking for some kind of link or clue to Maura Walsh. Being a journalist was easy for me. It was the rest of my life that was so difficult.

The cases in the file I'd taken from Frank Walosin's office weren't easy to figure out. None of them included names. Each one was just labeled with a case number at the top, and the people in the documents only as Surveillance Targets A, B, C, etc. Walosin had clearly gone to great lengths to keep secret the identities of his clients and the people he was investigating. Probably in case someone else ever got their hands on his files (like I did now).

I kept reading through the details of each case, looking for some kind of connection to Maura Walsh.

And I finally found it.

One of the reports in the file talked about him staking out the 22nd Precinct and following two police officers from there on their nightly rounds.

It included details about the precise movements of a woman cop who obviously must have been Maura Walsh as she made her patrol rounds with her partner during several nights of duty. Including the night she died.

Which raised an obvious question: if Walosin was following Maura Walsh for some reason, did he see who shot her in Little Italy? Did he know who her killer was?

"I've got another potential buyer for this information," he'd told me that day on the phone. "I'm offering that buyer the same deal as you. I'm open to the best offer. It's a seller's market."

But I still had to figure out where that link led.

Walosin's file certainly provided a detailed account of Maura Walsh's illegal activities. All the payoffs and money she took and where she got it from. It never mentioned Maura Walsh by name – just referred to her as Surveillance Target B. But it clearly was Maura Walsh from the description of her actions.

Walosin had nailed down an airtight case of corruption against Maura Walsh.

But why?

Who hired him to follow her?

He never named the client either in the file. Instead, he employed the same code he did elsewhere – using a letter in the alphabet. The client was simply listed as "Surveillance Target B Buyer". I needed to figure out a way to find out who that client was. And eventually I found one.

I got lucky.

Walosin turned out to be not quite as efficient as I thought he was at hiding the identity of his client. Yes, he'd meticulously removed every name from the file and replaced them with code names like "Surveillance Target B" and "Surveillance Target B Buyer." He'd gone to great lengths to hide the identities of everyone he was involved in tracking and the person who hired him to do it.

But he'd forgotten one thing.

Attached to the back of one of the documents about Maura Walsh, I found a cancelled check.

It was for ten thousand dollars and it was made out to Frank Walosin from someone named Linda Caldwell. There was an address listed on the check too. The address was in Queens. Who the hell was Linda Caldwell? I sure didn't know her, but I needed to find her to see why she apparently hired Frank Walosin to follow Maura Walsh.

There were a lot of Linda Caldwells from the New York City area online. Even more L. Caldwells. I checked out a few of them without success. But, when I figured out the answer, it was the address – not the name – that was the key. I googled Linda Caldwell's address in Queens on a real estate website, and I found out the property was listed as being owned by William Renfro. Billy Renfro, Maura's partner.

It didn't take a whole lot longer for me to determine that Renfro's wife's name was Linda.

And, after more digging, I established the fact that her maiden name was Linda Caldwell.

And then the connection with Frank Walosin and his private eye services all made sense to me.

Billy Renfro's wife had hired Walosin.

But Walosin wasn't following Maura Walsh.

He was following Billy Renfro.

CHAPTER 30

"What made you decide to have lunch with me?" Sam Rawlings asked.

"I told you the other night that I would see you."

"You said you might."

"Okay, I'm here now."

"I'm glad."

We were sitting in a booth at Ted's Montana Restaurant, a steak place near Rockefeller Center and down the street from the *Tribune* office. The steaks were good, and so were the hamburgers. Rawlings had ordered a cheeseburger with everything on it along with a side of fries. I decided to order the same. Even though eating something messy like a cheeseburger was a tricky proposition on a first date, I've found. Assuming that this lunch was a first date, of course.

I thought it might be a good idea to lay down some ground rules to him right at the beginning.

"Don't get your hopes up too high," I said.

"What does that mean?"

"This is just a lunch. No more."

"Meaning?"

"I'm not going to have sex with you," I blurted out.

"Okay." He smiled. "Well, I'm glad we got that settled before eating…"

"I'm serious."

He picked up his cheeseburger and took a big bite.

"Do you always do this when a guy is interested in spending time with you, Jessie?" he asked.

"Do what?"

"Go into attack mode, instead of just enjoying the moment."

"I don't do that."

"Sure, you do."

I sighed. "Yeah, I guess maybe I do."

"My current plan," he said slowly, "is to eat more of this terrific-looking cheeseburger. Then maybe have coffee – or even dessert – with you. After that, we'll see where everything goes between us. If something more does happen at some point, that's great. If not, well… let's not ruin this nice lunch."

We talked about a lot of things after that.

He asked me about my job. More about the Central Park attack and the more recent incident there where I finally solved the case. About my brief, ultimately unsuccessful bi-coastal romance with Logan, who I'd met doing that story. And, when he asked me more about my romantic past, I even told him about Gary, my ex-fiancé.

"This guy Bettig actually said he didn't want to be saddled with the burden of taking care of a cripple?" Sam asked.

"It was even a bit harsher than that."

"Hard to believe."

"I know, but he said it. I remember it all too well. I was there. Lying in that hospital bed when he walked out on me."

I wanted to stop talking so much about me, so I asked some questions about him. Like where he lived, for instance. He said he had an apartment in a high rise off Second Avenue in the East 70s, just a few blocks from where The Hangout restaurant was located. I knew that was a pretty expensive area to live.

"I thought struggling writers were supposed to live in garrets or something," I said.

"That's kind of a myth. Besides, garrets generally don't even have electrical outlets. No place to plug in or charge a computer."

"Hemingway never used a computer."

"Hemingway actually wrote everything out longhand," Sam said. "Did you know that? Well, the descriptive stuff anyway. He used a typewriter when he was doing dialogue. He said the typewriter captured the pattern of the way people speak. You know – a rat-a-tat-tat kind of thing. I read that once."

"You're a big Hemingway fan?"

"How could an aspiring author not be? Hemingway wrote something else about being a writer that I've thought about a lot. He said the thing you need to do is find out at some point whether or not you have what it takes to be a writer. Sometimes a person digs deep down inside himself and finds out that the talent simply isn't there. He quits his job, tries to write the Great American Novel and comes up empty. Hemingway said that disappointment can be enough to kill a person."

"Is that what you're afraid of? That you'll find out someday you're not good enough to be a writer?"

"There's something that scares me even more than that."

"What?"

"That I do have the talent, but no one else besides me will ever know."

"I don't understand…"

"Let me tell you my big nightmare. I think about it when I'm really depressed about my writing career. It goes like this: I spend my whole life writing novel after novel and none of them ever gets published. All these manuscripts sit in some drawer or closet in my apartment for years, and no one reads them until I die. Then somebody finally says: 'Wow, this guy could really write. Too bad he's not still alive so we can tell him.' Or even worse, no one ever reads the damn things. They just get thrown away as garbage after I'm gone. I have had no impact whatsoever on the literary world. I've wasted my life."

I laughed. "That is pretty scary, but probably unlikely?"

"Hey, you asked the question."

"Would you let me read something you've written?"

"Do you really want to?"

"Yes. Then if I like it, I can tell you what a great writer you are before you're dead."

"What if you don't like it?"

"I'll lie."

"You've got a deal." He grinned.

It turned out to be a long lunch. A nice lunch. But, at the end, the inevitable question came up. Could he see me again?

"Look, I'm going through a lot right now," I said. "I'm kind of on emotional overload. Everything from what happened in Central Park. The Maura Walsh story. And some personal stuff too involving my family."

Or my lack of a family, I thought as I said it.

"Is that a 'no' then?"

"Um…"

"Well, that's better than 'no'."

"I need time to sort all these things out before I'm ready to start seeing someone again."

"How long will that take?"

"I'm not sure."

Sam took out a piece of paper and a pen, then wrote something down.

"What's that?"

"My phone number."

He handed it to me.

"Call me when you're ready," he said.

CHAPTER 31

It turned out – after I did some more checking – that Billy Renfro's wife had left him a month and a half ago. That was about the same date on the check she'd paid to Frank Walosin to spy on her husband. But what exactly was she looking for from Walosin? Evidence of Billy's police corruption – taking bribes and payoffs – that she could use as leverage against him in a divorce settlement, perhaps?

I needed to talk to Billy Renfro again. I had a lot more questions for him now than I did the first time we met.

But first I wanted to talk to his wife about Frank Walosin.

Linda Renfro – or Linda Caldwell as she called herself now – was living in Edgewater, N.J. There was no easy public transportation to get there from Manhattan, so I rented another car to make the trip. I figured Danny wouldn't be happy about that expense. That's why I didn't tell him – or anyone else at the paper – what I was doing. I'd worry about it later when I filed my expense account. If I came up with a big story out of this for the *Tribune*, they'd be happy. If I didn't… well, no one would be happy. Including me.

She lived in a high-rise apartment building with a view of the Hudson River and the Manhattan skyline across the water. I wasn't sure at first if she'd be willing to talk to me. But she invited me over. I soon found out why.

"Where's the photographer?" was the first thing she asked me when I showed up.

"What photographer?"

"Don't you want to take a picture of me?"

"Why?"

"For the interview you're going to print in the *Tribune*. About me. Everything I had to put up with being a police officer's wife and all that?"

I'd given her a cover story when I called to set up the interview about why I wanted to talk with her. I said it was because her husband's partner Maura Walsh had died in the line of duty and I wanted to get a better picture of the stress and worry and dangers of being a police officer through the eyes of his wife. Or some kind of crap like that.

"I'm not writing an article about you, Mrs. Renfro. I'm here to ask you questions about your husband. I'm trying to piece together information about the events leading up to Maura Walsh's death, and I thought maybe you could help."

"What would I know about that?"

"Nothing, I'm sure. But maybe you could tell me a bit more about the effect it had on your husband."

She looked disappointed.

"Well," she said huffily, "I wish you had told me that before you came here."

She was a dark-haired woman who must have been in her fifties (based on what I knew about Billy Renfro's age and their children), but was trying hard to look a lot younger. She had on a silk top that was too tight, a skirt that was too short and heels that must have been six inches high. It did give her a kind of sexy look, I suppose. But there was also something about it all that seemed… well, desperate.

"What happened between you and your husband?" I asked.

"We split up."

"When?"

"Oh, a few months ago."

"And you moved here then?"

She nodded.

"I told him he could keep on living in that damn house. Our kids are grown up and have moved out. I didn't want to live in Queens anymore. I wanted to grow as a woman and as a person. So he agreed to rent this place for me to live in. It's fine for now. But I'd like to move into Manhattan so I can grow even more. It's very important for a woman to keep growing as a person. I'm sure you understand that."

I didn't understand anything this woman was saying. It sounded like something from a "self-help" book she had read. But I didn't want her to stop talking. So I simply nodded and smiled.

"I'm taking a painting class. I'm taking dance lessons. I belong to a singles club here where I've met a lot of nice men. Men who appreciate a woman like me. Not like my husband, who never has time for me anymore. I hope to travel soon too. I'm enrolled in a night school course to learn Spanish. I want to be able to speak the language when I go to exciting places like Cancun and Rio de Janeiro. I've spent my entire life taking care of Billy and raising a family. Now it's my time to live. And that's what I'm going to do. Watch out world, Linda Caldwell is coming!"

I thought about telling her that Rio de Janeiro was in Brazil, where they speak Portuguese – not Spanish – but I kept my mouth shut. No point in ruining this woman's fantasy.

"Why exactly did you leave your husband after twenty-five years of marriage?" I asked her.

"He was cheating on me."

"There was another woman?"

"Damn straight there was. I found out about it. He denied everything, of course. But I knew about what he was doing."

"Who was the other woman?"

"That little bitch who was his partner."

"Maura Walsh?" I said in amazement.

"Yes."

"Are you sure about that?"

"A wife always knows. Billy had a romance going on with her. I confronted him about it – and then I left."

Wow, I thought to myself. *Maura Walsh and Billy Renfro? I didn't see that coming.* But it sure explained a lot. Including why Mrs. Renfro had hired a private investigator like Frank Walosin. She was looking for dirt on her husband. And found out Renfro and Maura were carrying on an affair. Or were they? I had some trouble believing it. I remembered the way Renfro had talked about Maura like a daughter, not like a girlfriend. But middle-aged men do get smitten with young women, maybe that's what happened with Billy Renfro and Maura Walsh on all those long, lonely nights in a patrol car?

"Did you hire a private investigator named Frank Walosin to spy on your husband?" I asked her.

"How do you know about Walosin?"

"That's how I tracked you down – I got your name from his records."

"Okay, I hired him. No harm in telling you that, I suppose. I knew my husband was carrying on with Maura Walsh and I wanted proof. So I hired Walosin to watch Billy on the job and get pictures and other evidence. I wanted to confront Billy with it. To show him he couldn't carry on an affair without me knowing about it. To make him feel guilty for his infidelity – and to feel guilty over the way he didn't appreciate me the way he should. After all I put into our marriage."

"Did Walosin get proof of an affair?"

"No, he claimed he couldn't find any. But he kept my ten-thousand-dollar retainer. Said he'd done everything he could do and now he needed to move on to some other big job. Can you believe that?"

The "other job" must have been selling the information he'd stumbled onto about Renfro and Walsh taking payoffs.

"I should have sued Walosin to get my money back," she said. "Maybe I still will."

"Too late for that now."

"What do you mean?"

"Frank Walosin is dead."

She seemed surprised to hear that. Or at least she acted like she was. I told her about his murder. If she made any connection at all between Walosin's murder and his work for her, she didn't show it.

"There's something I still don't understand," I asked her. "You said Walosin told you he didn't find any evidence of an affair between Maura Walsh and your husband. And yet you seem convinced there was one. Why?"

"Like I said, a wife knows. My husband denied it every time I confronted him about her, but I knew it was true. Don't worry though, one day he'll realize what he lost with his tawdry little affair. He'll come begging me to take him back. That's why I left him. To show him how much he'll miss me when I'm gone."

I wasn't really sure how to answer that.

"I don't think Maura Walsh was having an affair with your husband," I said finally.

But she really wasn't listening to me.

She was staring at herself in a mirror and smiling.

"I'm thinking about going blonde," she said, talking to herself more than me. "Wouldn't that look nice? The men at my singles club will love it. And Billy will be so jealous the next time he sees me. He'll realize what he lost. The best woman he ever had."

She was still staring at herself in the mirror when I left the apartment and went back into the heat outside.

I got into the rental car, turned up the air-conditioner full blast and thought about what I'd accomplished in there. Not much really. Yes, she'd hired Walosin the private investigator. But it was supposed to be for a sex scandal. Instead, Walosin had stumbled onto the corruption scandal, which he thought could be a big payday for him. Except now he was dead.

So who could tell me more about that?

Well, maybe Billy Renfro could.

I'd suspected he was hiding secrets the first time I talked with him, I just had no idea how big these secrets might be.

My second conversation with Billy Renfro should be a lot more interesting than the first one was.

I drove up to Fort Lee, N.J., then across the George Washington Bridge into New York City. I was around 72nd Street when I saw a police car behind me. I watched it in my rearview mirror, then tried to ignore it.

Second police car I'd been aware of in the last few days.

But there were a lot of police cars in New York City.

Sure, I never noticed them before like this. But all the talk about police corruption and the rest had made me a bit jumpy and nervous, I guess.

Talk about paranoia.

It's just a police car, nothing more, I told myself.

And, sure enough, when I looked back into the rearview mirror again, the police car was gone.

CHAPTER 32

The Central Park nightmares – the ones I'd been having since the attack on me more than twelve years earlier – weren't the only nightmares that were keeping me awake at night.

It was two a.m., and I'd just woken up from another hospital nightmare.

Only it wasn't me who was the patient in the hospital this time. It was my mother.

I knew why I was having this nightmare about her too. I'd been thinking about my mother – and my confusing, troubled relationship with her – ever since the DNA/genealogy conversation I'd had with Ellen. I thought about it earlier that day when I went back to the *Tribune* office after my meeting with Linda Caldwell. I thought about it while I was working out on the treadmill for an hour, doing fifty sit-ups, a hundred leg curls and swimming a mile of laps at the swimming pool in my gym. And I was still thinking about it when I went to bed, going over and over in my head the questions I had about the father I never knew – and the mother I knew too well.

Which was why I was sitting at the desk in my apartment in the middle of the night – having given up on trying to fall asleep for now – and logged on to one of the genealogy sites I'd signed up for after my conversation with Ellen.

I'd found out my grandparents were originally from Pittsburgh, although they later moved to Cincinnati where my mother had grown up. And their parents – my great grandparents – had come to this country from Ireland. I even managed to get the date and number of the boat they traveled here on – and then the town in Ireland where they had come from.

But none of this really helped me find out what I was looking for – more about my father.

With that, I kept running into dead ends.

And the more I went through all this stuff on the website, the more unhappy memories it brought back about me and my mother.

Like I said earlier, I didn't have a very happy childhood. On the one hand, my mom enveloped me in motherly attention, but she also never really included any love in that relationship. It was almost, I used to feel, as if I was an object for her to show the world how wrong my father was to leave her. She was constantly pushing me to be the best – no, even more than that, to be perfect – in anything I did. Which I never was, of course. And so I was constantly disappointing her.

The culmination of our dysfunctional relationship came after the attack on me in Central Park. We didn't talk a lot after that, even after I recovered and began a new career as a newspaper reporter at the *New York Tribune*. When I began getting front-page stories, I rarely sent them to her. And, when I did, she never responded.

I hoped one day we could work it out and somehow salvage a mother and daughter relationship between us – even a strained and not so great one.

But then she got sick. The last time I saw her she was in critical care in the hospital. I flew there – I felt it was my duty, just like when she came to see me in the hospital. But I was not prepared for the emotions I felt when I saw my mother, the only family I've ever known, in that hospital bed hooked up to life support equipment.

She knew I was there and seemed happy about that. Or at least I thought she did. I couldn't tell for sure because she had a breathing tube down her throat that wouldn't allow her to speak.

On the night I arrived, the nurse told me she believed my mother wanted to tell me something. And it sure seemed like she did. Except she couldn't speak, and she was too weak to even hold a pen in her hand to write a note. I tried to communicate with her as best I could. Throwing out words or suggesting topics to which she could only reply with a slight nod or shaking of her head. It was very slow going. But at one point I said the word "father" and she nodded her head. I couldn't get any more out of her that night though, no matter how hard I tried. She became more and more agitated over being unable to get her message to me – whatever that message was – and the whole thing was so upsetting that I finally decided to leave for the night. I told her I'd be back in the morning.

That was the last time I saw her alive.

And that's what my nightmare was about. In the nightmare, I'm always hoping that I'm going to get my mother to reveal her secret to me this time. What it was that she wanted to tell me about my father at the end. But then – just as I think she's about to tell me – I wake up and realize all over again that my mother is dead.

Taking with her whatever she wanted to tell me about my father – or anything else – in her last moments on this earth.

I've dealt with all this by putting it out of my mind most of the time. But now it all came rushing back as I went through the details I had of my mother's life and background. It left me feeling sad and depressed. And, I suppose, a bit guilty too because I hadn't really been there for my mother when she got sick and needed me – just like I'd been so angry at her for not being there for me when I needed a mother. Now I had no one left in my family. No mother. And no father. Unless I did something about it.

I managed to get a few hours of sleep, but I was up at six a.m and exercising when I called Ellen.

"What the hell are you doing up at this hour?" she said sleepily into the phone.

"I'm on the treadmill."

"Oh, jeez."

"Long night?"

"Yes, it was. Unlike you, I have a social life."

"I have a social life."

"Okay, unlike you I have a *sex* life."

I didn't say anything.

"Speaking of that, whatever happened with you and that Sam guy?"

"That's not why I'm calling."

I asked for the details of the investigative genealogist she'd told me about. I said I'd pretty much determined that I couldn't do the search for my father alone. I needed professional help. She put me on hold, checked around for the information and then gave me a name and phone number.

I thought about calling the investigator right away, but it was too early.

Maybe I'd call later when I got to the office.

Or maybe not.

In the meantime, I got back on the treadmill and ran as fast as I could for as long as I could in hopes of pushing all the thoughts about my father and my mother and Maura Walsh and her father and all the rest out of my mind.

It worked too.

For a while anyway.

CHAPTER 33

Before I'd left Billy Renfro's wife in New Jersey, I got her to give me directions from Manhattan to their house. I checked first with the 22nd Precinct to see if Renfro had gone back to work, but they said he was still on sick leave. So I went to where Renfro lived in Queens.

The house was on a quiet, tree-lined street about a mile from the Long Island Expressway. Nice, but not ostentatious. Just middle-class American families. *And how was your day at work? Fine, I shook down three people and made $1000 in bribes. Oh, good – now could you take out the garbage?*

It was a white Cape Cod, with weather-beaten brown trim and shutters. I knocked on the front door. Nothing happened. Off in the distance, I could hear a dog barking. Somewhere I heard a car engine idling.

I walked around to the side and knocked on another door. Still nothing. From there I could see a large structure of some kind in Renfro's backyard. I realized it was a boat. He'd been building a boat, probably the one he planned to sail in Florida as soon as he retired.

I walked back around to the front and tried the door there again, knocking as loudly as I could. Then I leaned over and peered in a window. No sign of movement inside the house.

"Hey, get outta there!" a shrill voice yelled.

I looked around and saw a middle-aged woman in a bathrobe and hair curlers sticking her head out of the door next door. She was scowling at me and shaking her fist.

I walked over to her porch and up to her door.

"Hi, I'm Jessie Tucker," I said pleasantly. "I'm a reporter for the *New York Tribune*. I'm looking for Billy Renfro."

"Haven't seen him," she said in the same shrill tone.

"Do you have any idea where I might find him?"

"No. Now please just go away. We don't want any trouble around here."

Then she slammed the door shut in my face.

I walked slowly back to Billy Renfro's house and stood in the driveway looking at it. The dog had stopped barking, but I could still hear the engine running. It seemed close by. I looked around, but I couldn't see it. It didn't seem to be coming from the street anywhere. More like from inside Renfro's house. Or from his garage.

I walked up to the garage door and listened. Sure enough, there was the sound of a car running inside. The garage door wasn't locked, so I opened it and went in. I was only inside for a few seconds before I had to back out again, coughing and choking. It was long enough to know what had happened.

The lady next door shoved her head out again and saw me.

"What are you still doing here? I told you we don't want any trouble in this neighborhood."

"It's too late for that," I said, still trying to catch my breath.

"Huh?"

"You better call the police right away."

I read once that death by carbon monoxide poisoning is the most pleasant way to go. Much better than jumping off a building or putting a gun to your head. They say it gives you a feeling of euphoria at the end. No pain, no struggles. You just quietly go to sleep.

I hoped for Billy Renfro's sake that was true.

While I waited for the police to arrive, I made my way through the fumes again and pushed open a door in the garage that led to the house. I knew I shouldn't be doing that. But I wanted to see if there was anything in there that might be relevant to Maura Walsh or anything else before the cops arrived.

The first thing I saw was a note on the kitchen table. It said:

TO WHOM IT MAY CONCERN:
I'm so sorry about everything.
God, please forgive me.
Billy Renfro
NYPD Badge 892

Below that he had written the words, "Courtesy, Professionalism, Respect."

The New York City Police Department motto.

On a table in the living room, I saw a pamphlet from the Police Department Benevolent Association that told about how to get help for job-related stress disorders. There was a quote on the first page that said: "You help people all day, don't be afraid to ask for help yourself." It gave a telephone number to call.

Someone, I assume it was Renfro, had written the words "today I make the call" next to the telephone number. Several other similar notes were below it. They were in different colors of ink, as if he'd written the words at different times while he tried to work up the courage to make the call. I wondered if he ever had. It didn't really matter now.

It was amazing to me how objective I could be about doing this. I mean, I'd just discovered a dead body in the garage. Later, I knew, the sight of seeing Billy Renfro like that would haunt me for a long time. It had to. But, for right now, I was just doing my job. Which meant trying to examine as much of this stuff in his house as I could before the police showed up.

Looking more around the room now, I saw a lot of awards and pictures.

Awards for bravery and heroism and outstanding work in the line of duty for Police Officer Billy Renfro. Like Ventura had said to me when I asked him about it in the beginning, Renfro was a good cop. Or at least he had been for a long time. Until it all ended tragically for him in a garage filled with carbon monoxide fumes.

The pictures were like a scrapbook of his life. Him and his wife in happier times. His three children, when they were young and later all grown up. The boat I'd seen in the backyard that he dreamed of sailing to Florida one day. Lots of pictures of him in police uniform. One of them was him and Maura Walsh, laughing and standing with their arms around each other outside the 22nd Precinct. That must have driven his wife crazy. Another picture from outside the 22nd was Renfro with another police officer I didn't recognize. Probably his previous partner, before Maura Walsh came along.

Renfro's house was a mess. Dirty clothes all over, dishes in the sink – it looked as if living alone without his wife and family hadn't gone well for him. In the kitchen, I found a frozen lasagna TV dinner inside the microwave. He had cooked it, but never eaten it. I stuck my finger into the tray, then licked some of the lasagna off. It was cold. So it must have been in there for a while. There was also a fresh pot of coffee and an empty cup there too.

Then I looked through the rest of the house. I found a note from his wife in which she announced she was leaving him. He'd kept that in a prominent position by his bed in the bedroom, for some reason. There were a lot of receipts in a drawer I opened that seemed to be far beyond a policeman's salary.

I went back into the other room and looked at the last words of Billy Renfro.

I'm so sorry about everything, Renfro had written in his note. *God, please forgive me.*

Did Billy Renfro kill himself out of guilt because he felt responsible for Maura Walsh's death?

Did he do it because he knew the corrupt activities he'd been engaging in – the bribes and the kickbacks and the payoffs – were about to be exposed?

Or was Renfro apologizing for something else in the note – some other secret I didn't know about – which pushed him over the edge to suicide?

CHAPTER 34

The cops showed up a few minutes later. The guy in charge was a lieutenant named Williamson. He was a muscular African American, about forty, impeccably dressed in a three-piece suit and yet as imposing physically as a linebacker for the New York Giants.

He had a lot of questions for me, starting with the most obvious one:

"What were you doing here? Inside Renfro's house?"

I told him how I'd come there to talk to Renfro about his partner Maura Walsh for a story I was working on about her death. That I'd heard the engine running inside the garage and then smelt the exhaust fumes inside. And then I went into the house afterward where I saw the suicide note.

I did not tell him the part about going through the whole house and looking through all his stuff.

Williamson was unhappy enough about the fact that I'd gone inside Renfro's house, without getting into that kind of detail.

"Did you know Renfro?" Williamson asked me when I was finished.

"I interviewed him a few days ago about the Maura Walsh murder. And I'd run into him on stories before that over the years."

"So you just decided to drop by and say hello tonight?"

"I'm working on a new story – a different angle – about Maura Walsh. I thought maybe he could help me with it."

"What's the angle?"

"I can't tell you."

"Why not?"

"That's privileged information."

"Tucker, you're not a lawyer. You're just a newspaper reporter." Williamson shook his head in disgust. "Look, I know who you are. Everyone in the department knows who you are. You've made a lot of news. But the only thing I care about here is that you've invaded my crime scene. I don't like that. I've never worked with you before, so I'm not sure if I can trust everything you're telling me. Do you know any of the other officers here?"

I looked around the room. I didn't recognize anyone. I told that to Lieutenant Williamson.

"I generally work out of Manhattan," I said.

"Is there someone in Manhattan I could ask about you?"

"Do you know a lieutenant named Aguirre?"

"Aguirre, yeah. We've met."

"He'll vouch for me."

Williamson walked a few steps away and took out his phone. He punched in a number, said something softly and then listened for a few minutes. When he was finished, he came back to where I was.

"Okay, I talked to Aguirre."

"And?"

He smiled. "Well, I wouldn't put him down as a character reference on any job applications."

"Meaning?"

"He says you're a troublemaker, a busybody and a real pain in the ass. He says he's glad you're causing problems for me instead of him."

"Oh."

"He also says you have a disturbing habit of turning up around dead bodies."

"Oh," I said again.

I couldn't think of any other response to that.

"However, he also said you're pretty straight. So I'll buy your whole story for the time being."

The Medical Examiner's Office was here now. They took Renfro's body out of the car and stuffed it into a green body bag. Then they picked it up, placed it on a stretcher and rolled it out to a waiting coroner's vehicle. I turned toward Williamson.

"What do you think happened here?" I asked him.

"What do you mean, what do I think? Renfro killed himself. Hooked up the hose to the car, stepped on the gas and bye-bye world."

"Maybe."

"Maybe?"

"Why would he do it?"

"He was depressed over the death of his partner. Blamed himself for it. I think it's pretty obvious."

Yes, that was the obvious cause.

But maybe too obvious.

"What about his dinner?" I said. "He cooked himself a lasagna dinner and made a fresh pot of coffee before he went into the garage and turned on that motor. I saw them both in the kitchen. Why would he do that if he was going to commit suicide?"

Williamson shrugged. "I don't know. Force of habit or something, I guess. He made his dinner, brewed some coffee and then decided he was going to end it all instead. People who commit suicide do strange things. I remember one woman who cleaned her house from top to bottom before shooting herself in the head. You can't figure these things."

"But it seemed like he was still *fighting* against suicidal tendencies, Lieutenant. I mean, he'd written down the telephone number for the police helpline. He sounded from the other comments he wrote that he was seriously considering make that call. Maybe he did. Can you check to see if there's any record of calls from him to that hot line?"

"We'll check it all out," Williamson said.

"I'm just not sure it was suicide," I told him.

"We'll check it all out," he said again. "We'll check everything out. We check everything out anyway in a case like this. But for now Billy Renfro's death is listed as tentative suicide. Okay?"

I nodded. It really was the obvious way for the police to go here. The only scenario that made sense.

Maura Walsh, Renfro's partner, had died because he left her alone. He blamed himself for her death. Even though he tried to go back to work, he was still so upset he needed to go back on sick leave. Probably he was under tremendous stress too because he feared Internal Affairs were closing in on him over the illegal payoffs he and Maura had been taking.

Suicide was his only way out, and he took it.

It made perfect sense on the face of it.

Except I didn't completely buy the suicide scenario.

I had a nagging suspicion there was something more to Billy Renfro's death.

CHAPTER 35

I'd called in the story to the *Tribune* even before the police arrived. Once I got finished with Lieutenant Williamson, I got back on the phone and added more details. Including the fact that the police were tentatively calling it a suicide.

I went online from my phone, clicked on the *Tribune* website and saw they already had a headline up that said: SLAIN WOMAN COP'S PARTNER KILLS HIMSELF.

I worked the scene a bit more, kept talking to Williamson and other cops there and then filed a lot more to add to that original story.

Eventually, after Williamson had left, I did too. I went back to the *Tribune* office, where I wrote an even more complete story that would appear in the print editions of the paper the next morning.

I went with the official police version of suicide, but I mentioned Billy Renfro's cooked dinner and his apparent attempts to seek help further down in the story. When I was finished with that, I wrote up a sidebar – about my earlier meeting with Renfro at McGuire's, his anguish over his partner's murder and also about how I discovered him dead inside that garage. It ran alongside the main piece on Page 1 under a headline that said: SAD, LAST DAYS OF TRAGIC COP.

Norman Isaacs and Danny Knowlton were still there, standing around the news desk. I walked over and sat down.

"Nice job," Danny said to me. "It all reads great."

Isaacs didn't look as happy.

"Does someone want to tell me exactly what you were doing out there?"

"Trying to come up with a new angle on the story, Norman."

"What story?"

"The Maura Walsh murder."

"How come I didn't know anything about it?"

"She's been working on this angle about Maura Walsh's partner for me," Danny said, even though that wasn't totally true. But I was sure Danny was happy to join in on the credit for my front-page story.

"I'm the city editor here," Isaacs grumbled. "I need to know what my reporters are working on."

"Do I have to clear *everything* with you, Norman?" Danny asked.

"It would be nice."

"Okay, Jessie was working on the story about Maura Walsh's partner Renfro for me. That's why she was at Renfro's house. And that's why we have this front page exclusive. Okay? I've cleared it with you now. But, like you said, you *are* the city editor."

Isaacs glared at him. This was the office politics battle that seemed to go on more than ever now – as Danny became more confident about his position at the paper. Isaacs, on the other hand, was getting more and more paranoid about his job security. Not as paranoid as Lorraine Molinski, but pretty close. Me, I was caught in the middle of all this office distrust and backstabbing. Sometimes I could make it work for me, but not when it got ugly like this.

"What are we going to do next?" Danny asked me now, emphasizing the word "we" as he continued to revel in taking credit for my scoop. A story that he had absolutely no part in. But that's what a newspaper editor does. Takes credit when his reporters do something good, then delegates blame when they screw up. Danny Knowlton sure knew how to work that process to perfection.

I told him and Norman about the Frank Walosin connection that had been the impetus for my going to Renfro's house to try to talk to him again. About how the murdered private investigator had been spying on Renfro and Walsh for Renfro's wife – and claimed he had information to sell about Maura Walsh.

"How did you find out all this?" Norman asked when I was done.

"I obtained access to Walosin's private files."

"How did you manage to do that?"

"You don't want to know."

"Are you telling me you did something illegal to get them?"

"Define illegal."

Danny smiled. Danny Knowlton was happy to get the information, no matter how I did it.

"What do you think it all means?" he asked.

"I don't know. But it doesn't really matter. I'll write another story for tomorrow laying all this information out about the PI Walosin's involvement, and we're way ahead of anyone else in the media. Plus, I think this gives us an opportunity to raise questions in print for the first time about what Walsh and Renfro might have been doing before their deaths. I don't specifically have to say they were on the take. But I can raise questions about their actions, especially on that last night of Maura Walsh's life. What do you think?"

"I think that makes sense," Danny said.

"Agreed," said Isaacs, which kind of surprised me. "It's a legitimate story."

"Okay, then." Danny smiled. "Let's go for it, Jessie."

It sure was nice to see everyone getting along, even if I knew it wouldn't last.

CHAPTER 36

"You stole the file out of the dead PI's office?" Michelle said in amazement.

"I didn't technically *steal* it. I mean, the building manager gave me access to the office. Even though I did lie to him about what I was doing there. And Walosin, who owned the material in the files, was already dead. I'm not sure of the legal implications of that. But the bottom line is what I did could be looked at in different ways. It's kind of in a gray area, legally speaking. I prefer to think of it as—"

"You stole the damn file." Peter Ventura laughed.

"Okay." I sighed. "I stole it."

We were back at the same bar again. A bunch of the reporters and editors were there with me – including Michelle, Peter and Danny. We were sitting at a round table, underneath a wall filled with pictures of famous front pages over the years, drinking from several pitchers of beer. My stories about the dead Billy Renfro and the private investigator and all the rest of it was the main topic of conversation when we started.

But then everyone started telling other journalist stories, especially Peter – who had an endless supply of them from the old newspaper days.

I never got tired of hearing them.

"The greatest obit writer that ever worked on a newspaper in this town was Daniel Fullerton," Peter proclaimed.

"An obit writer?" someone asked.

"Not *an* obit writer. *The* obit writer. Fullerton turned obituaries into an art form. It was the only thing he ever did. Death was his beat, I guess you could say. People said he even looked like an undertaker."

He took a big drink of beer.

"Now, this was long before my time. I think he retired in the sixties or seventies, after one of the big newspaper strikes. But there were still all sorts of stories about him in the newsroom when I was starting out. A lot of them were about how he hated it whenever they took the death of someone famous away from him on the obit page and made it a news story up front. He thought the obits – all the obits – should be him. Just him, no one else.

"Anyway, on the day John F. Kennedy was assassinated, Fullerton supposedly came into the newsroom and saw everyone raving around, stripping wire copy and putting new leads on assassination stories. So he walked over to the managing editor and said: 'Does this mean you'll be taking the Kennedy story for Page 1?'"

Everyone at the table laughed, including me. "Who was the toughest editor you ever worked for?" Danny asked.

"Eddie Slotnick."

That got shrugs from everyone. No one knew him.

"He used to be city editor here. Before Norman Isaacs."

"Before Norman?" Danny laughed. "God, that's ancient history."

"Was he any good?" I asked.

"Yeah, but a real ball-buster. He used to write these brutal memos. One time a columnist's wife died. The guy did a column titled 'My Wife' that was a long, personal memory of the woman. It really had no place in a newspaper."

"Slotnick killed it?"

"No, he let it run."

Peter took another sip of his beer as everyone waited to see what was going to happen next.

"Now a couple of days go by and it's time for the guy to turn in his next column. This one's titled 'My Wife: Part 2'. Slotnick kills this one and sends the guy a memo. Know what it said?"

Everyone shook their head no.

"One wife, one column."

There was more laughter.

"Who was the most colorful guy?" Michelle wanted to know.

"Larry Egan. The greatest rewriteman of all time."

"Why?"

"Because he'd do anything to get a front-page story. Of course, every once in a while he went too far."

"Such as?" I asked.

"One time there was a big hostage drama and Egan told the city editor he'd gotten an exclusive telephone interview with the gunman. The paper put it on Page 1: THEY'LL NEVER TAKE ME ALIVE, GUNMAN VOWS. The next night the gunman gives up without firing a shot – and it turns out he's a deaf mute. The city editor demands an explanation. Egan says: 'Gee, boss, he never told me that.'"

"Yeah, I guess that was going too far." Danny laughed.

"Just a little bit," Michelle said.

"It's a tough call sometimes," Peter said. "How far do you push a story before you cross over that line? The one between aggressive reporting and doing something really unethical."

"Give us an example of something really unethical," someone said.

"Janet Cooke."

"Who?"

"She was a reporter for the *Washington Post*. She did a series of articles a few years ago about an eight-year-old drug addict that won her a Pulitzer Prize. Only it turned out there really was no eight-year-old kid. She'd made it up. They had to take the Pulitzer Prize back."

"Where is she now?" Michelle asked.

Peter shrugged. There were blank looks all around the table. No one knew what had happened to Janet Cooke.

Before we left, someone asked me what I planned to do next on the Maura Walsh story. Of course. Every reporter always wants to know what the next story was going to be. Well, I had an idea about that.

There was a quote I'd used in the Billy Renfro sidebar story I'd done that stuck in my mind. Something he said to me that first day in McGuire's about Maura's death. "She was my partner, and I let her down. I'll have to live with that for the rest of my life. She's dead, and I blame myself for not protecting her better. A police officer is always supposed to be there for their partner. But I wasn't there when Maura needed me. I was off somewhere buying a damn pizza!"

A police officer always stands by their partner, no matter what.

That's one of the unwritten rules among the men and women who belong to the NYPD.

Yep, no question about it, the bond between partners for cops on the street like Billy Renfro and Maura Walsh was an incredibly strong one.

Except I realized now that I'd completely forgotten about another partner.

Billy Renfro's ex-partner.

The one I'd presumably seen in the picture with him at his house.

Maura had been Renfro's partner for six months before her death. But Sam and the others had told me that Renfro had been picking up payments at their places before that. With his previous partner.

So what happened to that partner?

CHAPTER 37

I called Capt. Florio at the 22nd Precinct.

"Who was Billy Renfro's partner before Maura Walsh?" I asked.

"Matt Wysocki."

"What happened to him?"

"He died."

"In the line of duty?"

If Renfro had two partners who died in the line of duty within six months of each other, then it could be more than a coincidence.

"No, a heart attack."

"Was there anything suspicious about it?"

"Now why would there be anything suspicious about a man having a heart attack?"

"Just wondering."

I managed to convince him to give me the address of Matt Wysocki's widow.

It was a small house in a middle-class neighborhood on Staten Island. A sad-faced woman opened the door.

"Mrs. Wysocki?" I said.

"Yes."

"I'd like to talk to you about your husband."

"My husband is dead."

"That's why I'm here."

"You people," she said, shaking her head, "if you people in the department paid this much attention to Matt when he was alive, maybe none of this would have happened."

"I'm not with the police department, Mrs. Wysocki."

"Whatever—"

"My name is Jessie Tucker, and I'm a reporter with the *New York Tribune*. I'm not here to hurt you or the memory of your husband. I'd just like to find out a little bit more about him for an article I'm working on."

Her face relaxed a bit. She opened the door and let me in the house. We sat down in the living room. There were pictures around of two children – a boy and a girl, both from when they were growing up and now as adults. There was an old wedding photo of Matt Wysocki and his wife on the mantel. And a shot of the entire family next to a Christmas tree, holding up their presents and smiling for the camera. The happy pictures seemed out of place in this house now. There was a sadness here – personified by Mrs. Wysocki – that permeated everything.

"Why are you here?" she asked.

"I'd like you to tell me about your husband's death."

"There's not very much to tell. You live with someone for so many years, and then they're gone just like that. In a matter of seconds. You don't even have time to say goodbye.

"We were in bed when it happened. I woke up and heard Matt gasping for breath. At first, I thought it was a bad dream. But then I realized something was terribly wrong. Matt was clutching his chest and moaning in pain. I was helpless. I couldn't do anything at all to save him.

"I ran to the phone and called 911. But it was too late. By the time I got back to him in the bedroom, he was gone. The ambulance people couldn't revive him. They told me he was dead, and then they removed his body.

"The thing is," she said, wringing her hands in anguish as she talked, "they say a heart attack like that is the best way for a person to die. There's no lingering illness or suffering or pain that can go on for months or even years like with cancer or some other kind of terminal illness. The problem with sudden, unexpected deaths, though, is it's so tough on the people who love them. Like I said, you don't even get a chance to say goodbye."

I felt badly about putting the woman through all this. I thought maybe there'd be something I could find out about Matt Wysocki's death, but there wasn't. People die like he did all the time. There was usually no hidden meaning or significance to any of it. Only for the people like his wife who were left behind to try to deal with the heartache and the loss.

"Had your husband been under a lot of stress?" I asked.

"You might say that."

"Because of his job?"

"Not just the job, it was the bullshit that went with the job. There was a lot of pressure on my husband before he died. Now I have to face all those problems by myself."

"What do you mean?"

"This house," she said, looking around the living room, "it holds many wonderful memories. Memories of my husband. Memories of watching my children grow up here. Now it's going to be all gone soon. I won't be able to live here anymore."

"Why not?"

"I can't make the mortgage payments to the bank."

"How about your husband's police pension?"

"There is no pension."

"There must be something—"

"The department says it's been frozen, pending a final investigation by the Internal Affairs Department into his conduct."

It wasn't hard to figure out what had happened. Internal Affairs discovered Matt Wysocki was on the take. A corrupt cop loses everything, even his pension. This had probably all been happening at the time of his death. But now his wife was left alone to face the consequences.

"Did Internal Affairs believe your husband was taking bribes as a police officer?"

"Yes."

"Was he?"

"I asked Matt that question only one time. He wouldn't answer me. He never refused to tell me anything else the entire time we were married. But he wouldn't answer this. He just walked away, went into another room and shut the door behind him. I could hear him crying in there. I never asked the question again. I guess I didn't want to know the answer."

She looked over at the wedding picture on the mantelpiece.

"Matt was so frustrated those last few years. He'd been a police officer for so long, but never seemed to get anywhere. He saw other people getting promoted, but it never seemed to work out for him. There were minorities, women, younger people – the department always cared about everyone but him.

"I think it got to him at the end. He was a good cop for most of his career until then. He just wanted something more for himself – he wanted something more for me and our children. I suppose that's why he did what he did.

"That last day, a man from Internal Affairs came to see him. He was very mean and uncaring. I didn't like him. He said he needed to talk to my husband in private. I don't know what they said, but my husband was very upset after the man left. He was so agitated that he barely touched his supper or spoke to me for the rest of the night. Then we went to bed, and that's when he died. Whatever that man told Matt, I think it caused the onset of his fatal heart attack.

"I'll never forgive the department for that. They didn't have to treat Matt that way. Matt was a good man. He was a good cop. Okay, he made a mistake. But no one is perfect, not even police officers. Why couldn't they have given him a second chance?"

Mrs. Wysocki began to cry now.

"Do you remember the name of the officer from Internal Affairs?" I asked her quietly.

"I'll never forget it as long as I live," she said. "It was Garrison. A man named Russell Garrison."

CHAPTER 38

The Internal Affairs section was located in a nondescript building several blocks away and across town from Police Headquarters.

Many people thought putting the office so far away was supposed to be a statement of sorts about its split from the official police bureaucracy. The guys in Internal Affairs always boasted that they couldn't be bought and they couldn't be influenced by the police brass. So what if other cops hated them? That meant they were doing their job.

Russell Garrison was in his forties, with slicked-back hair and a closely cropped mustache. He knew who I was as soon as he heard my name. He didn't seem particularly excited by my appearance there.

"What do you want?" Garrison asked as I pulled up a chair in front of his desk.

"I understand that you went to see Matt Wysocki on the same day that he died of a heart attack."

"So?"

"His wife says you weren't very nice to him."

"Maybe Matt should have thought about that before he decided to break the law."

"Wysocki was dirty?"

"That's right."

"Can you prove that?"

"I don't have to anymore, he's dead."

"But you're still trying to keep his pension away from the widow."

"That's what happens to dirty cops. Hell, you should know that better than anyone. You're supposed to be such a hotshot police reporter. Don't go acting all naive with me about cop corruption."

"What did you say to Wysocki?"

"I simply spelled out for Matt Wysocki the gravity of his legal situation and laid out for him a possible solution to his problems."

"You wanted him to cut a deal and give up the other dirty cops that he knew about?"

"Something like that."

"Do you have any idea of the pressure that put on the guy? Rat out his friends and fellow officers or take the rap by himself? We're not talking about a murderer here, Garrison. This was a guy who screwed up for the first time in his goddamned career. Maybe he deserved a second chance."

Garrison shrugged. "Why are you here asking me questions about Wysocki?"

"I'm working on a story about Maura Walsh."

"What does that have to do with Wysocki? They never worked together."

"No, but they shared the same partner. Billy Renfro."

Garrison didn't say anything.

"Were you investigating Renfro for corruption too?"

"No comment."

"Which means you would have been investigating Maura Walsh before she died. She was Renfro's partner now. The new Matt Wysocki. What exactly did you find out about Maura Walsh? Was she as clean and wholesome and heroic as everyone thought she was? The golden girl of the force? The police commissioner's daughter who died a hero?"

"I'm not talking to you about any of that. I don't give a goddamn about how many important people you know in the department from what happened to you in Central Park or how you used to hang out with the mayor. You want to write a story about Maura Walsh for your paper, then go write it. Why are you here busting my balls?"

"I only want to tell the truth about Maura Walsh," I said quietly.

"Sorry, but I can't help you," he muttered, looking down at some paperwork in front of him.

"I know Maura was dirty," I said.

That got his attention.

"I know she was taking payoffs from restaurants and other businesses in her precinct," I said. "I'm not sure how widespread this was. But I assume it was not something she started or something she was doing on her own. I think Maura got caught up in something after she transferred to the 22nd and she used some bad judgement and did some things that were wrong. Just like Matt Wysocki did when he was at the 22nd. I'm still hoping you can tell me more."

"Everything I know will be in my report," Garrison said.

"Where does that go?"

"To my superiors."

"In other words, it probably winds up on the desk of Deputy Commissioner Walsh."

"Give us a little credit here, huh? If we did have evidence against Maura Walsh, and I'm not saying we do, we're certainly not going to send a report on a corrupt cop to her own father. Even if he is the deputy commissioner. It's called a conflict of interest."

"In other words, you're going around her father on this one?"

"Once again, I have no comment."

"Does anyone else know about this yet?"

"About what?"

"About Maura Walsh being crooked."

"Are we finished here?" Garrison asked.

I decided it was time to go. I was getting nowhere. I stood up and glared at Garrison, who was still doing his best to ignore me.

"Maura Walsh was a good person," I said.

"Whatever you say."

"She's dead now, Garrison. Why not just leave her alone?"

He looked up from his paperwork.

"Can we go off the record here?"

"If you want to."

"I have your word on that?"

"Yes, you have my word whatever you tell me will be off the record. And I take my word as a journalist very seriously."

"Okay, you wanted to know about Maura Walsh? I'll tell you about Maura Walsh," Garrison said. "If she wasn't dead now, she'd probably be indicted."

CHAPTER 39

I was still driving the rental car I'd used to go to New Jersey to see Billy Renfro's wife.

After I left IAD headquarters, I made my way across town toward the East River Drive, which would take me north. The traffic wasn't bad, but I noticed one car behind me in my rearview mirror – a blue police car. I couldn't be sure it was the same police car I'd seen a few times before. They all look pretty much alike. But I sure had a sinking feeling that it was.

I made a turn onto the entrance of the East River Drive, and the police car stayed behind me as I got in the northbound lane. It continued to follow me there until we were almost at Houston Street. Then it turned on the siren and flashing red light, pulled up alongside me and motioned for me to pull over at the Houston Street exit. I did.

Two cops got out of the squad car. I recognized them right away. Shockley and Janko, the two who'd given me the warning about not digging too deeply into the Maura Walsh story when I'd been at the 22nd Precinct. I'd checked them out afterwards. Luther Shockley and Vic Janko. Shockley was a thirty-year veteran. He had a half-day's growth of beard and a good-size pot belly spilling out over his pants as he walked toward me. Janko had been on the force five years. He was in better shape than Shockley, but there was something creepy about his eyes when he looked at you. *Crazy eyes*, I thought to myself.

They both came over to my car with hard stares on their faces and their hands on their gun belts.

"Step out of the car," Shockley said. "And let us see your driver's license."

I opened the door and got out.

"Is there a problem?" I asked as I passed him the license.

"Yeah, there's a problem, Ms. Tucker," he said, glancing down at it and then back at me. "The problem is its only fifty mph back there on the East River Drive. You were breaking the speed limit."

"I wasn't speeding," I said quietly. "I just got on the highway a few minutes ago. I wouldn't have had much time to start speeding, even if I wanted to. Which I didn't. I was barely doing forty mph when you pulled me over."

"I clocked you at sixty-one mph. My partner here can verify that. Vic, can you verify that for Ms. Tucker?" Vic Janko nodded. He still had that crazy look in his eyes, which scared the hell out of me. "See, that makes it two to one that you were speeding. You against both of us. So you lose. Get the picture?"

"I think I'm starting to."

"Also," he went on, "you've got a defective right taillight back there. Very unsafe. I'm going to have to give you a ticket for that too. You need to take better care of your vehicle, Ms. Tucker."

"It's a rental car," I said. "Not mine."

"You're still responsible for making sure it's in a safe and legal operating condition when you're driving it on a highway."

I walked around to the back of the car and looked at the right side where the taillight was. It looked fine. I walked back to the open window of the car, reached in and clicked on the turn signal. Then I checked the taillight again. It was flashing just like it should. Worked like a charm.

"My taillight's not broken," I said.

Shockley turned toward his partner Janko, who kicked it hard with his booted foot. The taillight shattered.

"Now it's broken," Janko said.

I sighed.

Then Shockley looked over at my purse, which was still on the front seat of the car.

"Show us what's inside that bag," he said.

"Why?"

"You also seemed to be driving erratically from what we could ascertain. Possibly due to the influence of some sort of drugs. That's why we need to examine the contents of your handbag. Will you show it to us?"

"What if I refuse?"

"You have the right to contact a lawyer, if you want."

"Maybe I will."

"But then we'd have to detain you, bring you back to the precinct and put you in a holding cell until the lawyer arrives."

I didn't have a lot of choices here. I just wanted to get through this with as little hassle from these two as possible. I gave them the handbag.

Shockley rummaged through it for a minute or so – and then took out a marijuana cigarette. He held it up in front of me.

"Tsk, tsk, Tucker. Look what's in here. An illegal substance."

"That's not mine," I told him. "You planted it."

"Possession is nine-tenths of the law." He smiled.

"You're not going to get away with that."

Shockley shrugged, then conferred briefly with Janko.

"Okay, we're going to let you slide on the illegal drug charge this time. But we will have to ticket you for speeding and your broken taillight. We hope we don't have to talk to you again. Next time we might not be so lenient as to let you off with just a few tickets."

He took out a pen and ticket book and began writing me up from the information on my driver's license. While he was doing that, I looked down at his badge number and his partner's. With their last names above the badges.

"Luther Shockley and Vic Janko. Those are your names, right?"

"Why?" Shockley smirked. "Do you want to file a complaint against us?"

I bit down nervously on my lower lip.

"You two are a real credit to the police force," I said.

Shockley handed me the tickets.

"Before you do anything else stupid, Ms. Tucker, remember that we're always out there watching for people like you. Think about that. Me and Janko here and a lot of our friends. You don't want to get on our bad side any more than you already are. Think about that if you ever consider impugning the integrity of the police."

"Why do I have the feeling this has something to do with Maura Walsh?" I asked.

"Maura is dead," Shockley said. "Let her rest in peace."

CHAPTER 40

The name of the genealogy investigator that Ellen had hooked me up with was Wendy Carruthers. She was a few years older than me, and she said she'd been doing this type of work for ten years.

Carruthers had a law degree, and she'd practiced law for a big New York City firm for several years. But then she said she'd done some genealogy checks on her own background, and she became intrigued by the field.

One of the things that made genealogy even more fascinating for her, she told me, was that she determined she was a foundling (an abandoned baby) when she started searching her family tree – or at least the ancestor of a foundling. A great-grandfather had been left on the doorstep of a church in Austria around the turn of the century, and so he never knew who his birth parents were.

Because of that, she had become obsessed with finding out answers – about herself as well as him. The law degree was important, although not essential, for a genealogy investigator, she said, because it helped open a lot of doors to the past. And, she told me proudly, she had even been able to track her great-grandfather's family history back to the birth mother who'd left him on that church doorstep.

Wendy Carruthers told me all this in one big burst of words that first day when I went to see her, barely pausing as she rattled off all this information about her and her background and the study of genealogy.

Normally, I would have found it extremely interesting – maybe even fascinating like she did – because of all her energy and passion and commitment to what she did.

I might have even thought about doing a story about her – and the whole idea of being a genealogy investigator – for the *Tribune* as maybe a big Sunday feature article.

But now I just wanted to deal with my own damn genealogy problem.

So I listened patiently until she was done, then gave her all the pertinent information I could about me, my mother and the man named James Tucker who had been my father.

That night, when I got back to my apartment and was trying to settle down after my stressful encounter with the police on the East River Drive, I found a message from her waiting for me on my home phone. It said she had some information about James Tucker. She did not say what that information was. In fact, she made a point of telling me that it was something she preferred to share with me in person.

Which mean it must have been pretty significant information.

And so I was now back in her office, waiting to learn more about the father I never knew and what had happened to him since he disappeared thirty-six years ago.

"Here's what I've found out," Carruthers said. "I've located the records for a James Tucker that seems to fit the profile of the man you've been looking for. This James Tucker was born in Raleigh, North Carolina in 1959, he attended college in Dayton, Ohio and he moved to Cincinnati after graduation where he worked as a marketing representative for an advertising firm. He married a woman named Susan Thorne from Pittsburgh, who he'd met in college. She gave birth to a child, a girl named Jessica."

Carruthers smiled at me when she said that. Susan Thorne was my mother's maiden name. And Jessica, of course, was me. My full name was Jessica Anne Tucker.

"Sometime soon after that, James Tucker disappeared. He was fired from his job for not showing up and not heard from again for a long time. But I was able to pick up his trail a few years later in Raleigh, his hometown. He filed for divorce from there with Susan Thorne Tucker, then married a woman named Jackie Stafford. They had three children, two boys and a girl. Based on all the evidence I've been able to accumulate, this appears to be the man named James Tucker that you wanted to find."

I nodded, still in a state of shock. I wanted to say something – anything – but no words came out.

This was the moment I had been waiting for.

The answers to all the questions I had about my father.

"Have you talked to him?" I finally asked, when I could pull myself together enough to actually speak.

"No."

"Why not? If we asked him why he left, told him who I was—"

"James Tucker is dead."

She showed me an obituary about him from the Raleigh newspaper. It said James Tucker had been killed in a highway accident about ten years earlier. He had been a schoolteacher, who taught social studies and civics at a local high school and also was an assistant coach on the baseball team there. A school bus carrying the team back from a game was rear-ended on Interstate 95. Most of the students survived, but three people died. One of them was James Tucker.

I stared at the words in front of me for a long time. I couldn't believe it. I just couldn't believe this was happening. After all this time, wondering about my father and dreaming about finding him one day and somehow reuniting – well, none of that really mattered. Because he was dead. Just like my mother was dead. Which meant I truly had no family at all anymore.

But then I remembered something.

"You said he had three children with his new wife. Two boys and a girl. That means I have brothers and a sister. At least… half-brothers and a half-sister. That's something. Do you think you can try to put me in touch with them? They're my family, after all. Maybe not the family I was looking for. But the only family I have."

Wendy Carruthers shook her head no.

"There's more," she said.

She looked extremely uncomfortable. But why? She'd already told me my father was dead. What else could there be?

And that's when I found out.

"James Tucker wasn't your biological father," Carruthers said.

"What are you talking about?"

"I found records that show at the time of your birth, James Tucker demanded a paternity test be taken. That was shortly before he left your mother and his job and everything else in Cincinnati. DNA testing was much more basic back then, but paternity testing was available. We don't know why he wanted a paternity test, but we do know the results. They were negative. Like I said, James Tucker was not your father."

"Then who was my father?"

"No one knows," Wendy Carruthers said sadly.

CHAPTER 41

I don't remember everything that happened after that.

A lot of it is still a blur.

I remember Wendy Carruthers telling me more about the DNA findings that confirmed James Tucker, the man my mother was married to when I was born, was not my biological father. I remember asking her questions without any real answers. And I remember leaving the building where her office was and finding myself out on the street again.

I'm not sure exactly what I did then.

I know I called the *Tribune* office at some point and said I was sick and couldn't come to work for the rest of the day. I'd never called in sick before. Even during my worst days with all the pain from my injuries after the Central Park attack. But this was a different kind of pain. And I couldn't face the people at the *Tribune* right now with my world suddenly turned upside down by Wendy Carruthers.

I called Ellen. She was the one person I could talk to about this. But she wasn't in her office. I left a message asking her to get back to me as soon as possible. But I didn't know how long that would be.

I went home for a while. But I didn't want to stay there. Not alone. So I went outside again and began to walk. Up Irving Place to Gramercy Park, then East over to Third Avenue and uptown after that. I walked for a long time. At 58th Street, I saw a little girl – no more than five or six years old – being carried on the shoulders of her father. She looked so happy. I know it sounds crazy, but I was jealous of that six-year-old girl. Why did she have a father and I didn't? Why did everyone else have a father except me? Even Maura Walsh had a father. She might have hated him by the end, but at least she had a father to hate.

I thought I'd had someone to hate like that all my life. James Tucker.

But I couldn't hate him anymore.

He was dead.

And he wasn't even my father.

It was all a lie.

I just couldn't get that harsh reality out of my mind, no matter how hard I tried.

I checked my messages. Still nothing from Ellen. I tried to call her again, but no luck. Where in the hell was she? I needed to talk to her. I needed to talk to someone. Well, not anyone. Someone I felt comfortable with and someone I could trust and someone I wanted to be with right now. If not Ellen, then who? I thought about calling Michelle or Lorraine or even Peter at the *Tribune*. But I really didn't want to involve the people I worked with there in something so personal for me. Besides, I'd already called in sick. No, I needed to stay away from the *Tribune* right now.

I kept walking. I was in the East 70s now. I pretended I didn't know where I was going. But I had a destination. The Hangout. The restaurant where Sam worked.

Except Sam wasn't there when I got to the Hangout. They said it was his night off. But Sam had told me he lived nearby the restaurant. And he told me I should call him when I was ready. I reached into my handbag, took out the card Sam had given me and called his number...

*

"What the hell is wrong, Jessie?" he asked when he opened the door of his place and saw me.

I was a mess. I was pretty tired too from all the walking I'd done. My legs kept buckling underneath me when I tried to stand. So I stood there holding onto his front door for support. Then, when I tried to go in, I stumbled on my bad right leg. Sam caught me and carried me to the couch.

He asked me if he could get me anything.

I said I sure would like a glass of wine, and he went to get it.

While he was gone, I thought about why I was there. How much should I tell him? How honest with him should I be about what I was feeling right now? In the end, I decided not to tell him anything about Wendy Carruthers or my father who wasn't my father or any of the rest of it. I would tell that all to Ellen when I found her. But not Sam.

No, I'd come here for a different reason, I realized now.

I was tired of being a victim. I'd been a victim in the park twelve years ago. Now I felt like a victim all over again because of what I'd found out about my family history from Wendy Carruthers. I couldn't do anything to change any of those things.

But didn't want to be the victim anymore.

I wanted to take control of my life, to do something on my own that was different and daring and exciting.

I looked around at his apartment. It was a two-bedroom in a high rise that had a doorman and even a concierge downstairs. Sam lived pretty well. I guess there must be good money in managing a restaurant. There were a lot of books around, just like my place. I liked that. I looked at some of the books on his shelves. Faulkner. Hemingway. Poe. Lots of newer stuff too. Stephen King, James Patterson, Janet Evanovich, Gillian Flynn and a lot of other popular writers. There was also a computer, a printer and a writing desk piled high with sheets of paper and notes on yellow legal pads.

"So this is the writer's lair, huh?" I said when he came with my wine and then sat down in a chair across from me.

"It's where I work." He smiled.

"Very nice."

I took a big drink of my wine. I was pretty sure I'd had wine earlier too at a place or two I stopped along the way in my walk. I kept drinking as we talked. When my glass was empty, I stood up and walked over to where the wine bottle was next to Sam. I poured myself another glass. I drank some more of it.

I was definitely starting to feel the effects of the wine now, both this and whatever I'd drunk earlier. Plus all the emotions running through me were making it even worse. The room seemed to be spinning a bit as I plopped down next to him. I reached over, took his hand and squeezed it. He squeezed back. I felt tired. I lay my head down on his shoulder. It felt good.

I picked my head up, leaned closer and kissed him.

He kissed me back.

"So is it too late to take back my no-sex decree I made at lunch the other day?" I asked him.

"I don't think there's any hard and fast rules binding you to that agreement." He smiled again.

"And you are a lawyer."

"*Was* a lawyer."

"Whatever."

I kissed him again.

"Let's do it then."

"You mean have sex?"

"Yes."

He looked uncomfortable. "I don't think we should do that right now."

"Why not?"

"It's just…"

"You're not gay or something, are you?"

"No, I'm not gay."

"Are all your working parts in order?"

"Last time I checked."

"Then don't you find me attractive?"

"I think you're very attractive."

"So what's the problem?"

"Look, you're upset about something, Jessie. You've been acting strangely ever since you got here. You're definitely very emotionally distraught. To be honest, I think you may be drunk."

I was starting to get mad now.

"So what?" I said. "You're an unpublished writer! Tomorrow morning I'll be sober and you'll still be an unpublished writer."

Of course, somewhere deep down inside, I knew he was right. He didn't want to take advantage of me in the condition I was in. I realized that later. But all I could think about at the moment was here I was offering myself to this guy, and he's telling me no.

"You can spend the night here if you want," Sam said. "I'll sleep on the couch."

"No, thank you."

I tried to stand up. The room definitely seemed to be spinning now.

"Then let me take you home," he said.

"I don't think so."

I grabbed my handbag and started for the door.

"At least wait while I call you a cab."

"I can find a cab myself," I told him.

Somehow, I made it out of the apartment, down the elevator and out onto the street by myself. I stood there for a while and let the fresh air help clear my head. As it did, I realized I was embarrassed by the performance I'd just put on back there. I thought about going back and apologizing, but I didn't know what to say.

I kept standing there for a long time hoping maybe he'd follow me out onto the street, put his arms around me and hold me for a while and tell me everything was going to be all right.

That's what I really wanted – just a man to hold me and show me some affection.

My fiancé Gary Bettig walked away from me.

So did Logan Kincaid, the guy from California.

Even my own father left me.

But Sam Rawlings didn't come chasing after me.

No one ever did.

CHAPTER 42

What was the point? What was the point of any of it? That's what I kept thinking about after I finally made it back to my apartment on Irving Place.

My apartment was normally a refuge for me from the crazy world that I lived in outside on the streets of New York City and at my job in the *Tribune* newsroom too. Here I had my books and my movies and my comfort foods in the kitchen and all the other good things in the life I'd so painstakingly built for myself after the horror of what happened to me in Central Park.

But, lying there awake alone in my bedroom now, I suddenly realized the utter hopelessness and futility of everything I'd done.

Because you can't change the past.

And you can't undo the terrible deeds that have been done.

No matter how hard you try to make it right again.

I guess I first discovered this difficult life lesson a long time ago when I was a young reporter starting out at the *Tribune*. I was full of self-righteousness and noble ideas and a naive belief that I could change the world and make it a better place back in those days.

That all evaporated during a conversation with the wife of a convenience store owner on a hot summer night in Brooklyn.

Her husband had been murdered during a robbery because he'd hesitated a second too long in opening a cash drawer. I was with the cops investigating the case and they tracked the holdup man to a nearby bar where he still had the stolen money. They easily captured him. I called in the story to the paper, and then I went back to the store to make sure the woman had heard the good news.

"They caught the man who killed your husband," I told her.

"I don't care about that," she sobbed to me. "I just want my husband back."

So in the end, even if we accomplish the things we set out to do, it turns out to be a hollow victory.

Like being attacked in Central Park will never leave my mind.

Or like finding out the truth about my father – that he never was my father at all – made me feel worse and more alone than I ever had before in my life.

And it's the same with Maura Walsh. Even if I do find out who murdered Maura, it will never bring her back to life.

So why did I keep trying?

Well, I was a reporter. And reporters went looking for facts and answers. Like I did with Central Park and my father. Now, hopefully, I would find out the answers about Maura Walsh too. And, when that was done, I'd start working on a new story and do it all over again.

I knew a reporter at another paper who once compared what we did to the Albert Camus story of Sisyphus, the mythical character forced by the gods to push a heavy rock up a hill, only to see it roll back down again every time he did it. The rock was always at the bottom of the hill, and all he could do was keep pushing it to the top again and again. This was his punishment, this was his life.

Was that what I was doing here?

With Maura Walsh?

My father?

My own life?

Okay, maybe it was.

But, like Sisyphus, I didn't know anything else to do.

So I'd just keep pushing the rock up the mountain for as long as it took.

CHAPTER 43

I had never visited the scene of the crime: the spot where Maura Walsh was killed. Oh, I knew it had been weeks since her murder. There weren't likely to be any clues or evidence still there after all that time. But I wanted to see it in person. I was desperate for any kind of a lead on this story. Why not start at the place where it all happened?

Little Italy, the neighborhood where Maura Walsh died, was in Lower Manhattan. An Italian enclave that's endured for years in this changing city. We sometimes think of it because of John Gotti and other mob figures. But for many years it was made up of hard-working Italians – some of whom lived in buildings that had been there for years.

Now though, just like a lot of other parts of the city, many of the old buildings were coming down and being replaced by co-ops, cafés and cappuccino stores.

I stood on the street there now – next to the alley where Maura Walsh's body was found – and wondered what happened to her during those last few minutes of her life.

The alley was next to one of the buildings that was being renovated or replaced. This one was a squat, gray, six-story structure with the windows boarded up and even some graffiti on the front door.

On the far corner, I could see a cappuccino store. Next to it was the pizza place called Delmonico's where Billy Renfro had gone on the night Maura Walsh died. Next to that was a store that sold T-shirts. I decided to talk to everyone. I started with the pizza place.

"Yeah, I remember the cop," the woman behind the counter told me when I asked about Billy Renfro. "I was here that night and gave him the pizza. I didn't know who he was or think much of it then. But the police came to question me afterwards, so I figured out the whole story of what happened to that poor woman cop in the alley down the street."

"Renfro just came in here, ordered his pizza, waited for it and left?" I asked.

"Sure, that's pretty much the way it happened."

"And you don't remember anything else?"

"Just that he acted real nervous."

"Nervous how?"

The woman shrugged. "You know, like impatient. He kept checking his watch and walking over to look out the window, as if he was waiting for someone. Then he paid for the pizza, and he left. A little while later, I heard all the sirens and knew something was going on. That's really about all I know."

The guy at the cappuccino shop didn't know anything about the murder. He hadn't even been there that night. He knew all about the building next to the alley though. He said there'd been construction crews inside, tearing apart the apartments. It was going to be turned into luxury co-ops that people said would cost at least a million dollars apiece. The cappuccino guy was happy about that, figuring the new tenants would be good business for him. But he didn't like all the construction work. He said the noise drove him crazy.

The clerk at the T-shirt shop wasn't very helpful either.

I went back to the alley and stood there again for a while. It was just an empty alley. This was where Maura Walsh had died. She didn't die quickly. It took her maybe as long as an hour to bleed to death. Someone left her there like that to die. Alone. Just like someone had left me to die alone a long time ago in Central Park. I'd survived. But Maura Walsh didn't. She died a lonely death in this alley. Far away from her friends and family and everyone else who loved her. Except for her partner, of course. He was next door buying pizza. And then he came over here and found her.

That was his story anyway.

It didn't make sense.

How did Billy Renfro find Maura's body here? He didn't first go to the cappuccino bar or the T-shirt place or any of the other likely spots. He came here to this alley once he started looking for her. Even if it took him nearly an hour to do that.

The conclusion was inescapable. Renfro knew all along where Maura had gone. And maybe why too. That was probably why he seemed so nervous and kept checking his watch and looking out the window while he waited for his pizza. But why? What in the world was Maura Walsh doing?

I walked up to the front door of the building being renovated next to this spot – and read the graffiti on the front door. Some of it was sex stuff. Some political slogans. I guess I was hoping to find something in the writing that might jump out at me as a clue. But I didn't. It was just a lot of graffiti, that's all.

I pushed open the door and went inside.

The lobby had already been gutted by the construction crews. The workmen had left behind some of their debris – empty boxes, paint cans and drop cloths. There was even a ladder still leaning up against one of the walls. No reason to think that any of this had anything to do with Maura Walsh's death outside. But I wanted to check everything.

After a few minutes in there, I couldn't think of anything else to do so I started to leave. I was just about out the door when I saw the label on the side of one of the boxes left behind by the people working there. It was the name of a private sanitation crew that must have been hired to clean up the mess.

I recognized the name right away.

Bennato Sanitation Services.

The company owned by mob boss Dominic (Fat Nic) Bennato.

The same man who owned two of the X-rated businesses that Maura Walsh had visited on the last night of her life.

CHAPTER 44

Tell it like you would in a bar.

That's an old newspaper adage they teach you as a young reporter. The idea is to simplify even a complicated story into its most basic elements. The best way to do that is to pretend you've just burst into a bar to tell everyone the information you have. That way you cut through all the bullshit and the extraneous information and get right to the point.

Let's say, for example, you see a horrible traffic accident on the street outside the bar. You don't run inside and begin an analysis of traffic flow problems on the streets of New York. You don't talk about rising auto insurance rates. You don't discuss the need for more driver education classes in our schools. You tell them what happened, which is:

1) There was a big accident outside.
2) At least two people are dead.
3) Several others are hurt.
4) It happened when a taxicab ran a red light, smashed into another car and careened onto the sidewalk.

I decided to do this with my story. Strip away all the non-essential information that was confusing me and deal with the most basic facts I knew. Just like I was telling it for the first time in a bar.

Fact No. 1: Someone murdered Police Officer Maura Walsh.

Fact No. 2: Someone murdered her partner, Police Officer Billy Renfro – unless you believed it was a suicide, which I didn't – a few weeks later.

Fact No. 3: Someone murdered Private Investigator Frank Walosin who had been spying on A) Maura Walsh and B) Billy Renfro before his own death.

The one thing that popped out at you when you looked at it like that was the obvious link between all three deaths.

Of course, they didn't have to be connected. Maura Walsh might have been the victim of a random crime, like the police theorized. Billy Renfro could have taken his own life out of guilt and depression over the loss of his partner. And Frank Walosin might have been killed by an angry client or someone else who was part of another case in his files.

When you looked at it like this, as three separate random cases, it eliminated a lot of suspects.

Except it didn't make sense to me that way.

And when you linked them up – when you made the assumption that Billy Renfro and Frank Walosin both died because of something they knew about Maura Walsh's murder – then everything started to fall into place. I'd been nibbling around that idea ever since this story started, but now it was time to embrace it wholeheartedly. Whoever killed Maura Walsh killed Billy Renfro and Frank Walosin too.

The next question, of course, was who?

Well, once you linked all three cases, it created a list of potential suspects. Corrupt cops who were afraid she might be working for her father. The people being forced to make payoffs to her – everyone from the bodega owner to Sam Rawlings. Maybe even her own father, who could have feared she was going to destroy the hallowed Walsh family legacy if her illegal acts were exposed.

And last, but certainly not least, mob boss Dominic (Fat Nic) Bennato, the most notorious of the people she was apparently involved with in the corruption.

I sure didn't see Sam as a murderer. Or any of the other shakedown victims I'd met at the various locations either, for that matter. It was just a cost of doing business for them. And I found it really difficult to believe that Deputy Commissioner Walsh might have anything to do with the murder of his own daughter. That left other corrupt cops – like Shockley and Janko and whoever else they worked for – but I wasn't certain even corrupt officers like that would murder one of their own.

Dominic Bennato seemed to be the most likely candidate.

I went through the articles about Bennato I could find quickly online. There were a lot of them. Murders, bribery, bookmaking, drug dealing – you name it. He'd become a mob superstar in the media. Everyone talked about him the way they used to talk about John Gotti or even Al Capone. He seemed to like the publicity too. There were stories and pictures of him showing up at parties, movie premieres and fancy restaurants. He was a celebrity – just like a movie star or a Super Bowl quarterback or a pop music idol.

I wasn't sure what any of this meant, but I was sure about one thing. Bennato was the only clear-cut connection I could find in all this. His name kept coming up in a lot of places.

Bennato was the key.

Bennato was the link.

Bennato was the man who might have all the answers.

I needed to figure out a way to talk to him.

And I could only think of one person who might be able to help me do that.

CHAPTER 45

"Do you want to get a cup of coffee with me at the Starbucks downstairs?" I asked Michelle. "I'm buying."

"Why?"

"Why what?"

"Why do you want to buy me coffee?"

"No reason. Just to chat."

"Jessie, we've worked together in this newsroom for quite a while now. You have never suggested we have coffee 'just to chat' in all of that time. You've always been too busy working on a story, and so have I. That's why I figure this has to be about some story you're working on."

"It is."

"Maura Walsh?"

I nodded. "I need another favor from you on this story, Michelle."

"Why didn't you just say that in the first place? All right, let's go get my free coffee."

A few minutes later, we were sitting by a window overlooking Sixth Avenue near where the *Tribune* was located. The streets were packed with tourists, vendors and ordinary New Yorkers. I really wished I could spend more time just appreciating the sights and sounds of this city sometimes, instead of always working so hard.

I was drinking a regular small coffee. Michelle, on the other hand, had ordered the largest size mocha and added whipped cream and fruit and other things to it.

"I realize I promised you a free drink here if you'd help me out with a favor," I said jokingly to her as I eyed it in all its enormity. "But that's a helluva big cup you've got there, Michelle."

"Well, I figure it's a big favor."

"All I need from you is some information."

"Topic?"

"Dominic Bennato."

Michelle did something I'd almost never seen her do before. She went silent. Stared down at her mocha for a long time without saying a word. I'd never seen Michelle silent about anything. I thought at first maybe she was afraid to talk about Bennato at all. But I was wrong. She was just collecting her thoughts about him to answer me.

"And this is about Maura Walsh?" she asked finally.

"Yes. Bennato owned several of the places Maura Walsh went on her last night. I think she was taking payoffs from him."

"And you figure that could have had something to do with her murder?"

"It seems like the most likely scenario for me at the moment. Unless you buy the theory that Maura Walsh's death was just a random murder."

Michelle nodded.

"Look, Michelle, you told me you met Bennato when you did that series on mob bosses a while back. I went back and read all your stuff in the clips. I want to find out more about him. And I want to try to talk to him too. But he never answers any of my calls to his office. How can I find Dominic Bennato to talk to him?"

"You don't find Dominic Bennato, he finds you."

"No, really, Michelle—"

"I'm serious. That's how I did it. His people hang out in a club down in Little Italy called Marcello's. I had to go there, tell his people I wanted to contact him for my piece and wait until he got back to me. A day or so later, a car picked me up and took me to meet him. I was a little freaked out, but I did it. I mean,

I'll do almost anything to get a story, you know that, Jessie. But this one had me worried more than anything else I've ever done. In the end, the interview worked out fine. I thought he might be upset about me writing a story calling him one of the city's top mob bosses. But all he really cared about what that I gave him top play over the other bosses, and made sure I said he was the most important of them. Go figure, huh?"

She shook her head and sipped some of the mocha.

"I've never told anyone about this. Certainly not anyone at the paper. But I took a favor from him when I did that article. I was desperate for an apartment. My sublet was over and I had nowhere to go. I mentioned it to Bennato that day in the interview. The next day I got a call from some real estate agency he was a partner in offering me a great apartment for an incredibly low rent. I took it. At least for a while. Until I found another place about six months later. I'm not proud of it, Jessie. But, like they say – or at least I told myself then – anything goes when you're trying to find an apartment in Manhattan."

"And Bennato never caused you any problems?"

"No, he couldn't have been nicer. The apartment was actually in the same building as the restaurant I just told you about. He even sent food takeouts up to me from the restaurant. The food was wonderful too. And, when I moved out, he got a moving van to take all my stuff up to the new place. I guess he must have really liked the article I did. Or maybe he just liked me because I was a newspaper reporter, and he thought that might be useful to him. But I never compromised myself in any way journalistically. I like to tell myself that made it all right. Even though I knew it really wasn't. But that's what I mean about him being scary. He can be really nice like that, and then you hear about all the violent criminal acts he's responsible for too."

I wasn't there to make a judgement about the ethics of what Michelle had done. I just wanted her help.

"My next question is—" I started to say.

"Would I go to Marcello's with you to try to set up a meeting for you with Bennato?"

"Exactly."

"That's a big favor to ask me."

"I know."

"A much bigger favor than just buying a mocha for a person normally gets you, Jessie."

I smiled.

"If you're uncomfortable about it, I understand. This could be very dangerous if he is Maura Walsh's killer."

"Aw, what the hell." Michelle shrugged. "I never planned on living forever anywhere. So let's go to Marcello's tonight."

CHAPTER 46

If Michelle and I had any hopes of blending in undetected at Marcello's, that evaporated the minute we stepped into the restaurant. We realized we were the only women in there. Well, except for a few here and there in bouffant hairdos and heavy makeup who were either girlfriends/wives or on their way to a casting call for *Mob Wives of New York*.

Everyone else in the place were men. Many of them big, tough-looking guys who might as well have been wearing signs that said, "I'm in the mob." That was unsettling enough. But what was even worse, everyone only seemed to have one thing on their minds right now. They were staring at us.

"Are we going to get out of here alive?" I whispered to Michelle.

"It'll be fine, Jessie."

She walked over to the bar as if nothing was wrong. My God, this woman was fearless. I followed her. What in the hell else was I going to do?

Michelle ordered wine for both of us from the guy behind the bar, who didn't seem happy to see us. But he didn't say anything. Just got our drinks and plopped them down in front of us without a word.

I looked around the restaurant again. Some of the men there had gone back to their food or drinks, but a few were still staring at us. Like they were waiting to see what happened next.

So was I.

"Shouldn't we tell someone that we want to talk to Bennato?" I asked Michelle.

"We don't have to do that."

"Why not?"

"They'll come to us."

"I don't understand…"

"Just drink your wine. Trust me on this."

I didn't really have a viable alternative plan, so I decided to trust that Michelle knew what she was talking about.

Sure enough, a few minutes later, a man walked toward us at the bar. He didn't look like most of the other mob guys in the restaurant, though. He was dressed in a plain brown suit and was short and frail-looking with a balding head. Not very intimidating at all.

It took me a few seconds but I finally recognized him from seeing him on TV news. It was Manny Edelman. Manny the Mouthpiece was the moniker the press used for him. He'd defended Bennato in a number of legal matters, usually managing to get him acquitted or the charges against him dropped even before a trial.

"Hello, Michelle," he said, smiling at her and then giving her a big hug. "Wonderful to see you. I hope the apartment was satisfactory and you're in an even better location now. We haven't seen you here in a while. You're missed."

"That apartment was just great," Michelle said. "I have a place uptown now, but I still miss being here. Especially those takeout meals I got from here while I lived upstairs. You don't get that uptown."

Edelman turned to me.

"And you brought a friend with you, Michelle?"

I stuck out my hand.

"Hello, I'm Jessie Tucker."

"I'm Manny."

"I know who you are, Mr. Edelman," I said. "I've seen you on TV acting as Dominic Bennato's" – I almost started to say "Dominic Bennato's mouthpiece", but I stopped myself – "I recognized you as the person who represented Mr. Bennato in a number of legal cases."

"You're a good observer, Ms. Tucker."

"I'm a reporter at the *Tribune* with Michelle."

"A reporter," he repeated.

"Yes," Michelle said quickly, "she sits next to me at the *Tribune*. And she told me today how desperate she is for an apartment. There is some kind of construction at the place where she is now and she has to move in a hurry. I told her how Mr. Bennato had helped me when that happened, and we were hoping she could talk to him too."

"About an apartment?"

"Yes."

"There's a lot of places to look for an apartment," Edelman said to me.

"But Michelle kept going on about how wonderful Mr. Bennato was at finding a great place for her. I'm hoping he could maybe do the same for me."

I was pretty sure that he knew I didn't want to talk to Bennato about an apartment. And I was pretty sure he knew that I knew he didn't believe me either. What I wasn't sure of was how he would react to all that.

But I also knew he was probably concerned about what it was I really wanted.

And the only way to find out what that was would be to set up a meeting for me to talk to Bennato.

In the end, he agreed to try and set up an appointment for me. I gave him my contact information. Then he picked up the tab for our drinks and offered to buy us dinner too.

"We've really got to be going…" I started to say.

"That sounds great, Mr. Edelman," Michelle jumped in. "I can't wait to have the chicken marsala and spaghetti again. And Jessie, wait until you taste the pasta primavera!"

After Edelman left, she said: "Remember, you told me once how you always drank coffee with the cops as a crime reporter? That it helped you bond with them. Well, it's the same with these guys. It's all about the Italian food with them. Even if you're not hungry, you eat it out of respect. They appreciate that." She grinned. "Besides, the pasta at this place is really, really good."

She was right about that.

Best Italian food I'd ever eaten.

We stayed there for another hour eating it and drinking more wine.

Everyone pretty much forgot about us after that. Nothing else happened that seemed particularly significant to me. No one shot anyone. No one took any underworld oaths or exchanged secret mob handshakes. No one sang any Mafia fight songs.

When we left, Michelle and I took separate cabs, and I went home to wait to hear about my appointment to meet the most dangerous and feared man in New York City.

Just another day at work for Jessie Tucker, crime reporter.

CHAPTER 47

Dominic (Fat Nic) Bennato had an office in downtown Brooklyn, not far from Borough Hall.

On the outside, everything seemed totally legit. There was a lobby with a directory that told me his office was on the ninth floor. I took an elevator up to nine, got off and walked down a long hall until I found a door that said, "Bennato Sanitation Services".

Inside, I found a secretary – a middle-aged, platinum-blonde-haired woman – who greeted me politely and then informed me that I could see Mr. Bennato in a few minutes.

I sat down and waited. There was an array of magazines on a table in front of me. Everything from *Time* to *The New Yorker* to *People*. Soft music from a female singer – I think it was Taylor Swift or Miley Cyrus, I wasn't sure which – played on a speaker.

Yep, it was all very businesslike.

Except I knew the truth.

Dominic Bennato's business wasn't sanitation services or looking for apartments or anything else legitimate. It was extortion, gambling, prostitution, drugs, loansharking, robbery and probably even murder – if you believed everything that had been said and written about him.

Sitting there now and waiting to see him, I started to wish I'd brought Michelle with me. She'd been damned impressive the way she handled herself at that restaurant. She'd offered to accompany me here now, but I'd said no. I told her it was better for me to meet Bennato one-on-one, under the circumstances. But now I wasn't so convinced that was a good idea.

I pondered what I should do and how I should act when I met Bennato. It was important that I observe the niceties of the introduction, no matter what happened afterward. So did I call him Bennato? Mr. Bennato? Fat Nic? I quickly discarded the last one as an option. But did I shake his hand? Did I smile at him? Did I kiss his ring finger like a scene out of *The Godfather*?

I knew it was probably a foolhardy move for me to just go to Bennato's office alone like this.

I knew I couldn't be sure I'd be safe – Bennato was still a cold-blooded killer, even if this was the front for his public façade as a legitimate businessman.

But that was the way I worked stories – like a bull in a china shop. I liked to just barge in and shake things up to see what would happen. And that's what I was doing here now with Dominic Bennato.

I tried to stay positive, but I kept thinking of worst-case scenarios. Him screaming at me. Him throwing me out. Him… well, I'd read about people disappearing after they went to meet with Dominic Bennato. Of course, nothing like that could really ever happen in an office building like this – with the secretary outside, the magazines and all the music playing, could it? I did my best to convince myself of that, but it wasn't easy.

"Mr. Bennato will see you now," the platinum-blonde-haired secretary said to me, interrupting my reverie of everything that could go wrong.

It was too late to back out now. I thanked her, followed her through a door that said, "Executive Office of Dominic Bennato" and went inside.

Dominic Bennato himself turned out to be everything I'd heard about him. He must have weighed nearly four hundred pounds, with slicked-back dark brown hair and wearing a suit that was too tight for all his bulk. He was sitting behind a desk that was covered with food. It looked to be various kinds of pasta and meat and even some pastries. It was ten-thirty a.m. Well, maybe Bennato liked an early lunch. Or else it could have been a late breakfast.

Michelle had told me at the restaurant how important it was to accept offerings of food from these guys to help bond with them, like I bonded with cops over coffee or beers. And so I was ready to join with him on the spread in front of me. But Bennato didn't offer me any food. He didn't shake my hand. He didn't even get up from behind his desk.

"What do you want?" he grunted, between bites of what looked to be linguini in some kind of meat marinara sauce.

So much for the polite niceties.

"I'm a friend of Michelle Caradonna," I said.

"I know that."

"She told me you'd helped her get an apartment."

"I know that too."

"I was hoping you could help me find an apartment for myself."

I'd decided to open up our conversation with the cover story and see how long I could maintain that with him. It turned out to be not for very long.

"An apartment?" he asked. "That's why you came to see me? For an apartment?"

"That's right."

"You went to all this trouble because you thought I could get you an apartment?"

"Uh, I guess…"

"You're a newspaper reporter, aren't you?"

"Guilty as charged." I smiled.

He didn't smile back.

There was an awkward silence.

"So then, do you have anything?" I finally asked.

"Do I have what?"

"An apartment for me."

"I'll tell you what I can do for you if you'll do something for me, Ms. Tucker."

"What's that?"

"Tell me the real reason why you're here."

He wiped some marinara sauce off his cheek, pushed the plate of pasta away and stared directly at me across his desk. Dominic Bennato was all business now.

"Maura Walsh," I said.

"Who?"

"Maura Walsh. She was a woman police officer. She was murdered a few weeks ago in an alley in Little Italy. It was in all the papers and on TV news. I'm sure you must have heard about it?"

"What does this police officer's death have to do with me?"

"The spot where she was killed was right next to a building which had materials inside that indicated you did sanitation service for the construction crews at work there."

"My company does sanitation removal at a lot of buildings around town. Do you have anything else that would make you think I know anything about this?"

"There is one thing. But you're not going to like what I'm about to say."

"Go ahead."

"You were paying Maura Walsh bribes from at least two of your businesses – an escort service and a strip club – to ignore violations and keep the places operating despite what I believe were illegal activities going on there."

I thought this was the moment when Bennato might explode at me, but he didn't. He did smile now. Well, it was a sort of a smile. Not like he thought it was funny, more like he was bemused by all of this and by me too.

"That's a pretty outrageous accusation to make," he said finally.

"I told you that you weren't going to like it."

I then went through everything I knew – or almost everything – about the payoffs at the escort service and the strip club. Also, about Maura Walsh taking payoffs at other businesses. And how I presumed some of them probably belonged to Bennato too.

"I have a lot of businesses," he said when I was finished. "I can't know what everyone in all of these businesses are doing. If they were making payoffs to a police officer, I wouldn't necessarily know anything about that."

"I find that hard to believe, Mr. Bennato."

"Are you saying I'm lying to you?"

"I think you're not telling me everything."

He kept looking at me as I talked. Staring even more intently now. The food on the desk in front of him was forgotten. Dominic Bennato was totally focused on me.

"You've got a lot of guts," he said. "Hell, if you were a man, I'd say you have a real pair of balls on you. Not sure how I say that to a woman. But not many people – man or woman –would walk in here and talk to me like that."

I suddenly had this recollection of a scene from an old *Mary Tyler Moore Show*. The first episode when Mary meets Lou Grant at a job interview. Mary talks back to him, and he tells her: "You know what? You've got spunk!" She's happy at first, but then he snaps: "I hate spunk!"

I wondered if that was what was going to happen now between me and Bennato.

"I like Michelle," he said. "I think I like you too. Do you know, I have a daughter about your age? She's a lovely girl. I would hate if anything bad ever happened to her, as I'm sure you understand. An accident. A crime. A fire. There's all sorts of bad things out there that I hope she never has to experience. Well, I feel the same way about you. I would hate if anything bad like that ever happened to you. I just wanted you to know that. Do you understand what I'm saying?"

Oh, I understood him. *Keep out of his business – or else.*

Once that message was delivered, he went back to shoving food into his mouth – as if I wasn't there anymore. It seemed like our meeting was over. I stood up, thanked Bennato for his time and made my way out of his fancy office – past the secretary, down the elevator and back out onto the Brooklyn street.

CHAPTER 48

Lorraine Molinski and I were eating lunch in the *Tribune* cafeteria.

"What's going on with the Maura Walsh story?" she asked in between bites of the chicken salad sandwich she was eating.

"I'm not sure what I've got." I sighed.

"Tell me about it."

"I've already gone through it all with Norman and Danny."

"Tell me about it," she said again.

I went through everything that had happened in the past few days, hoping maybe she could make some more sense out of it than I'd been able to do so far. My meeting with Dominic Bennato. My encounter with the two rogue cops, Shockley and Janko. My bizarre conversation with Russell Garrison at Internal Affairs.

"Then there's all the other stuff," I said. "The discovery that Billy Renfro's wife hired the murdered PI Walosin to spy on her. And Renfro's own death, which the cops are calling suicide but I suspect he might have been murdered. Plus, we've got that whole strange business about Maura Walsh investigating her own little brother's death in Saginaw Lake before she was killed."

"But what's the story, Jessie?"

"There's a lot of stories there."

"Yes, there are. All very interesting stories too. But just pieces of the Maura Walsh story, not the whole story. Those pieces don't fit together. Right now, it's simply a bunch of interesting pieces of information. I don't see a complete story there. You still need to find out the key answers about Maura Walsh. Who killed her – and why?"

"I know," I said with a sigh.

"The cops haven't confirmed anything about the Walsh woman taking payoffs before she was murdered?"

"No. Aguirre won't even talk to me about it. No one at the 22nd Precinct wants to hear anything about it either. There was that bizarre comment from the guy at Internal Affairs, but that was off the record. And I'm not sure what the hell it means anyway. So this is all I've got at the moment."

I plucked a crouton out of the Caesar salad I was eating with my fork and popped it into my mouth. I didn't care that much about food when I was working on a big story. Eating was just a way to put fuel into my body so I could keep going on the job. I was consumed by the Maura Walsh story right now. Except I wasn't sure where to go next on it.

"You're missing something," Lorraine said.

"Like what?"

"If I knew what it was, I wouldn't be asking you about it."

"There's nothing else, Lorraine."

"Sure, there is. You just haven't found it yet."

Lorraine had finished off her sandwich and was working her way through a plate of French fries. She was a big woman, and she had a prodigious appetite. She was wearing a loose-fitting blazer over her blouse and a pair of baggy slacks. I wondered again about the stories of her carrying a gun. Maybe it was under the blazer she was wearing right now.

"What's the status of that interview you were supposed to get with Deputy Commissioner Walsh?" she asked.

"Uh, that doesn't seem too likely anymore."

"Because of going to the Walsh house and talking to his wife?"

"Yeah, Norman was able to smooth some of that over and keep me out of more trouble with the newspaper owner Jonathan

Larsen, who it turns out is Walsh's big pal. But, if Walsh does give an interview to someone – and, based on his record, I doubt he will go public – it probably won't be with me. I've still got an official request in through my source. But I'm not holding my breath over it."

"Let me see what I can do," she said.

"What do you mean?"

"I'll check with a source of mine about trying to get you that interview."

"You have a source who might be able to do that?" I said in amazement.

I didn't mean it quite to come out like that, but she didn't seem to mind.

"I have a source," she said.

I wondered if maybe she was talking about Jonathan Larsen himself. I'd heard all the stories about how Lorraine might have slept with someone important at the *Tribune* – maybe even Larsen – to get promoted to managing editor so fast. I'd dismissed them as just office gossip until now. But maybe they were true? And maybe she could use her personal influence on Larsen – or someone else – to get me an interview with Walsh. Hell, I didn't care; I just wanted that damn interview.

"Sure, let me know."

"I'll get back to you on it."

Lorraine nibbled on one of her French fries, seemingly lost in thought.

"Have you gone through everything online and in the *Tribune* library on this?" she asked. "Everything that's ever been written about Maura Walsh? Her father? Corruption scandals? Anything you can think of that could give some kind of a clue what was happening here. Why this seemingly model cop – the daughter of the deputy police commissioner and a member of a revered NYPD family – would suddenly go bad. And whether that – or any of the rest of the material you've uncovered – somehow played a role in her murder?"

"Of course I've done that, Lorraine."

"Then do it again."

"C'mon, that seems like a waste of my time…"

"Go back and look at everything that's out there on any – or all – of these topics."

"What's the point?"

"Maybe you'll get lucky and find something this time."

"I don't know," I said. "It sounds like a real longshot."

"You got a better idea?"

On the elevator ride upstairs to the newsroom after we left the cafeteria, I asked Lorraine the question I'd wondered about for a long time.

"Do you carry a gun?"

"Why?"

"Some people think you do."

There was no metal detector at the *Tribune*. Lorraine could be packing heat every day she went to work here, and none of us would ever know.

"What do you think?" Lorraine asked me now after I finally posed the gun question to her.

"I'm not sure."

"Do you want to frisk me?"

"Huh?"

"You've covered the police beat for quite a while, right? You must know how they frisk a person for a gun."

"Oh, I actually did a feature on it once. They taught me how to do it. How to look for a weapon on a suspect. So yes, I know how to frisk a person for a gun just like a police officer does it."

"Then pat me down right now and tell me if I'm carrying one."

I laughed, but she was serious. I finally ran my hands up and down her body looking for the bulge of a weapon. I didn't find anything.

"Satisfied?"

"Well, at least I answered that question."

The elevator doors opened. As they did, I saw a flash of movement out of the corner of my eye. I turned around. Lorraine was standing there with a small pistol in her hand.

"Where'd it come from?" I asked when I regained my composure.

"Ankle holster," she said.

"I didn't check down that far."

"I thought you said you'd learned how to frisk someone."

"I did."

"I figured you'd find it."

"I guess I wouldn't make a very good cop."

CHAPTER 49

The most important trait for a newspaper reporter has to be persistence. Intelligence, deductive ability, good instincts and even luck, they're all important. But none of it compares to persistence.

I learned this lesson from Peter Ventura when I first came to the *Tribune*. A number of years earlier, he exposed a massive kickback scandal involving members of the City Council. It led to the impeachment and eventual indictment of six Councilmen; a revision of the Council's ethical standards and guidelines; and a slew of journalistic awards for Ventura. It was the story that cemented his reputation as one of the legendary reporters in New York City.

The key to breaking the story was the testimony of a City Council aide who knew all the details of the scandal. It was an exclusive interview Ventura did with this aide that set everything in motion and led to everything else that happened.

I asked Peter how he got the aide to talk. She was a sixty-five-year-old woman who was fiercely loyal to her boss despite the things she saw going on around her. No one had been able to get her to reveal what she knew.

Peter said that he called her each morning for fourteen consecutive days. Every time she hung up on him. Sometimes she didn't say anything. Other times she threatened to report him to the police for harassing her. Once she screamed profanities at him and told him to go to hell. On the fifteenth day, she didn't hang up on him. He asked her to meet with him. She did, and the rest was journalistic history.

I've thought about that whole sequence of events a lot. I don't know too many reporters who would have made that fifteenth call. A lot of them would have given up after the first hang up. There are still people around in the newspaper business who say Peter Ventura just got lucky with that big exclusive. Well, sometimes you do get lucky. But other times you make your own luck.

That's what Lorraine was telling me about this story.

I decided to take her advice.

Like she said, what did I have to lose?

I started in the *Tribune* library by going through Maura Walsh's file all over again.

Most of that stuff was online now, of course. But the *Tribune* still keeps clip files from the print editions too. I'd already done an online search about her at the beginning. But now I wanted to make sure I saw and read everything, and going through the actual print stories seemed the best way for me to do that.

She'd only been on the police force for a few years, but there were a lot of clips and articles about her. The first one was a feature that ran when she graduated from the Police Academy. The headline said: TRUE BLUE! DEPUTY COMMISSIONER WALSH'S DAUGHTER IS A CHIP OFF THE OLD FAMILY BLOCK. There were pictures of her in a classroom at the academy; shooting on the pistol range with other recruits; and at the graduation ceremony where she finished first in her class.

There were more articles chronicling the highlights of Maura's police career. Arrests. Rescues. Awards.

Then, at the end, came all the stories about her death. Including the stuff from me.

Her father's clipping file was much bigger. It went all the way back to his early days on the force, faded stories and pictures that had been stored away in some dark corner for years and years. It was all there, though – the account of Walsh's illustrious career as he rose through the ranks to the top of the NYPD hierarchy. The man who'd gotten the nickname of "Prince of the City" and become a legend for everything he had done to stamp out police corruption.

I read through everything I could find on the police department too. Corruption scandals. Internal investigations. Political wars with City Hall. Controversial arrests and cases. It was a tremendous amount of information, and it took me a long time to get through it.

I didn't find anything at all that helped me.

On the other hand, I didn't have the slightest idea of what I was looking for anyway.

When I was finished with all the newspaper clippings, I went through the picture files too. Some of the pictures were the same ones I'd seen in the clips. But the *Tribune* photo department also saved a lot of other pictures that never made the paper just in case they ever needed to use them again. That's what I concentrated on. Or tried to concentrate. My head hurt, my eyes ached and my brain felt like it had turned to mush.

I almost missed it. It was in Maura Walsh's picture file. It had been taken on the day she graduated from the Police Academy, but never ran with the article. A casual shot of her and three other police recruits. They were in the background of the shot, and you couldn't see their faces as clearly as Maura. They weren't identified in the caption.

But I had a nagging feeling that I recognized something.

I studied the three faces of the student police recruits behind Maura Walsh more closely. At first, I didn't see it. Then it hit me. Of course, he looked a lot different these days than he did in the picture. His hair was longer now, he had a beard and he'd probably put on a few pounds.

But there was no question about it.
I knew this guy.
Hell, I'd almost slept with him.
Sam Rawlings.

CHAPTER 50

"We need to talk," I told Rawlings.

"Look, I'm sorry about the other night."

"That's not what I want to talk about."

"So what do you want to talk about?"

"You."

"What about me?"

"How about we start by you explaining how come you didn't tell me you used to be a cop?"

We were sitting in a booth in the back of his restaurant. Rawlings didn't say anything at first. He just sat there looking at me across the table with a stunned look on his face.

"I've never been a cop," he said finally.

"Wrong answer."

"I really don't know what you're talking about."

"Maybe this will help refresh your memory."

I took out the picture of the Police Academy graduation and put it on the table in front of him.

"What about this picture?" I said. "That's you and Maura Walsh. You graduated from the Police Academy at the same time as she did."

He stared down at the picture for a long time without answering. Trying to figure out the best way to respond to this, I assumed.

"Okay, I used to be a police officer."

"But you're not anymore."

"That's right."

"Why not?"

"I didn't like being on the NYPD very much."

"Or the NYPD didn't like you."

I took out my iPhone, called up a file I'd downloaded earlier with notes I'd gotten from someone in the personnel office at One Police Plaza – and began reading from it.

"*Samuel Rawlings*," I said. "*Graduated from the Police Academy in March, 2015. Assigned as a rookie patrolman to the 22nd Precinct in Manhattan. Suspended in 2017 on charges of taking payoffs from businesses on your beat. Brought up on departmental charges. Agreed to plead guilty in return for no criminal charges being filed. Dismissed from the police force in June 2017.*"

I put the phone away and looked at Rawlings.

"The 22nd Precinct," I said. "The same precinct where Maura Walsh and her partner Billy Renfro were taking payoffs. And she just happens to come here and start taking money from you now. Hard to believe that all happened by chance.

"There's more too. I did some checking on who actually owns this place where you work, The Hangout. It turns out to be a company called Riviera Management. Riviera Management is part of another company called Cumberland Real Estate. And – here's where it really gets interesting – both of them are part of a bigger holding company owned by none other than mob boss Dominic Bennato. Which means you work for Bennato.

"Lots of connections, huh? And lots of lies by you. All of which make me suspect you might know a lot more about Maura Walsh's murder than you're letting on. For all I know, you played some part in it. So talk to me, Samuel Rawlings. Tell me the damned truth. Or is that something you're not used to doing very much? You certainly haven't ever done it with me. So please… no more lies about you being a goddamn aspiring novelist or all the rest of that crap."

I sat back and waited for his answer.

"You've got a few things wrong, Jessie," he said.

"Such as?"

"Well, first off I am a writer. I am trying to write a novel. I wasn't lying about that."

"Good for you."

"And I was a lawyer too. I went to law school before the Police Academy. I applied for a job on the police force when I was twenty-eight. One of the oldest recruits they ever had, I believe."

"Okay."

"And I don't know anything about what happened to Maura Walsh or who killed her. You've got to believe me about that."

"I'm not sure I do."

"What can I do to convince you?"

"Tell me the truth."

"I am telling you the truth about that."

"Tell me the truth about everything."

He hesitated for a few seconds, then shook his head no.

"I can't do that."

"I didn't think you would."

"I'm really sorry."

"So am I. Sorry I ever met you."

I stood up, started for the door – but then turned around one last time to look at Sam.

"I'm going to find out what happened to Maura Walsh and why," I told him before I left the restaurant. "Then I'm going to print the story. And if that brings down you and your corrupt cop friends back at the 22nd Precinct and your boss Dominic Bennato… well, then you're going to be really sorry about that."

I stormed away from him and back out onto the street, just like I had that night at his apartment.

He didn't chase after me this time either.

But I didn't want him to anymore.

I was just glad I found out about Sam Rawlings in time.

Before I did anything stupid.

Like fall for him.

CHAPTER 51

Lieutenant Thomas Aguirre called and said he wanted to see me.

"I'm going to do you a big favor, kiddo," was the way Aguirre put it to me over the phone.

"Kiddo?"

"Well, you got mad when I called you 'honey'."

"My name is Jessie."

"Do you want to find out the favor I'm going to do for you or not?"

I decided I could live with him calling me "kiddo".

"Okay, what's the favor?"

"Nah, it's gotta be in person. Come on over to my office right away."

When I got there, I could tell Aguirre had something good for me. There was this irritatingly smug look on his face. I'd seen that smug look before when he knew something that I didn't. The only thing I could figure was there had been some kind of a break in the Maura Walsh case.

I soon found out I was right.

"We've got a suspect in the Maura Walsh murder," he announced. "A real suspect this time. We think he did it."

I sat and waited.

"Don't you want to know who it is?"

"Who is it?" I asked, playing along with his little game.

While I did that, I tried to run through in my mind all the possible suspects I had. *Dominic Bennato. Other corrupt cops. Was Sam*

Rawlings really involved in her death? Or maybe even her own father, as crazy as that sounded? Could Frank Walosin the PI have murdered her for some reason before he died himself? Did Billy Renfro kill his own partner over some fallout in the corruption they were both involved in? Did—

"Charlie Sanders," Aguirre said.

"Her boyfriend?"

"*Ex-boyfriend.*"

"But he was across town on a stakeout in the Bronx."

"That was his alibi. But we broke it. He filled out a false report of a stakeout and then got his partner to back him up. We believed him, at first. But then the partner got cold feet and came to us with the real story. Sanders had disappeared for more than an hour that night. Want to know where he disappeared to?"

I was getting tired of playing this game with Aguirre, but I needed the information.

"Where?"

"East 86th Street in Manhattan."

At first, I didn't recognize the location. But then I remembered. East 86th Street was one of the spots Maura and Renfro had stopped at during their patrol that last night. It was listed as a meeting with an "informant". But now it sounded as if she was meeting with Charlie Sanders. And that meeting took place just before she was found murdered.

"Sanders heard rumors that she was having an affair with someone," Aguirre said. "He called her up, and she denied it. But he demanded a meeting with her. So he drove to Manhattan and confronted her in a bar on East 86th Street. They got in a big argument and she stormed out. We've got a witness now – once we went back to 86th Street and asked more questions – who saw some of that. And shortly after that, she turns up dead. That makes Charlie Sanders our prime suspect."

I remembered asking Charlie Sanders if he thought Maura might be seeing another man. He could have been jealous, I suppose, but murderous jealous? Sanders still seemed like a nice guy to me, not a killer. Then again, love does make people do crazy things sometimes. Including murder.

"What does Sanders say?"

"He admits to meeting her and having the fight. He says he went back to the Bronx afterward. When he heard she had been shot to death, he realized he'd be a suspect and came up with the phony alibi to throw any suspicion away from himself."

"Is that enough to charge him with the murder?"

"Not yet. For now, he's only suspended from the force for obstruction by lying about his whereabouts. But he looks good for it. We're all over this now. It's the first real break we've gotten on this case. And I'm giving you the story first. I'm doing a big press conference later this afternoon. But you can get this out online right now so the *Tribune* – and you – will get the credit for the exclusive. That's a pretty big favor I'm giving you, huh?"

He was right. It was a big favor. But, of course, I had a question for Aguirre about it.

"Why give me the story first, Lieutenant?"

"Hey, you made me a big media star after the Central Park stuff. Oh, I know I saved your life too. But I figured I'm going to be making big news here again today. So why not give it first to my friend, Jessie Tucker. Simple as that."

I knew it wasn't as simple as that. If I broke this story now, it would get us even more publicity because of our history together. Then he could still meet with all the rest of the press and get himself publicity there too. But, by coming to me first, he'd get even more attention. It was a win-win situation for him. He was doing me a favor, but he was doing himself an even bigger favor by making sure he got the biggest play possible for all this in the media. That was what it was all about for an egotistical cop like Lt. Thomas Aguirre. But what the hell, it was all right with me. An exclusive was an exclusive, no matter how I got it.

Before I left, I asked him a few more questions. Especially about why Sanders thought Maura was having a romance with someone. But he said all Sanders knew was he'd gotten an anonymous phone call telling him about it – and saying where Maura was. Sanders was jealous enough about the possibility of Maura seeing another man that he believed the caller was telling the truth. Which was why he'd gone to confront Maura.

All in all, it sounded like a good motive for murder. Jealousy usually was.

And Aguirre sounded confident that they'd soon have accumulated enough evidence against Sanders to charge him with killing Maura Walsh.

"Do you really think she was having an affair with someone else?" I asked Aguirre when he was done.

"Maura Walsh? Not that we know of. We've questioned a lot of people who knew her. But no one had heard of anything like that. They said the last man she'd been with as far as they knew was Sanders. And her psychiatrist said the same thing."

"Maura Walsh was going to a psychiatrist?"

"You didn't know about the psychiatrist?"

"No, I didn't."

Aguirre smiled smugly again. He was enjoying this.

"What's the psychiatrist's name?"

"C'mon, I can't tell you that."

"Sure, you can. We're friends, remember? I do you a favor, you do me a favor."

Aguirre laughed.

"Aw, what the hell?" he said. "I might as well give you the name. She's not going to talk to you anyway. She hardly talked to us."

"Thank you. I appreciate that."

"Just make sure you spell my name right in your story."

CHAPTER 52

"Wow, when it comes to men, I sure can pick 'em, huh?" I said to Ellen.

"You do have an uncanny knack for zeroing in on the wrong one at the wrong time, Jessie."

"Thanks for your support." I smiled.

"I'm serious. This was your worst ever. A corrupt ex-cop who lied to you about who he was and what he was doing and who he worked for. And he could even be a murder suspect in the death of Maura Walsh."

"I'm pretty sure he didn't murder Maura Walsh, if that matters."

"Okay, let's take 'murderer' off the table for now then. But it still leaves him as a corrupt ex-cop; a liar and a guy working for mob boss Dominic Bennato. Not exactly prime dating material. I gotta tell you, your screening process for choosing men leaves a lot to be desired."

"You're having a lot of fun with this, aren't you?"

"When something like this happens, what else can you do but laugh?"

We were sitting outside at a bar in Rockefeller Center, not far from the *Tribune* offices. The temperature had gone down to something more manageable in the eighties, at least for now, and it wasn't that bad not being in an air-conditioned place. Even better, most of the tourists who normally populate the area had stayed away tonight because of the heat wave we'd been enduring in the city. So the bar was relatively empty.

I had the front page of the *Tribune* in front of me. My story – the exclusive I'd gotten from Aguirre about Charlie Sanders – was the lead story on Page 1. The headline said: COP LOVER EYED IN WALSH MURDER. The story included everything I knew about Sanders's concocted alibi, the meeting he had with Maura on 86th Street just before her murder and his jealousy over the fear she was seeing another man. The *Tribune* had beaten the hell out of everyone else in town on this story. And I was a big star again in the office because of it. Norman was happy. Danny was happy. Lorraine was happy. I should be happy too, and I was. Sort of.

"You figure this Rawlings guy was part of whatever corrupt scheme was going on which involved Maura Walsh and his boss, Dominic Bennato? That he tried to get close to you when you found out about what Maura was doing? Then kept his eye on you so he could warn Bennato and the dirty cops at the 22nd Precinct if you got too close to the truth?"

"That's the only reason I can think of why he kept chasing after me the way he did."

"Maybe he really liked you."

"Well, he said he did."

"So?"

"He's a liar, remember?"

"Okay, no one's perfect." Ellen laughed.

"I'm just glad I didn't sleep with him."

"Why would that have been so bad? You might have had fun. No matter who he was. As for the lying, I've slept with a lot of men who've lied to me about a lot of things. It's not that big a deal."

"It is to me."

"Why?"

"I don't want to sleep with anyone I don't respect."

"Well, that sure cuts down your dating pool by quite a bit."

We talked then about a lot of other stuff. Including the unsettling conclusion of the search for my father – my non-existent father, as I found out – with the genealogy investigator she'd set me up with. My emotional trip to Sam's apartment that night when I'd unsuccessfully offered myself up for sex with him. And then back to my front-page story in the *Tribune* that was sitting in front of us.

"Do you think Sanders did it?" Ellen asked me.

"I still have trouble believing that. I met the guy, Ellen. He seemed to love Maura Walsh very much. Oh, I know that emotional passion like that can lead to murderous passion too. But I didn't see that in him. He was sad about Maura and him, more than he was angry at her. I know how bad it looks that he made up that phony alibi for the time of her murder. But they haven't actually charged him with the murder yet. Which means they don't have any direct evidence linking him to her death or the crime scene."

"Of course, if Sanders is guilty," Ellen pointed out, "that means all the rest of it doesn't mean anything. The payoffs; corrupt cops; mob involvement; and the troubled relationship between Maura and her father. All of that becomes irrelevant to the story if Sanders murdered her in a jealous rage."

"I understand that."

"Which is maybe why you don't want to believe the really simple answer of Charlie Sanders that's right in front of you."

"I plan to keep working this story," I said. "Until I find out more about Sanders and about all the rest of it."

Ellen nodded.

"What are you going to do next?"

"Go see Maura Walsh's psychiatrist."

"A psychiatrist isn't going to talk to a newspaper reporter like you about a patient."

"I know that."

"And, even if she did, what could she possibly tell you that is important to finding out who killed Maura Walsh?"

"I know that too."

"Then why waste your time?"

"Because another journalist once told me when I was starting out in this business that I needed to always ask questions – no matter how futile and unimportant they might seem – because—"

"Because that's what a reporter does," Ellen finished.

"Exactly."

"I can see I taught you well, Jessie," she said with a smile.

CHAPTER 53

The psychiatrist's name was Kowalski. Julie Kowalski. She had an office in a medical building on Madison Avenue in the 50s. I made an appointment to go see her there.

My plan was to pretend I was a patient, make up some story about why I was there for psychiatric counseling and then – when I thought the time was right – ask her about Maura Walsh.

I knew it wouldn't be easy getting medical information about a patient from a doctor. But at least this way I'd be inside her office when she said no – not at the other end of a phone or trying to get a message through her receptionist.

But that plan went off the rails as soon as I walked into her office because she recognized me from all the media attention I'd gotten recently over my own Central Park case.

She immediately assumed I was there to get professional help for all the emotional turmoil I'd endured – and maybe that wouldn't have been a bad idea for me to do. But I had no desire to open myself up emotionally to this woman about my real story, only the fake one I'd concocted for this visit.

Now that plan wasn't going to work. So I resorted to doing what I do as a reporter to get a story when I can't think of any other alternative: I told the truth.

"I'm not here to talk about myself, Dr. Kowalski," I said. "I only said that so you would see me. I'm working on a story for the *Tribune* about the murder of Maura Walsh. While doing this, I've uncovered a lot of disturbing information. I've also learned that she was a patient of yours. I understand the concept of doctor/patient confidentiality in most cases. But this isn't most cases. Also, Maura Walsh is dead now. The information you have from her could help find out who killed her and why. Will you help me do that?"

Dr. Kowalski was middle-aged, attractive, with short brown hair – but very professional-looking too. More than professional, she had a "no-nonsense" look to her. She looked like a psychiatrist. Or at least my idea of what a woman psychiatrist would look like. If I saw her on the street and didn't know anything about her, I'd probably guess she was some kind of a doctor. And because she was a doctor – a professional, no-nonsense doctor – I wasn't surprised by her answer.

"I cannot divulge information about any patient of mine to you," she said.

"But Maura Walsh isn't your patient anymore. She's dead."

"The death of a patient does not alter the doctor/patient relationship. What she might have told me about herself remains sacrosanct. It cannot leave this office – even after she is no longer alive."

"I understand, but—"

"Ms. Tucker, I have other patients to see. If you're not here as a patient, you have to leave. I will not discuss a patient with you."

"But in this particular case—"

"You can ask me the question as many times as you want, but my answer will remain the same. And that answer is 'no'."

I needed some kind of a Hail Mary to get through this woman's resistance to talk. So I tried one.

"Did you care about Maura Walsh, doctor?"

"I care about all my patients."

"No, I mean did you have any special emotional attachment to her?"

"Why would you ask that?"

"Because I do. And I never even met her. But, in looking into her short life, I developed tremendous empathy for this young woman and all she went through. Maybe because I went through a lot too. She's not just another story for me, Dr. Kowalski. I want to find out the truth for Maura's sake. Even if it is too late to help save her. But maybe I can save myself by doing that."

Her face softened a bit.

"I wish I could help you, Ms. Tucker. I really do. But I simply cannot talk to you about a patient. Even a former patient."

"What if I talk to you about a patient?"

"Excuse me?"

"Let's say I make up a hypothetical patient. No name. And I tell you what I think has been going on in her life. You wouldn't be breaking any confidentiality to listen to me talk about this hypothetical patient. Will you do that?"

She didn't say anything. I took that as a yes.

"Okay, this hypothetical patient," I said, "comes from a highly respected family with a long tradition of public service. She's followed this family line all her life, doing what was expected of her and always making the family proud of her. But then suddenly she stops doing that. She turns on her family, breaks off relations with them and then does unexplained things that will embarrass her family if they became public. I'm not sure why she did it. But I think it had to do with something she found out about a tragedy that happened when she was growing up. It involved the death of her brother. In a little town in upstate New York. She went back there and whatever she found out seemed to set a lot of other things in motion. Does that sound like a reasonable scenario, Dr. Kowalski? Hypothetically speaking, of course."

Dr. Kowalski nodded.

"Saginaw Lake," she said.

"Yes."

"She talked about Saginaw Lake the last time she was here. I couldn't tell you any more even if I knew it, but I don't. I never found out what she discovered there in Saginaw Lake that affected her so much. All she said was she had to make everything right. She needed to deal with it. I asked what she meant, but she wouldn't tell me. That was the last time I saw her."

"When was that?"

"Six months ago."

Six months.

Six months ago was when she'd transferred into the 22d Precinct, her father's old command, and partnered up with Billy Renfro to begin taking bribes and kickbacks and payoffs.

That had to be more than a coincidence.

"And that was the last time she ever came to see you?"

"Yes, I reached out to her several times after that, but she never returned my calls or emails."

"I wonder why."

"I think – and this is just my hypothesis, although I believe it's a reasonable one – that what she found out in Saginaw Lake was so devastating to her that she decided she didn't want to share it with anyone, even me."

I talked a bit more to Dr. Kowalski, but that was all she could tell me. I was surprised she'd opened up to me at all. But I think she was the kind of doctor who went by her instincts – not always by the rules – and her instincts told her that I was on Maura Walsh's side. Just like she had been.

I liked Dr. Kowalski.

If I ever did go see a shrink about my own emotional troubles, she would be a good choice.

Maybe that was something I should think about doing one day.

One day.

But right now I had a story to do.

CHAPTER 54

I was going to get an interview with Maura Walsh's father, after all.

My source at the NYPD called to tell me the next morning that the deputy commissioner was willing to meet with me in his office at One Police Plaza at threee p.m. that day to answer questions.

I was surprised.

But I was even more surprised when I found out how the interview came about.

"It wasn't me," my source said. "I tried, but couldn't convince Walsh to cooperate. Then someone from your newspaper contacted someone very close to Walsh – and he agreed to do it."

"Who was it from the *Tribune*?"

"A woman. The managing editor. Lorraine…?"

"Lorraine Molinski?"

"Yes, she's the one responsible for getting you in to see Walsh."

Damn. Lorraine Molinski. Well, she did say she had sources. But who? Not that it mattered, of course. All that mattered was that I was finally going to get a chance to meet with Walsh.

I was a little concerned at first that Walsh might have heard about what I was doing – checking into his daughter taking payoffs and all the rest – and he wanted to warn me off the story in person.

I mean, I'd already gotten threats from the police about pursuing my Maura Walsh investigation.

Not to mention a warning from mobster Dominic Bennato too.

So why not a personal message along the same lines delivered directly from Deputy Commissioner Walsh himself?

But that wasn't it at all, according to Lorraine.

"He actually liked the piece you did about Maura for the *Tribune*," Lorraine said when I went to see her about it. "The interview with her partner about what a great cop she was. The stuff from others about her dedication to the job and to the entire Walsh family tradition. And he even thought you handled the quotes from his wife well, under the circumstances. Anyway, he wants to talk to you himself now. I think he realizes he has to talk to someone about it at some point. And you've been the lead reporter in town on this story recently. So he'll do the interview with you."

Should I ask her how she'd managed to get me the interview? Probably not.

But it sure reaffirmed my belief that she was a damn interesting woman.

Deputy Commissioner Walsh's office was even more of a shrine to the Walsh family than the living room in his house had been.

The walls behind his desk and around the room were filled with pictures of him and all of the members of the Walsh family who had served in the NYPD. There were a lot of them. From beat cops to detectives to precinct captains to the one who'd been commissioner a number of years ago. There were all sorts of awards too – honoring him and the other Walsh NYPD officers.

On his desk was a picture of Maura in her police uniform – and another of her dressed the same way standing with him in front of the 22nd Precinct. They looked happy in the picture. I wondered if that was just for the camera, though. There was also a picture of a little boy dressed in a police hat with a badge. His father's hat and badge. Patrick Walsh, who must have died not long after this adorable picture of him was taken.

Walsh himself seemed even more stiff-necked and more officious in person than I remembered him from the awkward and emotionless screen appearance I'd watched the day after Maura died.

He got up from behind his desk – dressed impeccably in his blue police uniform – and walked over to me.

I wasn't sure whether to shake his hand – or salute him.

I shook his hand and introduced myself.

I'd decided to start off with something easy for him to answer.

"The police have named Charlie Sanders, who your daughter had been dating until recently, as the prime suspect in her murder. Do you believe Sanders was the one who killed her?"

He moved to his desk and sat down.

"My daughter's murder is still under investigation," he said. "I can't make any comment on the status of that investigation until it has been completed. I have the utmost confidence in the NYPD investigators to determine the facts about my daughter's case."

Okay, so much for that.

He picked up a sheet of paper now and began reading from it.

"My daughter, Maura Walsh, exemplified the best of the New York City Police Department. From her youngest days growing up, Maura always wanted to be a police officer and help her community. That's what she did for the past five years. She won awards, honors and – maybe most importantly of all – she won the admiration of her fellow officers and of the people in this city. Every police officer knows the risks he or she takes with this job. Maura certainly understood that. But she was willing to take those risks because she was so dedicated…"

He looked over at me. I wasn't doing anything.

"Why aren't you writing this down?" he asked.

"I can't use any of it for the article I'm working on for the *Tribune*."

"Why not?"

"Because I've heard all that before. Everyone has."

"You said you wanted to know more about Maura. I'm telling you about Maura."

"Not the kind of things I need to know though. I'm trying to get to the real story here. That's why I need to ask you some questions."

"What kind of questions?"

I took a deep breath. *Here we go*, I thought.

"First off, what was your relationship with your daughter like before she died?"

"She was my daughter. I loved her."

"Did she love you?"

I talked about the fight I'd heard about them having at the 22nd Precinct. How several people told me she never wanted to talk about him or their relationship. And even about the things his own wife had said about him pushing her into being a police officer as a young girl growing up.

"There's nothing wrong with a father who wants their child to follow his career. But there seemed to be much more going on between you and Maura. That's why I'd like you to talk about your father-daughter relationship."

"Next question."

"Excuse me?"

"Next question. I'm not going to talk to you or anyone else about my relationship with my daughter. My dead daughter, I might point out. I think that's very inappropriate for you to bring something like this up right now."

I tried to ask about it again in a couple different ways, but got the same answer from Walsh. So I moved on to the death of Walsh's son – Maura's little brother – a long time ago in Saginaw Lake, New York. I pointed to the picture of the little boy I'd seen on Walsh's desk.

"I was in Saginaw Lake and I wanted to ask about what happened that day."

"I will not talk about my son."

"But I have some questions about the circumstances of his death. I think your daughter had questions about it too. She was looking into the details of exactly what happened right before she was killed. Do you have any idea why she was doing that?"

"That's none of your business."

"But—"

"Next question."

I sighed.

"I came here to ask you questions. I can't do that if you won't answer any of them."

"Not these questions. Do you have any another questions?"

"I do. But it's a big one. And I don't think you're going to like it either."

Walsh just glared at me.

"I think it's only fair for me to tell you that I'm working on a story about corruption in the 22nd Precinct," I said. "Your former command. I'm pretty sure your daughter was involved in the corruption currently going on there."

I went through the highlights of what I knew – including the payoffs she'd been witnessed taking and the money she'd spent on a fancy car, a condo and other expensive items.

"I think we have to consider the possibility at this point that your daughter's death wasn't random at all but somehow connected to the bribes and payoffs she was a part of. Do you have anything to say about that?"

At first, I thought he hadn't heard me clearly. But then I realized he had. The calm, emotionless expression faded from his face. He got up from his desk as if he was going to attack me. But then he just stood there hunched over and confused-looking, like a punch-drunk fighter desperately trying to stay on his feet after taking his opponent's best left hook. His eye twitched, he was sweating and I thought he might faint. But then – drawing on some hidden reserve – he pulled himself erect, jutted out his jaw and said defiantly:

"My daughter died a hero."

That's the way I left him. Standing there in that office with the pictures of all the Walsh family members through the years. Seventy-five years of police tradition. And now it was over. His daughter was dead. His son had died years before. For a second, I almost felt sorry for him. But then I thought about the man who came home from work one day and threw out his daughter's most prized possession – the fish in her aquarium that she loved so much – and my sympathy drained away.

"My daughter was a hero," I heard him say once more as I walked out the door of his office.

CHAPTER 55

"I want to go back to Saginaw Lake," I told Danny, Norman and Lorraine when I got to work at the *Tribune* the next morning.

"Why in the world do you want to go to Saginaw Lake again," Danny asked.

"Because I think that's where the answers are to the Maura Walsh story."

I was grasping at straws here, I realized that. There were all sorts of leads and investigative paths to pursue floating around in front of me right here in New York City on Maura Walsh. Dominic Bennato. Shockley and Janko and the dirty cops from the 22nd Precinct. Charlie Sanders. Sam Rawlings and other business people she was taking money from. The answers to what happened to Frank Walosin and Billy Renfro. And then, of course, there was Deputy Commissioner Walsh himself.

I had written a story for the *Tribune* front page that morning about my interview with Walsh. It was pretty dramatic stuff, even if he hadn't really answered any of my questions. "MY DAUGHTER WAS A HERO" the headline said. This story was the day after I had broken the Charlie Sanders exclusive for the paper. I was on a roll at the moment, no question about it.

All I had to do was sort through all these angles – Sanders, Bennato, Walsh and all the rest – to find out who killed Maura Walsh.

And why.

But I had this crazy feeling – a reporter's instinct, I preferred to call it – that the real answers for the Maura Walsh murder were back in Saginaw Lake where a little boy died a long time ago.

I believed that whatever Maura Walsh had figured out during her trips to Saginaw Lake had somehow set in motion a series of events that led to her own murder.

A peculiar configuration… as the cop once told me about another summer murder.

A perfect storm.

Now all I had to do was persuade Danny and Norman and Lorraine to let me loose on this. I was sitting in an office at the *Tribune* with all three of them. I'd asked to meet with them together, saying I had a possible big break on the Maura Walsh story. I was tired of playing this office politics game. They all agreed, which was one of the few times I'd ever seen them agree on anything. I guess they all had gotten excited about the idea of a big break in the Maura Walsh story, and they all wanted to be in on it with me.

But right now they looked confused.

"I know I'm stating the obvious, Jessie," Danny said, "but the Maura Walsh murder was in New York City – not Saginaw Lake in upstate New York."

"And whatever did happen in Saginaw Lake happened years ago," Lorraine said.

"I don't understand," said Norman Isaacs, which was probably the most astute comment of all.

I didn't understand either. Not yet. I told them that.

"Okay, maybe I'm crazy. Maybe Maura Walsh just had nostalgia for the old place where she spent summers as a young girl. Maybe she still had a childhood friend or something up there she wanted to reconnect with. Maybe she just wanted to get out of the city for a while. But she went back there – several times – during the time leading up to her murder. I'm betting there's a connection. That's what I need to find out.

"I want to look into little Patrick Walsh's death all over again. There were five people I know who had some involvement with the case when it happened. Walter Palumbo, the Saginaw Lake Chief of Police; Greg Stovall, his deputy; the two EMT workers who took the body to the hospital and then to the morgue; and the friend who Maura Walsh supposedly was with at the time.

"Chief Palumbo is dead, and I've already talked with the deputy. That leaves three names for me to track down – the two EMT people and the friend of Maura Walsh. I want to find them and get their story."

Isaacs shook his head no.

"That sounds like a wild goose chase, Jessie. Plus, you're still messing around with the personal life of Walsh – and you know how that's worked out in the past. I want you to keep working on this story, but I want you to do it here – not in Saginaw Lake."

Danny and Lorraine both nodded. Jeez, I liked it better when they were fighting with each other. At least that way, I usually had one of them on my side.

I was ready for this response though. I'd come prepared with a Plan A to deal with it. And, if that didn't work, I had a Plan B too.

"I'm going to do this story," I said to them. "I'm going to do it any way I have to. For the *Tribune* – or for someone else. If I have to quit, I'll do that. Or, if you decide you want to fire me for disobeying your direct orders, that's okay too. But I am going back to Saginaw Lake. I'd prefer to do it for the *Tribune*."

I was bluffing, of course. I wasn't prepared to quit the paper for this story. And they weren't going to fire me either. I knew I was bluffing. They knew I was bluffing. Everyone knew I was bluffing. So much for Plan A.

I switched to Plan B.

"Norman, you remember a few months ago when I didn't believe the official story of what happened to me in Central Park? All of you thought I was crazy. But you let me do the story, Norman. And we wound up breaking a huge exclusive all because you had faith in my instincts. Show some faith in me again. Let me do this story the way I want to do it."

Norman Isaacs didn't say anything right away. Neither did Danny. But then Lorraine, bless her heart, was the first one to back me up.

"Aw, what the hell!" she said. "Jessie's a great reporter, we all know that. So let's let her report. Sure, she could get us in trouble nosing around Walsh's personal life like this if it turns out there's nothing there. But I'm willing to take that chance. Let's send her back to Saginaw Lake and see what happens."

I heaved a sigh of relief. As managing editor, Lorraine had the authority to make the decision on her own. But I wanted Danny and Norman on my side for this too.

I figured Danny was all right about me going, but didn't like the idea of sharing the glory if I broke something with Norman and Lorraine. He would have preferred being the only editor working with me. So he'd go along, but he wasn't happy about it.

Norman, on the other hand, was still wary of the potential pitfalls of focusing like this on Deputy Commissioner Walsh, because of his ties with powerful political figures as well as the owner of our own newspaper. I wished I could reassure him about that, but I really couldn't.

"How much do you need to focus on Walsh himself for this story?" he asked.

"Walsh is the story, Norman."

"I know, but—"

"I think he's the key to Maura Walsh's murder."

"Wait a minute, are you saying—"

I was. I'd been building up to this idea for a while now. I'd kept rejecting it though because it seemed so unbelievable. But now, after everything I'd found out, it was the only scenario that made sense to me. Maura Walsh had gone back to Saginaw Lake seeking to uncover long-buried secrets about her family. Specifically, about the death of her seven-year-old brother, Patrick. Which presumably would have reflected badly on her father, the deputy commissioner. Maybe even curtailed his career. And then she wound up murdered before she could tell anyone about it.

Okay, it was – on the face of it – an unbelievable scenario.

An unthinkable one.

But I'd been thinking about it anyway.

"I think there's a real possibility Walsh murdered his own daughter," I said.

CHAPTER 56

There was a message on my voice mail when I got back to my desk from Wendy Carruthers, the genealogy investigator.

My God, the last person in the world I wanted to talk to again was Wendy Carruthers. She said on the message that it was important she talk to me. What could be so damn important? She'd already told me the man I thought all my life was my father wasn't really my father. Was she going to tell me my mother wasn't my mother either? I did not want to deal with this anymore.

But I'm a reporter.

And a reporter hates unanswered questions.

So I called Wendy Carruthers back to find out what she thought was so important.

"Jessie, I know you were upset when you left my office. Extremely upset. But, as I tried to tell you then, this is sometimes a very long and frustrating process."

"What process? My father's dead. And he's not even my father. End of process. Period."

"No, James Tucker was not your biological father. But someone *was* your biological father."

"How do I even know that? Maybe I was a test tube baby. Maybe my mother got the sperm from some anonymous donor in a lab and then made up all the rest of it. That's the kind of thing my mother would do. You didn't know her. She was—"

"You had a biological father, Jessie."

"Says who?"

"Says the DNA results I'm looking at on my desk right now."

I sat there in stunned silence, waiting for what she would say next.

"I believe I know who your biological father is, Jessie. He is alive. And I know how to find him. I figured you'd want to know that."

I hadn't really thought about this possibility. Or, maybe I had. But, in my anger and frustration and disappointment over the news about James Tucker, I'd pushed it out of my head. It was the logical next step, though. If James Tucker was not my father, then someone else was. And that someone might still be out there.

"How did you find this out?" I asked her, ignoring the obvious question for the moment of exactly who this man was.

"We got lucky," she said. "Do you remember we talked about the DNA results from the genealogy websites? How if you found someone who matched your DNA sample – or even a family member of someone who did – that could help track a missing parent like your father. Sure, it was a long shot, but I wanted to try. And it paid off.

"A little girl in New Jersey got a DNA kit as a birthday present. She got very excited about tracking her family roots and submitted her DNA sample as part of that process. She even got other family members to help her by doing it too. Including her grandfather who lives in Florida. That's the person we're looking at."

"His DNA is a match for me?"

"Without question."

I sat there silently for what seemed like an eternity.

Never saying a word in response to this shocking news.

But I realized I was squeezing my phone so hard it had begun to hurt my hand.

"Don't you want to know, Jessie?" Wendy Carruthers asked.

"Know?"

"Who he is?"

"Yes," I heard myself say mechanically and without emotion, almost as if my voice was coming from someone else.

"His name is Nathan Wright. He's sixty-three years old, which is certainly the right age. He went to college at Dayton with James Tucker. In fact, they were roommates there. And he lived in Cincinnati later when your mother and her husband, James Tucker, were living there. So that all matches.

"Oh, by the way, Nathan Wright is a writer too. Like you. He's an author of historical books. Lived right here in New York City for a long time. Hell, you could have passed by him on the street without having any idea who he was. He moved to Sarasota, Florida, a few years ago. Wright has a son and a daughter, and three grandchildren. Including the one who sent the DNA sample in for her genealogy tracking. His wife died a few years ago.

"He knew your mother and her husband very well at the time of your birth, Jessie. In fact, they were all close friends. Let's assume he impregnated your mother and James Tucker, her husband, found out. Maybe James Tucker demanded a paternity test because he suspected he wasn't the father. In any case, once he found out the truth, he left your mother. And that's when she made up all those stories about what happened to him. That's just a scenario, but it makes sense. It would also explain why James Tucker never contacted you. Because you weren't his child."

"What about this Nathan Wright guy? Why didn't he do something? Why couldn't he have tried to find me or contact me during all these years?"

"Maybe he doesn't know."

"What do you mean?"

"If you were the result of your mother carrying on an affair with this man – or maybe only sleeping with him once or a few times – he probably wouldn't have realized that he, and not James Tucker, was the father of her baby. Maybe your mother wanted to keep up the pretense that you were her husband's daughter, not the result of an affair she had with her husband's best friend. And, when that failed because James Tucker figured out the truth, she made up all those other stories to make it sound better to the world. Nathan Wright could just be as surprised about who you are as you are surprised at who he is. I know this is a lot to take in for you, Jessie. But I believe there is a strong possibility that this is what happened when you were born thirty-six years ago."

I nodded, still numb from the news. "Have you contacted him yet?"

"No. And I won't, unless you ask me to do that. Or you can contact Nathan Wright yourself, if you'd prefer. This is a very delicate thing to deal with so I always leave the decision on how to proceed up to the client. That means it's completely up to you what you do next."

She sent me the specific information she had about Nathan Wright.

Historical author.

Lives in Florida.

Has a son and daughter and three grandchildren.

Plus, of course, one daughter he might not even know about.

After I hung up with Carruthers, I sat staring at that information for a long time. I went online and googled Nathan Wright. He certainly was an historical author. I found stuff there about his books. Civil War, Revolutionary War, he appeared to be pretty acclaimed in his field. There was a picture of him too. A gray-haired man in his sixties. Not bad looking, not great looking. He looked just like an ordinary man, so much different from the rakish, handsome picture of a young James Tucker I'd carried with me all these years as the image of my father. Like Wendy Carruthers said, I could have passed by him on the streets of New York City and never given him a second glance.

There was contact information too. A Twitter handle. A Facebook page. Even what seemed to be a working email.

"This is your decision, Jessie," Wendy Carruthers had said. "Whatever you decide to do, it's up to you."

I shut off my computer, put the information I'd gotten from Wendy Carruthers in a drawer and went home to begin packing for my trip to Saginaw Lake.

I'd opened too many doors already.

I wasn't ready to see what was behind this door.

All that mattered to me right now was the Maura Walsh story.

CHAPTER 57

The name of Maura Walsh's teenaged friend back in Saginaw Lake was Melissa Soroka. She still lived there. In a pleasant, split-level ranch not far from the same neighborhood in Saginaw Lake where she'd grown up.

She was a computer consultant who worked from home and her husband had some kind of a sales job that kept him traveling a lot. They didn't have any children yet, a decision they'd made partly because he was away so much. But he was in line for a new job that would keep him closer to Saginaw Lake, and then they planned to start a family. Four children, she told me. Two boys and two girls. Of course, you could never count on that, but it's what they were hoping for.

I let her talk about this – and a lot more – and pretended like I was interested. I've always found this was the best way to conduct an interview. Let the person talk about whatever they wanted to talk about. Until it was time to talk about what I wanted to talk about.

"I understand you and Maura were good friends when she used to come up here in the summer with her family," I finally said to her.

"Oh yes, we were the best of friends during the summer. Melissa and Maura. We used to call ourselves the M-girls! We had a lot of good times, Maura and I."

"Tell me what you remember about her."

I'd told her that I was there because our readers at the *Tribune* wanted to know more about Maura as a person, and I was hoping to write a full profile about her in life. Including the time she'd spent growing up when she was in Saginaw Lake. Which was sort of the truth. Just not the entire truth.

"We only saw each other during the summer, of course, when her family came up here. But we had so much fun. Especially Maura, I think. Her father wasn't around much, he would come up here on weekends to be with the family after working at his job in the city. So Maura got to do a lot of stuff she couldn't do when he was around. And we sure did some wild, crazy stuff for a while. We went out on our first dates together back then. We smoked our first cigarettes together. We drank alcohol for the first time together. Jeez, we had great times. Until, well… until Maura stopped coming here."

"You mean when the family sold the house after her young brother died?"

"Right. It all happened so fast. One minute she was here, then she was gone. The whole family. What a terrible tragedy that was for them. And, of course, I was so close to it all."

Now we were really getting down to it.

"So, Maura was at your house that day when Patrick died?"

"Later she was."

"What do you mean?"

"We were at Maura's house first. We were both pretty out of it though as we'd drunk a lot of booze that day. That's what I meant when I said I was so close to it. The Patrick Walsh death. I mean, it could have happened right in front of me. I used to have nightmares about that day. Thank goodness, we left when we did."

I was confused. There was nothing about this in the police reports I'd read or in the accounts I'd seen elsewhere. Only that Maura was at Melissa Soroka's house when it happened. And there was nothing about Melissa Soroka being at the Walsh house. Chief Palumbo had gone to interview Maura after the Walsh boy's death, and presumably talked to Melissa too. But no one ever found out exactly what they told him. Except now I was going to find out.

I asked her a few questions, but mostly I just let her tell the story herself.

The story about the day Patrick Walsh died.

"Like I said, Maura and I were pretty wild and crazy in those days when we were teenagers. And one of the things we wanted to do was drink. Neither of us were very experienced at it. But we were young and looking for thrills. So that day we broke into her family's liquor cabinet and started drinking what was there."

"Wait a minute! There was alcohol in that house?"

"Lots of it."

"But her father doesn't allow stimulants of any kind – not coffee or sugar, and certainly not alcohol – for members of his family."

"Well, he did then. Maura and I got snookered on what we found. Her worse than me. That's what caused the problem. Maura was supposed to take care of her little brother that day. At least for a few hours. Her father was busy doing something and her mother wanted to run out to the store for some things. But then I came over, and Maura and I found the liquor. I know it sounds irresponsible now, but we figured Patrick was fine. He was in another room playing like he was Superman. I always remembered that – he was dressed in a Superman outfit. He was so cute. Then we started drinking, and we both drank too much. Way too much. Maura actually blacked out at one point. She told me later that she never remembered anything about... well, she couldn't remember any of it."

Oh my God, I thought to myself. *This was the secret. Maura Walsh got drunk and allowed her little brother to die? Or maybe, even more horrifying, she got drunk and accidentally shot her little brother?*

"Her mother came home to find us like that. She got really upset with Maura. For good reason, I guess. They had a huge fight and Maura walked out with me. She was still pretty out of it so I took her back to my house. She crashed on my couch and fell asleep. Until we found out from the police about what had happened back at her house."

"Where was Patrick Walsh when you and Maura left the house?"

"He was fine. Absolutely fine. I remembered that afterward. Who knew what was going to happen? But afterward Maura blamed herself for her brother's death."

"You just said she wasn't there when he died?"

"But she didn't know that. Not then. She never found out until a few months ago. All these years she thought Patrick got the gun and shot himself with it while she was there but blacked out. That it happened when she was supposed to be watching him."

"Why did she believe that?"

"Because that's what her father told her happened."

I was confused.

"But you said she wasn't even there when Patrick shot himself. That he was fine when you and she left the house. Didn't you tell her that?"

"I never saw Maura again after that day. The family disappeared after that. I always assumed she knew the truth. But she didn't. She didn't remember anything that happened after all the drinking. She believed what her father told her. That she got dead drunk and wasn't watching her little brother like she was supposed to when he found the gun. That's why she thought her brother's death was her fault. She'd been living with that guilt ever since."

"How did you find out about this? You said you never saw her again after that day because her family moved away so quickly."

"I didn't then, but I found out differently from her few months ago. When Maura came to see me. My God, it was such a surprise to find her at my door after all this time."

Of course. Maura Walsh would have come here for answers, like I was doing right now.

"That's when she told me the story of how she'd blamed herself for Patrick's death all this time. And her father had too. She'd spent her whole life trying to make it up to him for costing the life of his son like that – the son he envisioned following him into the NYPD one day. That's even why she joined the police force, she told me. Her father demanded that she become a police officer like all the other members of the Walsh family before her. She didn't want to do that, she wanted some kind of a different career. But he said she owed him this because of letting her brother die. She had to take his place. So she eventually gave in and joined the force. She desperately wanted to do anything for her father to make up for what she had done that day which allowed her brother to get his hands on the gun. Until she found out the truth recently. She knew now she wasn't responsible for her brother's death. She knew now she wasn't even there when it happened. Her father had lied to her all these years, and he made her feel guilty. Maura was furious at her father and wanted to quit the NYPD, she said. But, before she did that, she also said she wanted to make her father pay a price for what he had done to her."

It was a pretty mind-boggling story that Walsh had done something like that to his own daughter, but it finally explained why she was so angry with him once she found out the truth.

There was another question I had. Why did Maura Walsh suddenly go looking for answers about what she did or didn't do that day her little brother died? Why now after all this time did she question the story she'd always been told? The story she believed all her life. Melissa Soroka didn't know. She said Maura only kept talking about how she'd been living all her life with the guilt that her irresponsibility in getting drunk caused her brother's death. Now she knew that wasn't true and had come to get Melissa, her teenage friend, to confirm the real events of that day.

"Back then, when this all happened, didn't you tell this story about you and Maura to the authorities? About how you had been at the house earlier, and Patrick Walsh was still fine and playing with his toys when you left?"

"I told the police when they asked me questions about Maura. I told them everything I just told you."

"Chief Palumbo?"

"No, it wasn't him."

"Who?"

"The deputy."

"Greg Stovall?"

"Yes, that was his name."

CHAPTER 58

Greg Stovall had been one of the first people I talked to about Maura Walsh. I thought I was done with him, but he'd lied to me. Stovall said he never got a chance to talk with Melissa Soroka because his boss, Police Chief Walter Palumbo, ordered him off it. Except I now had found out that wasn't true. So what else had Stovall lied to me about?

I knew where to find Greg Stovall again at his landscaping firm in Elmira, but I decided to wait before confronting him. I wanted to talk to the two EMT workers first.

Except there was only one now. One of the men on the two-person EMT team had died of cancer several years earlier, I discovered. Timothy Fenton, the other EMT at the Walsh house that day, was still around though. He'd left the EMT job to go to medical school and he was now a doctor at a hospital in the Saginaw Lake area. I met with him in the hospital cafeteria.

"Sure, I remember the Walsh boy's death," he said to me. "I wasn't an EMT for very long – I always knew I wanted to do something more in the medical field, so it was just a starting point for me – but I saw a lot of traumatic stuff on those EMT runs. Never worse than the Walsh house though. The father crying and screaming at us, the mother pleading for someone to save her son – and that poor little boy lying dead on the living room floor. God, it was horrible. I still get chills when I think about it. But that was all a long time ago. Why are you writing about this now?"

I told him about the murder of Maura Walsh in New York City, and gave him my cover story of doing a profile on the family.

"That's terrible," he said when I told him about Maura. "That sure is a cursed family. Both children gone now."

"Did you see her that day in the house?"

"The daughter?"

"Yes."

"Nah, no one else was there except the mother and father. I didn't even know there was another child. Of course, we were pretty frantic – trying to see if there was any way we could save the boy and all. But it was hopeless. He was dead by the time we got there."

Fenton went though more details, which seemed to go along with the account I'd read in the police report on the Walsh boy's death.

"Anything else you remember from that day which was… well, unusual?" I asked.

"There was one thing," Fenton said. "I'm sure it didn't mean anything. At least in terms of the boy's death. But on the ride to the hospital – and then to the morgue – with the body, I noted bruises on the boy."

"Bruises? But he was shot, right?"

"Oh, yes. His whole head was pretty much blown away. That's not where the bruises were that I saw. They were on his arm and other parts of his body. It looked to me like his arm might have been broken at some point in the past, although I couldn't be sure. But the bruises and scars were all from a while ago so – like I said – they couldn't have had anything to do with his death."

"What do you think caused them?"

"Well, in a case like this, I normally would have said some kind of abuse."

"Someone had hit him?"

"There were signs of that kind of physical abuse. On more than one occasion."

"From who?"

"I never had enough information to make that kind of judgement."

"Could the bruises have been from his father?"

"Well… yes, I assumed – based on what I saw from the body – that the boy might have been beaten in the past by his father."

"Did you tell anyone about this?"

"Of course I did. I put it in my report."

"Your report…"

"Oh yes, I was very conscientious about putting everything into the medical records on my EMT job. I guess I was getting ready to be a doctor already back then. But it was all in my report, if you want to read it. Not that it really means anything, of course. The only thing that mattered at that point was the gunshot wound to the little boy's head that killed him."

"Was there ever an autopsy done to officially determine the cause of death?"

"I don't think so."

"Isn't that routine procedure in a death case like this?"

"Usually. But it was pretty obvious the boy died from the bullet wound in his head. And I'm sure the father used a lot of his NYPD pull with the authorities in Saginaw Lake to make sure their little boy wasn't cut up for an autopsy. I remember they just wanted to bury him. I could understand that."

So no official cause of death.

And bruises on the boy's body from some time earlier.

This was getting weirder and weirder.

There was something else that didn't make sense to me too. I'd made copies of all the documents in the police file about Patrick Walsh's death, including the reports from the EMTs. I'd brought them with me for the interview. I took out Fenton's report now and read through it quickly, looking for the part about the bruises. I couldn't find anything. I read it again, more carefully this time.

Nope. Nothing there. Just a straightforward account of them arriving at the house, finding the boy dead of a gunshot wound on the floor and transporting the body to the hospital.

"There's nothing in the report about the bruises on the body," I said to Fenton.

"Sure there is."

"I'm reading it right now. No mention of any bruises."

"Well, I wrote the report, and I included my observations about earlier bruises on the boy's body."

I handed him the report. It had been signed and dated by him on the day of Patrick Walsh's death. All very official. Except it turned out that it wasn't at all.

Fenton read through his long-ago report – casually at first, but then his eyes widened with surprise.

That's when I knew.

I knew for sure how far someone had gone to cover up the true facts of Patrick Walsh's death.

"This is not my report," Fenton said.

"You signed it."

"That's not my signature," he said. "And not what I said. Someone filed a false report under my name."

CHAPTER 59

Greg Stovall wasn't as friendly to me as he was the first time. I think he must have figured out that I knew about him now when I pulled up again in front of his landscaping business in Elmira. Once I told him I needed to talk to him again about the Patrick Walsh death, he said he was too busy to spend any more time with me. I said that wasn't good enough. I said it was urgent we discuss Patrick Walsh right now.

"What's so urgent about a simple accidental death case that happened a long time ago?" he asked.

"I don't think it was that simple anymore. And I'm not even sure it was accidental."

That got his attention.

"What do you want from me?" he asked warily.

"The truth."

"I told you the truth. I told you everything I know about that case. It was Chief Palumbo who did it all. Whatever happened – or didn't happen – was because of Palumbo. Like I told you before, I had more questions about that case too. But I never got any answers. That's why I left the force."

Of course, he'd told me all that. It had been his plan all along. Make me think he was the good guy, and Chief Palumbo the bad guy. Or at least the only bad guy in this. I wasn't sure Palumbo was a bad guy. Or Stovall either. But I did believe they had not done their jobs properly. And that was because they'd succumbed to tempta-tion. In Palumbo's case, the temptation had been a chance to join the NYPD – his lifelong dream. So what was Stovall's temptation that got him to cover up evidence in the investigation of Patrick Walsh's death? Looking around at the landscaping business he had here, I had a pretty good idea it had to have been money for him.

"I've been to see Melissa Soroka," I said. "The woman you said you never got a chance to interview. Only thing is, she remembers talking to you. She says she told you everything she knew about that day of the shooting."

I figured that would shake him up, and I took a chance and hit him up with something else too.

"I talked to the EMT guy on the scene that day. Timothy Fenton. He filed a report on everything he knew that went into the police file. Except… well, the report in the police file isn't the one he submitted. Someone substituted a fake report there. Do you want to comment on that?"

I wasn't sure that it was Stovall who had switched the EMT reports in the file. It could have been Palumbo. But I knew I'd hit pay dirt by the way Stovall responded to me.

"Look, I don't have to talk to you at all. You're not a police officer or anyone official. You're just a lousy newspaper reporter. You have no authority whatsoever. You want a comment from me? Okay, here it is: I don't know what you're talking about. Now get the hell off my property! Or I will call the police!"

"Really? I'm not sure I'd do that if I were you. I mean, most police are honest and responsible and want to hear the true story. Not like you and Chief Palumbo were when you were on the Saginaw Lake force."

"Screw you…"

He pretended like he was taking out his phone to call the cops on me. I just waited him out. He started to punch in a few numbers, then stopped. No, he didn't want the police here. I figured maybe I could use that to get him to open up to me about what he really knew and had done.

"I'm not here to make trouble for you. I only want answers from you. You're right when you say I have no official authority to ask you questions. But I do have the power of the press. I can write an article in the *New York Tribune* about all of this. Then the police would definitely be interested in you. I'm not sure what the criminal penalties are for what you did – or if the statute of limitations has run out – but I think it would pretty much mess up the nice little life you've built here for yourself," I said, looking around at the landscaping company he owned. "All I want is the truth. Give me some truthful answers, and I'll be gone. Okay?"

He didn't answer me.

"What happened to Patrick Walsh?" I asked.

"I don't know any more about the shooting that day. And that is the truth."

"What about the bruises they found on the boy's body?"

"What about them?"

"Did they have anything to do with his death?"

"Not that I'm aware of."

"So you do believe the Walsh boy's death was accidental?"

"What else could it have been?"

"You tell me."

"I'm telling you, I don't know anything."

"But someone did convince you and Chief Palumbo to put a lid on the investigation, to avoid an autopsy and even to alter the official police report to make sure the death looked just like a 'simple, accidental shooting', as you put it so eloquently before.

"Now in Walt Palumbo's case, it's easy to figure out what happened. Someone with authority in the NYPD – and that would have to be Walsh – pulled strings to get him a job there. A job Palumbo always wanted. Or at least thought he did. Even got him assigned to Walsh's favorite precinct, the 22nd where he'd been commanding officer.

"But what about you? You didn't join the NYPD. Despite all your claims the last time we talked about how much you loved your time on the force and missed being a police officer. No, you opened this landscaping business. Which must have taken money to do. But where did you get the money?"

"I told you – I'm not talking to you about this. You're right about Walsh and Palumbo. He did get him on the NYPD. That was the quid pro quo. But that's all I've got to say."

"You've told me this much, why not give me the rest?"

"I can't."

"Who gave you the money for this company to cover up stuff about Patrick Walsh's death? Was it Walsh? Did he first offer you a job with the NYPD like he did for Palumbo? But you didn't care about that, did you? You wanted something more than a job with the NYPD. You wanted money. And you used the money to make this business here for yourself. Isn't that right?"

"You'll get nothing from me about that."

"Aren't you afraid I'll go ahead and write that article for the *Tribune* if you don't come clean with me?"

"I'm more afraid of what would happen to me if I did."

"Why are you so afraid of Walsh?"

"It's not Walsh I'm afraid of."

And that's when I knew.

I knew there was only one person in all this who could invoke that kind of fear in a man like Greg Stovall.

Dominic Bennato.

CHAPTER 60

I'd been seeing police cars in my sleep for a while now because of the Maura Walsh story. I saw them when I was wide awake too. And I was getting increasingly paranoid about whether the police might be watching me. Especially after that encounter of mine with the two rogue cops, Shockley and Janko.

That's why, after I left Greg Stovall and saw a police car on the street behind me, I wondered if it might be Chief Palumbo. Okay, it was his father that had helped cover up facts about the Walsh boy's shooting, but maybe the son, Dale Palumbo, was looking out for his legacy or whatever. I was getting pretty nervous about this damn police car business.

But then I remembered I was in Elmira, a hundred miles away from Saginaw Lake where Dale Palumbo was the chief. No one in Elmira was following me. And, sure enough, very soon the police car turned off and began going in another direction away from me.

The same thing happened when I got closer to home in the city. There was an NYPD car on the West Side Highway as I came down it. Could this be Shockley and Janko again? Or else some of the other corrupt cops from the 22nd or wherever? But, when I checked again in my rearview mirror, that police car was gone too.

I made it home without any more sightings and quickly ran upstairs to my apartment and locked the door.

Okay, it was probably just my paranoia. But all the stuff with Bennato and the dirty cops and the rest was freaking me out. And it didn't help when I saw how afraid Greg Stovall seemed to be of

Bennato. Even locked away here in my apartment, I couldn't stop this rising panic I felt at the moment. I didn't feel safe anymore. Crazy, right? Or maybe not.

Which was why I really got nervous when I heard a knock on my door.

I wasn't expecting anyone.

So who the hell was out there?

"Who's there?" I said through the closed door.

"Jessie, open up."

I recognized the voice.

It was Sam Rawlings.

Who I now knew worked for Dominic Bennato.

"Go away," I said.

"I need to talk to you."

"No."

"Please, it's important."

"Go away, or I'll call the police!!"

"I am the police," Rawlings said.

"You got it all wrong, Jessie," Rawlings said when I finally relented and did let him inside. "I am a police officer. I'm working undercover."

"Why should I believe that?"

"Take another look at that picture you showed me. The one from outside the Police Academy."

I walked over to my desk, found the picture and brought it back to the living room where Rawlings was sitting.

I studied it again. No question about it, that was Rawlings graduating at the same time as Maura Walsh. They knew each other back then. And now they were sharing in illegal payoffs, all connected to a mob boss like Bennato. I told that to Sam again.

"Look at the instructor," Sam said.

I hadn't really thought about that. There were several recruits and an instructor. I had picked out Samuel Rawlings and Maura Walsh. But I hadn't noticed anyone else. I stared at the picture of the instructor now. The man who had been teaching the two of them while they were at the Police Academy. And I recognized him too.

"Russell Garrison," I said.

"We all knew each other back then," Rawlings said. "That's why I was working with Garrison. I've been undercover for a while now. Ever since we – Garrison and I – came up with the phony story about me being booted from the force for taking payoffs. That was my cover. We needed that to make people like Bennato believe I was okay to work with. I'm telling you this because I think you need to know the truth. I'm not the bad guy, I'm one of the good guys. But you can't print anything about this, or else people's lives will be jeopardized, including mine. I need you to agree to that before I tell you anything more, Jessie."

I nodded numbly.

"Okay," I said.

"And it's not what you think about Maura Walsh either."

"You were going to arrest her sooner or later for corruption, weren't you?"

"No."

"What were you going to do – give her another award?"

"We weren't after her."

"But…"

"Maura was working with us too, Jessie."

"Maura Walsh was undercover?"

"Yes."

"For six months?"

"Yes, taking payoffs and doing other illegal acts. It was part of the cover. We had to convince people of that, even if she was the deputy commissioner's daughter. So we set up phony purchases for her of a fancy sports car and other expensive things so everyone would be convinced she really was on the take. Just like they had to do with me. It was harder with Maura Walsh because of who she was and her family background. We had to go to great lengths to make her look dirty because of that. That's the only way it could work."

I still didn't understand it.

"Why her?" I asked. "Wouldn't it have been easier to put another officer undercover?"

"We had no choice but to use her. She was the one who came to us first with the incriminating information involving corruption in the department. She said she'd only work with us under the condition that she was directly involved in the case. She volunteered for the assignment, Jessie. She insisted on doing it."

"It must have been a big assignment for her to want to get involved and devote six months of her life to an undercover investigation."

"It is."

"How big?"

"We're talking about corruption at the highest levels of the department."

The highest levels of the department.

"Is her father involved in this?" I asked.

"Yes."

"How deeply?"

"Deputy Commissioner Walsh is the target of the investigation, Jessie."

CHAPTER 61

The corruption in the police department had been going on for a number of years, Sam said.

Little things at first. Special favoritism being shown to some business and real estate projects. Money winding up where it shouldn't be. A tendency to look the other way and ignore violations of some laws and city codes for certain individuals. No one paid much attention to it for a long time.

It was Maura who first came to Internal Affairs and said she had obtained information about a pattern of systematic corruption within the police department in connection with its dealings with a prominent New York City mobster.

The mobster was Dominic Bennato, who in addition to his sanitation company owned many other businesses around town.

"These businesses were paying off police officers for protection from the law to do anything they wanted. No arrests, no raids, not even any tickets or summonses. Some of the businesses were legit on the surface like The Hangout was. But many of them were escort services and X-rated clubs and gambling or drug dealing operations. Even the supposedly reputable operations like The Hangout were involved in activities like money laundering. A lot of cash went into that restaurant and then into Bennato's pocket. Whatever he paid for the police protection was minimal compared to the huge profits he was making from all his illegal operations. Without any interference from the police, Bennato had a free hand to do whatever he wanted in New York City."

A special elite unit was set up within the Internal Affairs Division to investigate the scandal, working under top-level secrecy because no one knew for sure at that point how far up the chain of command the corruption spread. It was eventually determined that Bennato's influence seemed to come right from the top – the deputy commissioner's office.

"And it was definitely Maura herself who came to you with this investigation and volunteered to go undercover against her own father?" I asked.

"Yes. At first, the Internal Affairs people rejected the idea of Maura's participation because of who she was. But she said she was a police officer first, and Walsh's daughter next. If he was guilty of a crime, she said, then he had to pay the price just like everyone else. She said it was her father who had taught her that a long time ago. Her enthusiasm and intensity and dedication finally won everyone over.

"The big problem we had was to convince the dirty cops – Renfro and all the others – that Maura was really one of them. I mean, they all knew she was the deputy police commissioner's daughter – and about his reputation for integrity – so everyone would be very careful not to do anything illegal when she was around.

"That's when we decided to create an obvious rift between Maura and her father. She deliberately picked a fight with him in the middle of the 22nd Precinct station house so that everyone could see it. She called him up, said she needed to see him there and then told him something that she said she knew would make him angry. It worked. Things were never the same between them after that.

"I know it was probably hard on her, but she never complained. She knew it was essential for her role in the undercover operation to work. The other cops had to truly believe that she and her father were on different sides. And, as it turned out, they were.

"Even then though some of the other cops on the take didn't trust her at first. But she kept telling everyone how angry she was at her father and how she wanted to get back at him somehow. She started taking payoffs from store owners on her own, without any help from anyone else. Finally the other dirty cops cut her in on their deal. Maura was very convincing. She played the part of a disgruntled cop like Meryl Streep.

"The rest you know about. When Renfro's partner died, we put Maura in there to gather evidence. No one knew what she was really doing. Just me and Russell Garrison in Internal Affairs. I got a job with the restaurant so I could work on Bennato from the inside."

"How about Billy Renfro?" I asked. "Did he know what Maura was doing?"

I told him about how strange Renfro had acted in the pizza parlor that night and how I was convinced he felt guilty for some reason about his partner's death.

"He did blame himself for it," Sam said. "We confronted him after the murder and told him the truth about Maura. He said he'd begun to suspect that she might be working undercover. He said he'd confided his fears to some other cops who were also involved with the bribe taking and payoffs. On the night that she died, Renfro was worried. He was afraid the other dirty cops might do something to her to keep her mouth shut. He couldn't tell Maura that though without giving himself away. And he figured that they wouldn't hurt her. Just try to scare her a little bit. But when she wound up dead, he blamed himself for letting his partner get killed. Especially when he found out that she had been lying there for as much as a full hour bleeding to death. He could have saved her. But he waited too long to start looking for her."

I took a deep breath as I tried to assimilate everything he was telling me.

"Do you think Maura Walsh was killed because of the under-cover work she was doing against other cops?"

"We're not sure."

"Is Dominic Bennato a possible suspect in her death?"

"Yes."

Then I asked him the unthinkable question.

"What about Maura's father? Is Walsh a suspect in the death of his own daughter?"

"Everyone's a suspect," he said.

CHAPTER 62

"Maura Walsh was working undercover?" Isaacs said.

"For six months. Pretending to be a corrupt police officer. But really working with Internal Affairs to expose corruption in the 22nd Precinct and other places in the department too. Including her own father, the deputy commissioner."

We were in Isaacs' office with the door closed. Me, him, Danny and Lorraine. I told them about everything Sam had told me. About everything I'd found out in Saginaw Lake. And about everything else I knew.

"Do the police think she was killed because someone found out she was working undercover?" Danny asked.

"That's certainly a strong possibility, they say."

"By her own father? My God, that's hard to believe."

"Or Dominic Bennato."

"That makes more sense."

"Or maybe Bennato and Walsh both. I think they were working together. My scenario – and it's just a scenario at this point, but I think it's a reasonable one – is that Walsh covered up things about the death of his seven-year-old son in Saginaw Lake. He desperately didn't want anyone to find out that the boy had been beaten by him numerous times before that. Bennato found out about this somehow. Presumably by paying off Stovall, the deputy on the case for the Saginaw Lake Police Force, and financing his landscaping business. In return, Stovall gave Bennato the authentic police report and other information about what happened to

Patrick Walsh. Bennato then used that to blackmail Walsh senior. To protect himself, Walsh gave Bennato free rein for all his illegal activities. There's no indication Walsh actually took money from Bennato, but he did look the other way when the cops at the 22nd and other places were making secret deals with him. Otherwise, Bennato threatened to reveal the details about what happened to the Walsh boy. The beatings from the father that had been covered up by the phony medical report. And maybe even more stuff that had been covered up about the circumstances of the boy's death. And that's what Maura Walsh was about to expose."

I looked around the room. Danny seemed excited by the story, Norman nervous about it and Lorraine... well, I couldn't figure out what she thought about it. She was always a big mystery.

"One thing I don't understand," Lorraine said now. "Why would this undercover cop Rawlings tell you all this? Why would he reveal it to a newspaper reporter? Doesn't that violate the code or whatever those undercover people live by?"

I wanted to say Rawlings did it because of me. He wanted to protect me from going off in the wrong direction on this story. He wanted to atone for the lies he'd told me in the past. He wanted to tell me everything now in an effort to re-establish our personal relationship, whatever that might be.

But I'd found out from him in my apartment the night before it was for a more practical reason.

"The Internal Affairs People – Garrison, Rawlings and the others involved – want to go public with this information. They want me to write a story. They want the *Tribune* to let the world know about it all. I can't reveal the undercover part about Sam Rawlings or Maura Walsh. Not yet. But they will give me information to write a sourced story linking Bennato to all sorts of crimes – including blackmail, extortion and possibly even murder. And that high members of the NYPD are believed to have participated in the cover-up of Bennato's crimes.

"Until now, there has been a tight security lid over this whole corruption operation. I'm not even sure Aguirre knows. And they sure didn't tell Florio at the 22nd, which was the center of the corruption. But now they're ready to move in on Bennato and the others. Except they don't have a hundred percent airtight case. Everyone knows how crazy and reckless and unhinged Bennato can be. They feel if he finds out the *Tribune* is going with a story exposing it all, it might push him over the edge to do something really stupid. Then they'll have him."

It was Norman Isaacs who first brought up the obvious. Norman was always the pragmatist.

"That could be very dangerous for you, Jessie. Bennato might go to any lengths to stop you from writing about this. And we can't print the story without running it past him first. We have to get a comment from him about all these allegations. And then he might do anything to retaliate. And I'm not just talking about legal retaliation. Your life could be in danger."

"I understand that."

"Did you tell Rawlings you had any misgivings about making yourself a target like that for Bennato?"

"He said it was my decision. They'd understand if I decided against it."

"You don't have to do this," Lorraine said.

"I told him I would."

Even Danny seemed a bit rattled by the potential consequence of me doing this story.

"We need to come up with a way to protect you," he said. "You really need to be careful about this."

"I'm way ahead of you," I said. "Believe me, I don't want to die on this story. I didn't die in Central Park and I sure don't plan to get knocked off by Dominic Bennato."

*

In *Deadline – U.S.A.*, Peter Ventura's favorite newspaper movie, there was a wonderful scene at the end where the paper's managing editor, played by Humphrey Bogart, was about to run an exposé about a mob boss that would send the guy to jail. The mobster calls Bogart and makes all sorts of threats while Bogart was in the press room getting ready for the presses to roll with the story. But Bogart just orders the presses to start rolling.

I thought about that movie now as I called Dominic Bennato to tell him about the story we were running and ask for any comment from him about it.

It took a while for me to get through to him on the phone, but I finally did.

Maybe because he'd met with me before that day in his office.

Maybe because he found me so charming.

Or maybe because he knew something was about to happen, and he needed to find out what it was.

I went through everything that we would be running in the *Tribune*. I said we were still gathering more information about it. He had twenty-four hours to get back to me with a response. Otherwise, we would run it without any comment at all from him. I said that seemed more than fair. Bennato obviously didn't agree.

"You can't print that story," he screamed at me when I was finished.

"That's not up to you, Bennato."

"You kill that story or you're in big trouble," he said.

"I'm sorry, but I can't do that."

"Big trouble," Bennato said again, then he slammed down the phone.

Danny was right.

I did need to be careful.

CHAPTER 63

I saw another police car the next morning. But not soon enough. And this time it was the real thing, not my paranoia. A blue and while NYPD squad car pulled in front of the *Tribune* building just as I approached. Shockley and Janko got out.

I tried my best to stay calm. I was on a busy Manhattan street in broad daylight with lots of people around, I told myself. Nothing bad could happen to me here, I told myself. I told myself wrong.

"We've been thinking again about that marijuana we found in your car," Shockley said. "We decided we let you off too easy then. So we're gonna take you to that jail cell, after all."

He looked over at his partner Janko and smiled. Janko smiled too. They were enjoying this. Shockley and Janko were the type of cops who enjoyed their work, even if what they were doing was not really police work.

"I don't have to listen to this anymore," I said, and I started moving toward the *Tribune* front door.

"Yeah, you do," Shockley said, and he grabbed me.

"Let me go!"

"Cuff her, Vic."

Janko pulled out a pair of handcuffs and put them on me. Then both of them began dragging me toward the squad car. All I could think of to do was scream for help. Which was what I did. I yelled at people passing by on the street that I was being kidnapped.

But these were cops. They just told everyone I was a psychotic mental patient they were picking up for my own safety. A few people stared, but most kept walking and ignored us. Like most New Yorkers do when they see something unpleasant happening on the street. I probably would have done that too.

They shoved me into the car and began driving away.

Headed away from the 22nd Precinct on the Upper East Side, where they worked.

Instead, we drove downtown and then across the East River into Brooklyn.

"What precinct are you taking me to?" I asked, even though I was afraid I didn't want to know the answer.

"You ain't going to any precinct, honey," Janko said.

"You ain't going to be going nowhere!" Shockley laughed.

I didn't say anything after that. There was nothing to say. We drove through Brooklyn to a deserted area along the waterfront. There was nothing there except a big old warehouse building. They took me out of the car and into the building.

There were a half dozen men inside. A couple of them wore police uniforms like Shockley and Janko. The others I assumed were mob guys who worked for Dominic Bennato.

But there was one person in the room that I gave the most attention to: Dominic Bennato himself.

All four hundred pounds or so of mob boss.

Sitting there in this warehouse building and glaring at me.

This was not the Dominic Bennato I met in his fancy, business-like office with the secretary, the plush rugs and the Muzak playing in the background. This wasn't the Dominic Bennato either who ran the Italian restaurant Marcello's with the wonderful pasta primavera and had takeout food delivered upstairs to Michelle when she lived there. And it wasn't the Dominic Bennato who told me in his office how much he admired "my balls" for standing up to him.

This was the real Dominic Bennato.

A vicious thug.

A killer.

"I've decided it's time to put an end to all this trouble you're causing for me," Bennato said. "You've refused to stop investigating everything about Walsh and Walsh's daughter and all the rest. That means I have to take matters into my own hands. Walsh is too important to me to allow you to mess up this deal. I have Walsh in my pocket, and he's going to stay in my pocket. So I'm going to have to shut you down, Jessie Tucker. You won't be telling this story to anyone."

Even in my current situation, I was curious. Still a reporter to the end, I guess.

"What damaging evidence do you have on Walsh?"

"That's none of your business."

"Is it about the death of his son?"

Bennato almost smiled now. "You are a pretty good reporter."

"You got the real story about his son's death from Greg Stovall, the deputy. You financed Stovall in his landscaping business in return for the information. And that's given you something to control Walsh – the man everyone always thought was the Prince of the City because he was supposedly so honest and incorruptible – ever since. Am I close?"

"Let's just say Walsh had his secrets that he didn't want to come out. And that's proved very profitable for me."

He nodded toward Shockley and Janko.

Something was about to happen.

The time for talk was almost over.

"I'm going to give you two options, Ms. Tucker," Bennato said. "Neither of them are very pleasant. But one is exceedingly less pleasant than the other. The first option is that you will write out and sign a note saying that you were wrong about this story; that you made all the facts up which were never true; and you did it because you wanted to stay in the media spotlight like you were with all the Central Park events. You will also say that the trauma over everything that happened to you all over again recently in Central Park has been too much to bear, and you just can't go on anymore. Yes, it will be a suicide note. Just like the one Billy Renfro left. That should be enough for the *Tribune* to not run your story. And, even if they did, no one would believe anything you said because of your clearly disturbed mental state from the suicide note. Then, once you have written this note for us – and signed it, officers Shockley and Janko will shoot you in the head and dump your body into the East River."

This can't be happening, I thought to myself as I tried to control the fear and the panic inside me. *I can't have my life end like this. Not after I survived everything I went through in Central Park. Did I go through all of that just to die in some crappy warehouse at the hands of a thug like Dominic Bennato?*

"What's the more pleasant option?" I asked Bennato.

It seemed to be the only logical response.

"That is the more pleasant option. The other option – if you refuse to write and sign the suicide note I just spoke about – is that Shockley and Janko will still kill you and dump you in the East River. But they will make it a very long and painful process for you. They're experts at prolonging pain like that, and they enjoy torturing a victim long and hard before the final kill. So make it easy on yourself. Just like Renfro did. Write and sign the note, and I promise you it will all be over very quickly."

I looked at Shockley and Janko. They were smiling even more now. Janko had that crazy look in his eyes again. Excitement maybe. Anticipation. Or both. Like Bennato had said, these two enjoyed their work.

I turned back toward Bennato.

"And those are my only two options?"

"I'm afraid so."

"Actually, I do have a third option."

"Really? What is that?"

Shockley and Janko weren't holding on to me, so I was able to move my handcuffed arms in front of me. I moved them up to my chest. Then I reached up to the top buttons on the blouse I was wearing.

"Here's my third option," I said, and began to open up my blouse.

Bennato just shook his head. He didn't understand what I was doing. Not yet.

"Sex? You're offering us sex for your life? I really don't see how that could make a difference. If we wanted to have sex with you, we could. And then go ahead and kill you anyway. So let's stop wasting time and—"

"Not quite," I said.

I unbuttoned my blouse all the way down now and pulled it apart so they could see what was underneath.

A recording device.

"I'm wired, Bennato. And you're screwed. Everything you just said and did was being recorded by the police. The real police, not these disgraces to the NYPD you have working for you. They're outside the building now listening. They should be arriving here very soon."

At first, I think they thought I was bluffing.

But I wasn't.

Suddenly, there was a smashing sound at the door of the warehouse.

Bennato turned around in a panic, lumbered to his feet and started to try to run, along with Shockley and Janko and the others.

But there was nowhere to run to.

A huge number of cops, including SWAT team members with automatic weapons, were inside the warehouse now and taking everyone into custody.

Sam Rawlings was there, which didn't surprise me. He was the one who came up with the idea to have me wired – and then followed – in case Bennato tried something like this.

Thomas Aguirre was there too, which also made sense.

But one of the other people there – one of the cops – was a surprise.

It was Walsh.

"What are you doing here?" Bennato yelled at him.

"My job."

"If I go down, I'm taking you with me!"

"I know."

"Then why—"

"This was something I should have done a long time ago," Walsh said.

CHAPTER 64

I was a media star all over again. Just like I'd been with Central Park. Everyone wanted to talk to me. I was on *Good Morning America*, the *NBC Nightly News* and the cable news channels. Newspapers, magazines and websites chased after me for an interview. And #jessietucker was trending like hell on Twitter and the rest of social media.

This all came after I broke the story first on the front page of the *Tribune*.

MOB BOSS BENNATO BUSTED
—AND THE *TRIBUNE* WAS THERE!
Top NYPD Officer Walsh Implicated in Crimes Too
By Jessie Tucker
Tribune Crime Reporter

Dominic (Fat Nic) Bennato, the legendary New York underworld leader, was arrested during a dramatic raid in a Brooklyn warehouse for murder and a host of corruption charges growing out of the death of policewoman Maura Walsh.

This reporter was there and actually participated in the stunning takedown of the notorious mob boss who has successfully avoided prosecution from law enforcement over the years.

Also taken into custody were NYPD Deputy Commissioner Mike Walsh, the father of the recently slain policewoman, and a group of allegedly corrupt officers from the 22nd Precinct in Manhattan who had been taking bribes from Bennato.

The *Tribune* learned that Maura Walsh was working undercover at the time of her death to expose those corrupt police officers – including her own father – who had been cooperating with Bennato on various illegal schemes and activities.

It is not clear yet if Maura Walsh's murder on a lower Manhattan street was connected to the undercover investigation. But Bennato and several of the officers from the 22nd Precinct have been tied to at least two other murders – Billy Renfro, Maura Walsh's NYPD partner, and Frank Walosin, a Manhattan private investigator.

It took a while to sort everything out. And, when that happened, it turned out to be even more incredible than I or anyone else could have ever imagined.

Some of it I already knew or had figured out.

Yes, Walsh admitted to Internal Affairs investigators, he had used his NYPD influence and connections to cover up the details of what really happened in the death of his son years earlier in Saginaw Lake.

He said he'd lost his temper and beaten the boy for bad behavior that day. He said he had beaten the boy for doing things wrong in the past too, once even breaking a bone in Patrick's arm. But the physical abuse hadn't really gotten out of hand, he insisted, until that last day. That's when he realized he had beaten his own son to death with a series of powerful blows to his head. He hadn't meant to hurt the boy that badly, he said, it was an accident. Just a horrible and tragic accident, he kept saying over and over.

It was what happened next that was truly unfathomable.

In order to hide the fact that the boy had died of injuries inflicted to his head, Mike Walsh took out his spare service revolver that he kept in a closet at the house and then – Walsh began to cry as he relived this movement – he shot his own son in the head. That way it appeared as if the boy died of a self-inflicted gunshot wound, not a beating.

Walsh – who had always seemed so impassive and unfeeling in the past – completely broke down in tears as he related this part. I remembered the EMT Timothy Fenton talking about how emotional Walsh was that day at the house too. And with good reason. He had just shot his own son. To cover up the fact that he'd already accidentally killed the boy with his fists in a fit of anger.

He then offered the police chief, Walter Palumbo, the dream job he'd always wanted with the NYPD and paid off his deputy, Greg Stovall, too. They made sure no autopsy was done; nobody asked too many questions; and they even switched the medical records in the report on the case.

Neither of them were aware he'd actually killed his own son, Walsh believed, but they knew he wanted details about what happened that day kept secret – or even altered, in the case of the medical report.

He said they thought he was trying to protect his teenaged daughter Maura by doing all this.

"When they found out Maura had been drinking while she was supposed to be watching Patrick, they assumed Maura had done something irresponsible that caused his death. That we had lied about her not being in the house when Patrick died to protect her. And they believed that was the secret I didn't want anyone to find out about. I did not disabuse them of that belief. I let them keep thinking that's what had happened – my daughter was responsible – rather than let them discover the truth."

But it seemed the money wasn't enough to buy Stovall's silence for good. Because it turned out he had a cousin who was involved with the mob, and he told the cousin about it all at some point afterward. The cousin got the word to Bennato, who saw an opportunity to get a top police official like Walsh, a man known for his integrity and refusal to accept any payoffs or gifts, under his control.

Bennato gave Stovall a lot of money for his landscaping business – much more money than Walsh had been able to afford. In return, Stovall told Bennato everything he knew about the death of little Patrick. When Bennato confronted Walsh with this information, Walsh realized he was in too deep now to back out of the lies he'd told. And so he reluctantly agreed he had no choice but to cooperate with the mob boss.

There was a dramatic video made during Walsh's interrogation by police investigators where he talked about his daughter, Maura. It eventually wound up on YouTube and trended all over Twitter and the rest of social media. But I got it first from one of my sources and we played it prominently on the *Tribune* website before anyone else did.

It was a terrific exclusive for me.

But it still pained me – and made me feel sad about Maura – to watch Walsh as he talked about his daughter. The man's cold, aloof exterior was gone now. Instead, all of his guilt and his remorse and his anguish over what he had lost because of his own actions were what we saw in the video as he talked:

"My daughter was consumed by guilt because she had gotten drunk when she was supposed to be watching Patrick," he said. "When I spoke to her afterward, she didn't remember anything – including the fact she had left the house while Patrick was still alive. She had gone into a total blackout.

"She was convinced it was she who had been at fault for her brother's death. That she had allowed Patrick to play with the gun. Or, perhaps even worse, she had taken the gun out of the closet and – in her inebriated state – accidentally killed her own brother. She really believed she was responsible for her brother's death – and that we had lied about where she was to protect her.

"I let her believe that. I let my daughter continue to believe she was the one at fault for Patrick's death. And that everything I had done to keep the facts a secret was to protect her, not to protect myself. Just like Palumbo and Stovall believed I was doing too. Even after they spoke to Maura's friend she'd gotten drunk with and left with that day, they assumed it was all part of the cover-up. Letting people like Palumbo and Stovall think Maura had acted irresponsibly to cause her brother's death just seemed the most effective way of making sure the real story never came out."

My God, I thought to myself, as I read the incriminating statement.

But there was even more.

"As Maura grew up, I used this information – information that wasn't true, of course – against her to get her to do what I wanted. Which was to join the police force. I had lost my son. The son that I desperately wanted one day to carry on the Walsh tradition of NYPD service.

"But Maura was headstrong and insisted she wanted to do something else with her life. That's when I used her guilt over Patrick to bring her back into line. I said she was the reason her brother wasn't here to take over that role, so she needed to join the force to make up for what she did. She acquiesced in the end, and she became a police officer. And then she died.

"I'm responsible for all of this. I'm not sure what punishment you'll decide on for me, but it can never be worse than the punishment I've been putting myself through every day."

"That's an amazing story, huh?" I said to Norman, Danny and Lorraine in the *Tribune* newsroom after I broke the latest exclusive on Walsh's confession.

Everyone nodded in agreement.

"Except for one problem," I said. "I just found out Walsh's story wasn't true."

"What do you mean?" Norman asked.

"Let me rephrase that: it wasn't the whole story."

I told them then how I'd gotten a call with the latest update from Aguirre and Rawlings and Russell Garrison on the questioning of Walsh.

"None of them could quite believe that Walsh – a man who had lived his life upholding the integrity of the police force – would have thrown all of that away so easily just to protect himself. And, after intensive questioning, Walsh has now revealed that he was protecting someone else – not himself."

"Who?" Isaacs asked.

"Yeah, who?" Danny said. "Who else was there? He's already made clear that his daughter wasn't even in the house when the boy died."

It was Lorraine who figured it out, even before I told them.

"But there was one other person in the house," Lorraine said. "His wife. Nora Walsh."

In the end, that was the real story of what happened that day in Saginaw Lake at the Walsh family house.

Nora Walsh had lived her life under the thumb of her domineering husband. She loved him, but she also feared his wrath and his anger. Most of all, she always desperately wanted to please him. Which wasn't easy with a man as demanding as Mike Walsh.

For a long time, Nora Walsh had felt a sense of guilt because she was not able to give him the son he wanted. Maura was already nine years old, and there was still no son to carry on the Walsh family tradition with the NYPD. Walsh and his wife tried a lot of birth methods for a period of years, and eventually they were successful with Patrick. Her husband finally had the son who would follow in his footsteps as a police officer one day, just like so many other Walsh men had followed the family tradition in the past.

But now Nora Walsh felt under tremendous pressure to raise Patrick to be everything her husband wanted him to be. No little boy could meet the high standards she – and she believed her husband – wanted from him. And so she began to feel guilty over that, blaming herself for not being a good enough mother.

As the stress and demands from her husband about little Patrick grew, she turned to the bottle for solace. Nora Walsh became an alcoholic. She drank constantly at home, even when she was supposed to have been taking care of Patrick. Which was probably the reason she'd gotten so mad at her daughter Maura that day for breaking into the liquor cabinet and getting drunk herself.

After the argument with Maura, Nora was so upset that she did what she always did when she felt that way: she began drinking.

She drank a lot that day.

So much that she completely forgot about Patrick in another part of the house.

The seven-year-old boy loved playing Superman. Which was what he was doing. Dressed in his Superman outfit and cape. But he wasn't old enough to understand what was real and what was fantasy. His hero Superman could fly. So he thought he could fly too. He climbed up onto the roof of the house, a superhero in a cape in his young mind – and leaped into the air. Instead, he landed head-first on the concrete driveway below.

When Nora Walsh found him dead, she panicked. All she could think about was that her husband would blame her because she was too drunk to be watching him properly. She didn't want him to know it was her fault.

And so it was Nora Walsh who used her husband's service revolver – the spare one he kept in the closet – to shoot the dead boy in the head and carry his body back into the house in an effort to eliminate the evidence of what had really happened.

To make it look like Patrick had accidentally shot himself with the gun.

That way, she reasoned to herself in her drunken state, it would be her husband's fault too because it was his gun and he would blame himself – not her – for having left the weapon in a place their son could reach it.

That was the story Nora Walsh first told her husband when he came home on that tragic day.

But afterward, when she sobered up and confessed to him the truth – how she'd lied to him, the EMTs and the Saginaw Lake Police about what really happened, Mike Walsh had done everything he could to protect his wife.

"She stopped drinking," Walsh said. "That was why I never allowed any alcohol, or any stimulants of any kind, in my house anymore. Because of my wife. She had a lot of emotional and mental issues, but I love her. I always will. She didn't mean to let Patrick die or do what she did afterward. I'm not sure she even knows what really happened, any more than Maura remembered anything about that day. You may find this hard to believe, but my wife and I have never talked about what happened since then. Not in all these years. You have to understand why I did what I did. I had already lost my son, I couldn't lose my wife too. That's why I was willing to do anything I had to do in order to protect her. But now that's all over. And my daughter is gone too. I've lost them all."

So what about the bruises and scars on Patrick Walsh's body? Who had beaten the boy in the past?

No one knew the answer to that for sure. Walsh insisted that was him, saying he'd lost his temper – but never meant to hurt his son. But investigators thought he might still be covering up for his wife. That she had beaten Patrick in her desperate efforts to make him the perfect son for her husband. Which would explain why he went to such great lengths to keep the beatings the boy had suffered a secret – to protect his wife, not himself. Or maybe they both had been guilty of physical abuse.

Either way, it was a tragedy of unimaginable proportions.

Mike Walsh had wrapped himself in the cloak of duty and loyalty and service to the NYPD as his family for all these years.

But, in the end, it had cost him his own family.

CHAPTER 65

"Internal Affairs is still interrogating Shockley and Janko and Florio the rest of them from the 22nd Precinct," Rawlings said to me. "From what I hear, they're all talking their heads off – trying to blame each other. At the same time, the DA's people have really zeroed in on Bennato. They think they've got the goods on him this time. His lawyer Edelman is trying to make some sort of a deal with Bennato flipping on other big mob names to cut time off of a prison sentence." He sighed. "There really is no honor among thieves, is there?"

"Did they kill Maura Walsh?"

Rawlings shook his head no. "Doubtful. They deny it and it looks like they're telling the truth about that. Apparently, none of them suspected Maura Walsh was working undercover, even though Renfro had begun to figure it out. But none of the other cops he mentioned his suspicions to took it seriously. That's how good her cover worked as a dirty cop taking big money payoffs. Everyone thought it was going fine. Until Maura got herself killed in Little Italy that night. We found out that she and Renfro had gone there to pick up another payoff from one of Bennato's people. That's who she was waiting for when Renfro went to get the pizza. But, when the person with the money showed up, she was already dead."

"And that's what set everything off?"

"Yeah. First there was the private detective Walosin. Now Walosin wasn't much of a private detective, probably had trouble finding his own coffee in the morning. His real specialty was blackmail. So when he stumbled onto the cops taking payoffs, he figured he could make some money out of it. He talked to you, but he also contacted Renfro – figuring blackmail might pay better than selling tips to a newspaper reporter. Only Renfro told his boss Florio, the head of the 22nd Precinct. Florio passed the information on to Shockley and Janko and Bennato. Bennato sends Shockley and Janko to pay a visit to Walosin's office. Bye-bye, private detective."

"What about Renfro?"

"He panicked. First, he still blamed himself for Maura Walsh's murder, then he found out Walosin had been killed. He decided he was in over his head, and he tried to go to the authorities. Only Shockley and Janko found out and got to him first. They then tried to make his death look like suicide."

Just like they wanted to do with me, I thought to myself. They must have forced Renfro to write that suicide note the same way they wanted me to do it. And it wasn't difficult to convince people that a police officer like Renfro would take his own life because he was depressed and feeling guilty over the loss of his partner.

"That still leaves us with one big question: who killed Maura Walsh?"

Rawlings shrugged. "We're back to square one. It's just like we figured in the beginning, it was probably a random kill. Had nothing to do with any of the rest of this. Funny how those things work, huh?"

Meanwhile, Rawlings said Maura's mother Nora Walsh was undergoing psychiatric care. She kept babbling about "my darling little boy" and how she had let her husband down and didn't deserve to live. It was a sad case on so many levels.

I asked him what he thought was going to happen to Mike Walsh.

"Funny thing about that, it looks like he never took a dime of money for anything. He just let it happen, without stepping in to stop the corruption he knew was going on. It's kind of tragic when you think about it. A man who supposedly dedicated his life to the integrity of his job and the NYPD. But he threw it all away to protect his own family secrets. I don't know if he'll get jail time for any of it, either the corruption or what happened with his boy in Saginaw Lake. There's a lot of mitigating factors here, including the fact that he cooperated with us at the end. But his life is ruined."

There was something else I still didn't understand though. Why did Maura Walsh suddenly start investigating what happened to her brother back in Saginaw Lake after all this time? Rawlings said he didn't know and neither did anyone else. Maybe there was no reason for why she did it. Maybe Maura Walsh just impulsively decided to go looking for answers about her past one day. Maybe she did the same thing I did with my father, and she found out things she didn't expect. No news story is ever perfect. There are always loose ends, unanswered questions. "I wonder what she really did want from her father?" I said. "The truth, I guess. And, when she found out she'd been lied to all of her life, she lashed out at him in the best way she could. It's very hard to spend your whole life believing something about your family that you've been told – and then to have your whole world turned upside down."

"So Maura's anger at her father – and everything she did – actually makes some kind of sense to you?"

"Yeah, I can relate to a woman being lied to all her life," I said.

I guess I should mention that Sam Rawlings and I were talking about all this while eating dinner at a restaurant on Madison Avenue.

"So is this a date?" Sam asked me over dessert.

"Why would you call it a date?"

"Well, you're a woman and I'm a man…"

"I can't argue with that."

"We're out together in a restaurant."

"Okay."

"That sounds like a date to me."

"It's not technically a date."

"What is it?"

"A business meeting."

"And our business together being what?"

"This is a follow-up to my story. You're a part of the story. We're talking about the story, that's our business here together. Ergo, this is a business meeting. Now do you understand?"

"Absolutely."

"Good."

"I love that dress you're wearing, by the way," he said.

"Thank you."

"You look really hot in it."

"Uh-oh."

"Your hair is very sexy tonight too."

"You're coming on to me."

"Is that a problem?"

"I'm not sure."

We sat there eating in silence for a few minutes.

"The truth of the matter is," Sam finally said, "I've been having second thoughts about not taking you up on your offer when I had the chance at my place that night."

"I was drunk. It would have been wrong."

"You weren't that drunk."

"I was definitely drunk and I was very emotionally upset. You did the right thing, Sam."

"Are you drunk or emotionally upset now?"

"No."

"Do you want to sleep with me tonight then?"

"Now I think we're officially on a date." I smiled.

*

I didn't really harbor any illusions that Sam Rawlings was Mr. Right for me and we were going to get married and live happily ever after.

I actually didn't know Sam that well, and what I did know about him wasn't promising. For one thing, he was an undercover cop – and I wasn't sure what would happen to him next. Some sort of other secret assignment. Maybe he'd even have to go into hiding and disappear forever if the mob came after him as revenge for taking down Bennato.

But he was here now, and so was I.

And that was enough for the moment.

"So what do you think?" Sam asked me as we lay there in bed together afterwards.

"Definitely a date now," I said.

CHAPTER 66

If I thought New York City was hot and uncomfortable in the summertime, Sarasota, Florida was absolutely brutal. The heat hit me in the face the minute I stepped out of the Tampa–St. Petersburg Airport and walked to my rental car. The air-conditioning in the car helped, but I was still sweating profusely from the heat and, most of all, the oppressive humidity, when I checked into my hotel.

I'd managed to locate the address of Nathan Wright, the man I now knew to be my biological father. I did some more old-fashioned sleuthing on him too. I found out he lived alone, his wife had died a few years earlier of cancer, he wrote during the day and then taught history classes at a local community college. After his class was over, he regularly stopped in at a place called Molly's not far from the school for a beer before heading home.

And so I was waiting in Molly's that night when Nathan Wright came in.

That was the easy part.

But I wasn't exactly sure what I would do – what I wanted to do – next.

I recognized Nathan Wright from the picture I'd seen as soon as he walked into the place. Gray hair, in his sixties. Somehow he looked even more ordinary in person than he had in that picture. He was wearing tan slacks, a white short-sleeved shirt and I noticed he had a bit of a pot belly under the shirt. He sure looked nothing like the dashing man in the picture my mother had kept. That was the image I always had of my father, not this man.

Wright sat down on a barstool, greeted the bartender and ordered a beer. When it came, he sipped on it while watching a baseball game on a TV screen in front of him. This was my father. Jeez.

I could have just knocked on his door where he lived, I suppose.

Or shown up at his class at the community college instead of tracking him down to this bar.

Just like I could walk over to Nathan Wright right here and now and announce to him: "Hello there, I'm your long-lost daughter."

But I wanted to check him out a bit first. Find out more about Nathan Wright before I sprang my big surprise and told him who I was. If I decided to tell him. I still wasn't sure about that.

I was still mulling all that over – sitting a few seats down from him at the bar, and trying to figure out my next move – when something completely unexpected happened.

Nathan Wright got up off his barstool and walked over to me.

"Hey, I know who you are," he said.

My God! He actually recognized me! After all these years…

"You're Jessie Tucker. That newspaper reporter from New York. I saw you on TV. That big story about the mobster and police corruption that made all the news shows. You *are* Jessie Tucker, right?"

Of course.

He didn't know me as his daughter.

He knew me as Jessie Tucker, media celebrity.

"Guilty as charged," I told him.

"What are you doing all the way down here in Florida?"

"Working on another story," I said, throwing out the first thing I could think of as an answer to that.

"A big story?"

"One can only hope."

"I guess you never know how big a story is until you actually do some investigating into it, huh?"

"That's what a reporter does."

"So some of them have told me."

"You know other reporters?"

"I've talked to a few people in the media over the years. Mostly book reviewers, though. I write history books – as well as teach history. My name is Nathan Wright."

He put out his hand. I shook it. I wasn't really sure how to handle this. He'd thrown me a bit off my game. I decided to just wing it in the conversation with him and see where it went. Of course, I had to pretend I didn't know anything about him. I had to pretend I didn't know this was my biological father that I was meeting for the first time. It wasn't an easy act for me to pull off.

"What kind of history do you write about in your books?" I asked.

"I concentrate mostly on the Civil War era. It was such a terrible and bloody period, but yet a fascinating piece of American history. I've read and written about it pretty much all my life. I've done a dozen books and a lot of essays and talks. My best-known book is called *Brother vs. Brother: The Real Story of the Civil War*. It actually made a few bestseller lists. Did you ever hear of it?"

"Oh, my gosh… I read that book! That was you?"

"You're interested in Civil War history?"

"Ever since I watched that PBS series from a long time ago about the Civil War."

"The one by Ken Burns," he said.

"Right."

I wasn't lying about that. I had watched the Ken Burns series on TV. And I'd read through some of Wright's books before I came down to Florida, including the one we were talking about. I'd wanted to research Nathan Wright – find out as much as I could about him and his work – before I met him. I sure was glad now that I had.

"There's a lot of people today who want to remove all the Civil War monuments and memories because they believe it glorifies a period in our country when slavery of another person – based on their race – was legal," Wright said, finishing off the beer he'd been holding since he came over to me.

"I know. I read recently about a city in the South that tore down a statue of Robert E. Lee there because Lee supported the slave owners' cause – and owned slaves himself."

"That's right. The mayor and people said Lee should not be remembered as a legendary general, but as a disgrace. What do you think?"

"Well, I understand what they're saying. But I still feel that the Civil War – and all the things we have from that period – are an important part of American history that we can continue to learn from today."

He nodded, so I figured I'd said a good thing.

I wasn't sure how much longer I could keep talking intelligently about the Civil War, but it didn't matter. We talked a few minutes more, and then Wright said he was leaving. That he came in here for one beer a night, no more.

"Nice meeting you, Jessie," he said. "And good luck with your story."

"Good luck with your books," I said.

He started for the door.

"Mr. Wright!" I called out to him.

"Yes?" he said, turning around with a quizzical expression on his face.

I didn't respond, I just kept staring at him.

"Was there something else you wanted to say to me?" he asked me finally.

There was a lot I wanted to say to Nathan Wright. I wanted to ask him about him and my mother. I wanted to ask him about him and the man I always thought was my father, James Tucker. I wanted to ask him if he loved my mother. I wanted to ask him if he was the reason James Tucker left her. I wanted to ask him why he didn't stay with her. And, most of all, I wanted to ask him if he knew he had a daughter from that long-ago relationship. A daughter who was standing in front of him right now.

But I didn't say any of that to him.

Instead, I just smiled and gave him a goodbye wave.

"Have a nice evening, Mr. Wright," I said.

Maybe one day I would tell Nathan Wright the truth.

Maybe one day I would have a relationship with the man who was my father.

But not tonight.

I wasn't sure exactly why I'd just let him walk away like that. All I knew was that I'd gone my entire life without a father. Now I finally knew who that father really was. And I knew where my father was – here in Florida. And – just a few minutes ago – I'd actually met the man who was the father I've been searching after for a long time.

That was enough for now.

CHAPTER 67

Lieutenant Thomas Aguirre told me that it looked like they were going to formally charge Charlie Sanders with Maura Walsh's murder in the next day or so.

"Do you really think he did it?" I asked.

"The DA's office does. They're the ones who make the decision on whether to prosecute."

"But do you?"

"It doesn't matter what I think. I just hand over the evidence I accumulate in the case. And that evidence points directly at Charlie Sanders, and no one else."

Aguirre shrugged.

"Jessie, there's three things you look for in a murder case. Means, motive and opportunity. Sanders has the last two. Opportunity, because he met up with her in a bar just before she died so he could have easily followed her downtown afterward. Motive, he was in love with her and she'd rejected him – lots of murders happen by spurned lovers. Plus, he lied in the beginning about his alibi, which makes him look bad. The only thing missing is the means. We've never found Maura Walsh's gun. But, except for that, the DA thinks they've got a pretty good case."

I nodded. It did all make sense. Except I didn't want it to make sense. I liked Charlie Sanders. And I didn't think he would have ever murdered Maura, no matter how angry he was. He loved her too much.

"I still keep thinking it could be someone else," I said to Aguirre.

"Who? We've determined that Bennato and his people didn't kill her. They killed the PI and Renfro – but not her. Walsh certainly didn't murder his own daughter, not after the way he stood up to catch Bennato at the end. Sure, the wife killed the little boy back in Saginaw Lake – but that was an accident, not cold-blooded murder like this. Besides, she's such a basket case she never even leaves her house, much less would trek into downtown Manhattan at night. Hell, we even checked out the ex-Saginaw Lake cop Greg Stovall you talked with. He admitted to us that Maura Walsh had come to see him too, asking the same kind of questions as you did. We thought maybe he got nervous afterward and was afraid she'd blow the sweet deal he had with Bennato that financed his landscaping business. But Stovall had an alibi, he was in Elmira when she died. And his alibi held up. He was attending a conference meeting of local business owners there. More than thirty people remember seeing him there. Stovall confessed to the rest of it, though. How he and Walt Palumbo covered up details about the Walsh boy's death. How Palumbo felt guilty about it afterward and that's why he left the NYPD job Walsh set up for him so quickly. But Stovall was happy to take the money – first from Walsh, then a lot more from Bennato. Yes, Greg Stovall is not an honorable person, but he isn't a murderer. So that's it. That just leaves Sanders. There's no one else."

Aguirre started talking then about how glad he'd be to get off this special assignment – the hunt for Maura Walsh's killer – and return to his normal job as a homicide detective. "We did pretty good again though, didn't we, Tucker?" He smiled. "We make a great team. Even though I did have to save your life again. Or at least help save it this time. Remember, I was there when we busted Bennato and his mob. That's the second time I've saved your life – so you really owe me—"

I was only half listening to him though. There was something bothering me. Something that didn't seem right. And then, all of a sudden, I realized what it was.

"There is someone else," I said. "You've left out one possible suspect who might have done it."

"Who are you talking about?"

"The person who called Sanders that night and got him to go confront her at the East Side bar."

"But we don't know who that was. Sanders never knew either. It was just a voice on the phone."

"Man or woman?"

"Sanders said it was a woman."

Of course.

"Think about it. Who would do something like that? Tell Charlie Sanders his girlfriend was having an affair with someone else. Try to make him jealous. Well, it likely was someone who was also jealous, but not jealous of the same person. Someone who could have been waiting at the bar too that night and then followed them afterward downtown to the pizza place in Little Italy. Someone who knew where Maura Walsh was because she was with this woman's husband."

"You mean…?"

"Billy Renfro's wife."

It all fell into place pretty easily after that. Linda Renfro – or Linda Caldwell, as she called herself now – had no alibi for the night and the time of Maura Walsh's murder. And later, under intense interrogation by authorities, she broke down and admitted she'd murdered Maura Walsh, the woman she thought was having an affair with her husband. They later even found Maura's gun when they searched Linda Renfro's home. She hadn't even bothered to get rid of it. That's how crazy and spontaneous this crime had been.

"I just thought about her with Billy," she said during her confession. "I couldn't get that out of my mind, no matter how hard I tried. That's why I told Sanders about them. I was hoping he'd do something to stop them, but he didn't. So I went downtown and watched them afterward. My husband got out of the car and went to get her food, like they were on a date or something. I couldn't take it anymore. So I walked over to the car where she was waiting and told her to leave my husband alone. She got out of the car to try to calm me down, and we started walking. She kept telling me there was nothing going on between her and Billy. But every time she said that – it just made me madder. There was a piece of wood lying in the alley from the construction going on next to it. When she turned away from me to head back to her car, I got so mad I picked up the board and hit her in the head with it. She fell to the ground. Then, when she was lying there still dazed, I reached down and took her gun. I pointed it at her. Just to scare her. That's all I wanted to do, only scare her. But then…"

"You shot her," the police interrogator said.

"Yes. The gun just went off."

"But you shot her twice."

"I don't remember."

"Was she alive when you left?"

"Yes."

"But you didn't try to get help for her. And you took her radio so she couldn't signal for help on it as she lay there dying. Why?"

"I wanted her to suffer. I wanted her to feel pain before she died. Real pain. Just like the pain I felt so much after she took Billy away from me."

"Maura Walsh wasn't having an affair with your husband. She was working undercover on a special assignment. That's all that was going on between them. Nothing personal at all."

"I know that now. But I was so angry when I thought she was… that's why I called Sanders that night and all the rest."

"But you had left your husband. You were living in your own apartment. It seemed like you had already moved on from your marriage. So why did it matter so much to you if Maura Walsh had been involved with him? There's a lot of things hard to understand about why you did what you did. But that's the biggest one. Why did you even care?"

She began to sob.

"I couldn't stop thinking about Billy being with her. It was driving me crazy. I thought that if she wasn't there, everything might go back to the way it was. I fixed myself up to look beautiful again, like I did when I was young. I bought sexy clothes. I did everything I could to get Billy to notice me again. I loved Billy, don't you understand? I just wanted him to come back to me."

CHAPTER 68

It was a hot, muggy night when I finally left the *Tribune* office after filing the story.

The sun was gone, but the humidity had remained. There were people sitting out on stoops in front of apartments I passed. Kids played in an open fire hydrant on one block. A group of teens sat on a parked car with music blaring at full blast.

Summertime in New York City.

The death of Maura Walsh had turned out to be a completely senseless crime – the result of a complicated series of events that began a long time ago. For years, all the isolated incidents had been dormant. Waiting for the right moment. Waiting for a catalyst to pull them all together. That catalyst had been Maura Walsh herself.

There had been so many what-ifs, so many interlocking pieces.

If Patrick Walsh hadn't died. If the police in Saginaw Lake hadn't covered up the real story of what happened. If Maura Walsh had been allowed to follow her dream of being a marine biologist instead of joining the police force. If she hadn't gone undercover to try to expose her father's wrongdoings. If Billy Renfro's wife hadn't hired a private investigator to see if her husband was cheating on her. If Matt Wysocki hadn't died so that Maura Walsh became Renfro's partner. So many ifs…

The results had been staggering. Three people were dead – Maura Walsh, Frank Walosin, and Billy Renfro. Other lives and careers – most notably, Deputy Commissioner Walsh – were ruined.

So many lives intertwined, so many repercussions.

The "Summertime Blues", as the cops in New York City called it.

Because so much crazy, senseless crime like this always seemed to happen here in the summer heat.

Almost like a perfect storm.

A storm that could be unforgiving at times, cutting a swath of death and destruction across the city. Like a hurricane bearing down on the island that Manhattan was. Some people died, some people lived. Just like it had always been in the summertime. Son of Sam's deadly terror spree. Robert Chambers strangling Jennifer Levin in the Preppie Murder Case. And the near-fatal attack on me in Central Park on a hot night twelve years ago. It was as if there was a price in blood that sometimes had to be paid, and the reasons for it never seemed to make much sense.

But it was August now.

In a few weeks, fall would be here.

The city had survived the storm.

So had I.

A LETTER FROM DANA

I hope you enjoyed reading *The Golden Girl*. If you'd like to keep up to date with all of my latest releases, you can sign up at the following link. Your email address will never be shared, and you can unsubscribe at any time.

www.bookouture.com/dana-perry

I was inspired to write this book because I work in the New York City media, and I wanted to show how a journalist – in this case, newspaper reporter Jessie Tucker – can become personally involved in a front-page story she's covering. As Jessie digs deeper into the baffling murder of police officer Maura Walsh, she begins to identify more and more with the slain woman – and finally goes looking for answers about her own life as well as answers about Maura Walsh. That's the story I wanted to tell in *The Golden Girl*.

If you have time, I'd love it if you were able to write a review of *The Golden Girl*. Reader reviews on Amazon, Goodreads or anywhere else are crucially important to an author and can spread the word to new readers. If you'd like to contact me personally, you can reach me via my website, Facebook page, Twitter or Instagram.

Thank you for reading *The Golden Girl*.

Best wishes,
Dana Perry

@DanaPerryAuthor
@DanaPerryAuthor

Made in the USA
Monee, IL
14 May 2021